PRINTHOUSE

A Turn of Kismet
Fiction

Kalandra St. George

To my mother, who always saw the picture in every abstract I've ever created. Thank you for holding my left hand in yours & teaching me the power of words.

A Turn of Kismet

Kalandra St. George

VIP INK Publishing Group, Inc.
Atlanta, GA.

Camille's world was just getting back to normal after losing the love of her life in a brutal hit and run accident a year ago. She was in no way ready for the complication of a new relationship when she met Sean.

Camille turns to her best friend, Rita, for counsel and the savvy Puerto Rican mami offers her support while revealing a secret of her own. The thread of pregnancy is the only thing holding her marriage to Hassan together. The two friends take a weekend retreat to the shore that brings about an unusual outlook on their sexuality.

Meanwhile Sean, with his West Indian accent and captivating looks, is out for seduction following the ugly break-up with his girlfriend, Nicole. Nicole on the other hand is determined to find harmony after the split and is thrilled when she meets a man that seems to be on the same page. However, Hassan turns out to be closer in her cipher than she ever imagined.

Truths begin to unravel at an alarming rate bringing devastation as they all find themselves intertwined in ways never imaginable. Destiny proves itself the victor as their lives shift under A Turn of Kismet.

Cover designed by SK7
Editor: Shelby Oates
ISBN: 978-0-9965701-45

Library of Congress Data

#201594914

Printed in the United States of America

Table of Contents

Table of Contents

Prologue

As she watched the man follow the woman out of the apartment building she felt like she was going to be sick.

"She's even more beautiful in person," Camille thought.

The moon, high in the November sky, illuminated the couple as they exited past the doorman. He spoke to both of them knowingly and tipped his hat, bidding them a good night. The evening was cool. The woman wore a mid-length black fur faux with matching gloves, a silk scarf, and a hat pulled to the side like a 1920's gangster. A silver belt fell low around her petite waist resting teasingly on her full hips. Her fitting blue jeans were tucked stylishly inside spike heeled, knee length, black leather boots. She stood almost even with 'Mr. Tall Dark and Handsome' at her side. He too had on blue jeans that fell neatly atop a pair of camel brown Durango boots. Below his cream leather coat flowed a matching camel brown turtleneck sweater.

His hair, locked neatly, adorned a fresh shape-up and a finely trimmed goatee that brought more attention to his already attractive face. As they waited by the curb, he placed his arm around the woman's shoulder pulling her close. He whispered in her ear while his eyes scanned the busy parkway behind her in an effort to settle the eerie feeling that they were being watched. Unaware of his apprehension and seemingly pleased by what he was saying she didn't loosen her grip around his tight waist until the valet pulled up before them. The man opened the passenger door of the silver Tahoe as the beauty placed her hand extravagantly in his sliding into the front seat. He trotted around the back of the vehicle unzipping his jacket with another long look over his shoulder before hopping in the driver's side. The truck sped away rapidly heading north.

After the SUV pulled off, Camille sat there for what seemed like hours. With each passing minute the hurt that burned inside of her boiled more and more into uncontrollable anger. Her face was tight from the river of dried tears on her cheeks; her head ached from the conjured up scenes her mind replayed of what possibly had gone on upstairs. Numb from the cold, her tight grip on the steering wheel turned her knuckles white. As she breathed, she did not notice the fog creeping up on the windshield nor the smoke coming out of her mouth. All she could see was the two of them together and that was too much to bear. She had a million vengeful thoughts running through her head at one time, all in a race to be the victor.

'*I'm gonna kick his door in and leave him a note telling him I saw him and what an asshole he is. No, you know what? I'm not gonna say anything. I'm just never gonna talk to his*

9

black ass again and let him figure it out. I wish he would try to call me. Nah, that's not gonna get it. I'ma wait 'till that nigga comes home - slice all four of his tires then bust his windshield out..." The more she schemed in her mind the more heated she got. Finally, she began to cry all over again. '*Why am I letting him get me like this? Why am I allowing myself to get like this? I gotta get it together.*' she thought. "I'm slippin'! For real."

The words struck the air like a rock smashing through a glass window. She looked around erratically, wondering how long she had been sitting there. "For *real* for real." she repeated while starting the ignition. Turning on the defroster, Camille hit replay on the radio and threw the gear stick in drive. No one paid attention to the sleek, navy blue Range Rover as she pulled away from the curb, bumping the Jay-Z classic *Song Cry*.

PRINTHOUSE BOOKS PRESENTS

A Turn of Kismet
Fiction

Kalandra St. George

Chapter 1
Camille

"You did what?!" Rita exclaimed.

Immediately Camille regretted telling her friend about the late night stakeout.

"I told you not to get caught up behind that nigga. Now look. You've gone totally Glen Close on me."

"Way to make me feel better Ree. And don't act like you're not the one that hooked us up in the first place."

"Hooked ya'll up? I was just tryin' to get you some. I didn't know you were gonna go ballistic behind the shit. I know you said it was good, but damn mami, was it *that* good?" Rita burst out laughing.

Camille could feel herself jumping on the defense.

"Look I'm not beat for no man and you know that. I just... I don't know. One minute I was just driving home thinking about him and the next thing I knew I was across the street from his house. I swear when I saw them come out together I thought I was gonna die. I was so heated."

"Well, did he see you?"
"I don't think so. No, he didn't."
"You're lucky, 'cause he seems like the type of nigga that would flip."
"I know. It's just that I can't stop thinking about him. I say I'm not going to call him and the next thing you know, I end up parked across the street from his house. I'm trippin'. I don't know what to do."

Camille pictured herself wrapped in Sean's arms. She could even smell him. The scent of his cologne seemed to float through her nostrils as if he were right there in the room.
"You know that right, Camille?" Rita stated.
"Huh? What?"
"I said you need to stop looking for 'Trevor'. He's not your son's father. I don't know why you expect him to love you like Trevor did. Sean has his own 'B.M.' Shit, you better face it, dear. You're the 'other woman'."

The words fell from Rita's mouth so matter-of-factly; Camille's face started to burn and her eyes welled up with tears. In her heart she knew Rita was right about Sean's baby's mother. Still, it was the last thing she wanted to think about, let alone hear right now.

"Rita, I gotta go. Jelani is calling me for his nightly peanut butter fix." she lied. "Tell Hassan I said, 'what up'. I'll see you in the morning."

She hung up the phone with tears streaming down her face in a salty downpour. Flipping over Camille buried her sobs in the king size canopy bed that Trevor had surprised her with for her birthday years ago. She ached to be loved again, but knew Sean was not in love with her. It was obvious he still loved his ex. Why else would she be at his house? How long had she been there? What was really going on? Camille was just with him two days ago. That explained why he had not called her today. He was too busy playing house.

Camille was catching feelings and it scared her. Sean was turning her into something she vowed she would never be-- second to another woman. It burned her up that she allowed things to go this far. The more she thought about it, the more her pain turned into resentment. She hated Sean for giving her his number and for being so damn fine. She hated that he bought flowers and left sweet notes on the bathroom counter. She hated how he rekindled emotions that were laid to rest long ago with her first love.

Her thoughts shifted to Trevor. She was still mad at him too for leaving them like he did. Camille placed her hand on the diamond cut heart charm that hung from the dainty Singapore necklace. It was a constant reminder of Trevor's broken promise that they would be together forever. To this day, one year and eight months later, although she tried not to be, Camille was still bitter about his passing. Each time she replayed the accident in her head she asked the same questions, more so to him than to herself.

How dare he get behind the wheel of a car after drinking? Didn't he know how much of a risk he was taking? Hell, he could barely drive when he was sober! What was he thinking? Didn't he know how much she and Jelani needed him?

As her mind raced back to that Thursday night, she felt the same sense of dread she'd felt that evening before going to bed. It was the playoffs and the game had just gone off. She knew Trevor wouldn't be leaving the bar for at least another hour, especially since the Knicks had won. Knowing in her heart something wasn't right, she forced herself to sleep, pushing the anxious feeling rising in her throat back down to the pit of her stomach. She told herself everything was fine and he would be home soon. Camille could still see the red glare of the clock that read 2 a.m. and she could still hear the piercing sound of the telephone as it rang in distress...

"Mommie..." Jelani knocked and opened the door, snapping Camille back into the present.

As usual, like the morning sun, Jelani's smile lit up the whole room. He was her angel, always there when she needed him. She tried to hide her tears from her four year old who was wise beyond his years. Little did she know he'd felt her emotions even before he opened the door.

Using the step stool for a boost, he scrambled onto the massive bed as Camille opened her arms allowing his spirit to engulf her.

"Mommie, what's wrong?" he asked, kissing her cheek.

"Nothing, baby. Mommie is just sleepy."

"Are you sad?" he fingered the necklace Camille had just released from her grasp.

"No, I'm ok," she attempted to change the subject.

"Come on. Let's go make you a peanut butter and jelly sandwich."

Jelani's face, brightening at the mention of his favorite snack, "Yessss," he piped, "I love choke and slides!"

"Jelani, what in the world is a 'choke and slide'?"

"You know, Mommie." he replied. "The peanut butter chokes you and the jelly slides it down," he motioned along his neck with his tiny fingers.

The unpleasant memories of the day faded into the back of Camille's mind as she followed her red headed, cornbread colored child skipping down the hallway.

The next morning was cool and windy, as Camille stood at the bus stop watching Jelani board his Pre-K shuttle. She tried to erase the scene from last night, but could still see Nicole laughing romantically at Sean. Her mood was as cold as the November air whipping around her, pushing her forcefully back toward the truck. Once inside, her cell phone rang an all too familiar ringtone.

"*I swear I'm going to de-program his number,*" she thought. Still, she flipped open the mobile.

"Hello?" Camille tried to sound hurried.

"Hello, woman." The sound of his voice made her wish she'd sent the call to voicemail. He made all of the hairs on her body stand on end and her temperature rise thirty degrees.

"'Ow was ya'r nite?" Sean's cool unwavering tone was that of a man with the world at his fingertips. Although his smugness made her cringe, his West Indian accent made Camille's stomach flutter.

Acting like she didn't hear the question, Camille blurted out, "Could you hold on a minute?" Pressing mute on the phone she thought, *"Let's see how he likes being put on hold."* After about thirty seconds she returned making sure her voice held an obvious annoyance.

"I'm sorry, now what were you saying?"

"I asked 'ow ya'r eve'nin went." Sean's tone didn't skip a beat and a short wave of disappointment washed over Camille's attempted victory.

"Not as well as yours, I'm sure." Her voice was full of cynicism.

This time Sean caught on, "What's that 'posed ta' mean?"

"Nothing. It was fine," she lied. "So, what did you do last night?"

"Not shit. I was able ta' get some long needed rest. I'm not as young as I used ta' be, ya' know," Sean chuckled.

"Well needed rest, huh? You make it sound as if you've been busy lately."

"I 'ave. Someone likes to keep me up 'till the wee hours of the dawn."

"I have no idea what you're talking about."

"Sure ya' don't. What'cha doin' ta'night?"

Her common sense was yelling, "Tell him you've got plans. Go ahead, tell him!" But, her heart spoke up instead. "Nothing. Why, what's up?"

"I'd like ta' see you, if possible."

See me my ass, Camille thought.

Trying to sound blasé, "Well, what did you need?"

"I don't *need* any'ting. I *want* ta' see ya'."

"Is that right?" She could feel her body getting warm and the anger subsiding the slicker he talked. "What did you have in mind?"

"I don't know. But, I'm sure someting' will come to me," He chuckled. "You know I like to let the chips fall where they may." Sean succeeded in talking her out of her anger.

"Yeah, ok. I'll call you later, dear."

"Later it is."

She hung up and rolled down the window to calm her nerves. *Why do I always put his wants ahead of my needs?* It was clear to Camille that Sean was satisfied with the relationship just as it was. No strings attached and no commitments. He saw her whenever and that was enough for him, while she, on the other hand, was in complete turmoil. Sure, the sex was great and she loved having a man around again, but this was becoming unhealthy. Camille knew she deserved more, but it had been so long since anyone had come this close to her she allowed herself to overlook the obvious.

"Did you call him?" It was the first thing Rita asked when Camille walked into the office. No 'Good morning' or 'How are you holding up?' The two had been best friends since the ninth grade when they were accidentally assigned the same locker.

Camille remembered it like it was yesterday. Rita was standing there unzipping her book bag when she walked up.

"Excuse me, sweetheart. I think you're in the wrong hall."

Pulling the schedule out of her back pocket, Rita eyed Camille from head to toe. Her face lit up as she checked out the crisp white Uptowns with NYC on the strap.

"Where did you get those kicks?" She asked.

Camille stared back directly in Rita's face which she didn't recognize. Although she was quiet, Camille wasn't beat for any drama on the first day of school. Normally, she didn't have to worry about beef with any of the girls at school. Growing up an only child, Camille had no other choice but to learn how to keep her guard up or else get chumped. The passive Sagittarian had no problems setting anyone straight who even thought about crossing her. With this attitude, rumors of her temper traveled. "From VIM's in the Bronx." She kept it short.

"They're tight as hell." Rita's compliment caught Camille off guard, but she nodded to say, 'Thanks' anyway.

"What's your locker number?" Rita asked.

"1152. Hall C."

"Shit, they gave us the same fucking locker."

Rita exhaled loudly slamming the flimsy metal door shut. "I knew this school was bootleg."

"Where you from?" Camille was unable to pinpoint anything behind the girl's thick Hispanic accent.

"Philly." Pulling her thick mane into her fist, Rita went on while staring at the ground as she wrapped the rubber band tight around her ponytail. "Look I just spent all morning in that hot-ass office…"

Camille cut her off. "Yo, don't worry about it. We can just share this one. I'm Camille."

"Rita, but call me Ree," she smiled, holding her arms open wide presenting Camille with the chance to give her a once over. There was something in her eyes that made Camille like her. She got a good feeling from the chick. Not like the rest of the 'wanna-be-hard' girls that had followed her from junior high.

With Camille's mother being so strict, Rita turned out to be a relief. She started meeting Camille every morning to walk to school, often saving her from Carole's sunrise lectures. After a while the two became inseparable. Camille spent most of her time at Rita's house marveling secretly at her many freedoms. Rita seemed to do all of the things Camille only dreamed about.

Rita lived with her grandmother, aunts and cousin. She never said much about her mom when they were young and taking it as something she chose not to discuss, Camille never asked. Ms. Anna, Rita's grandmother, was a gem with a heart of gold. She spoiled Rita, letting her do damn near whatever she wanted. A lot of times Rita's aunts complained, but Ms. Anna shooed them away, saying her baby was special and too smart to do anything stupid.

The first time Camille got high, she was sitting on the floor in Rita's bedroom sulking over a midterm she'd bombed. Rita, who blew weed on the regular, handed her friend the joint jokingly to interrupt her monologue on the "ramifications of not passing World Literature". To her surprise, Camille snatched the tightly rolled papers bringing the spliff to her lips.

Rita told Camille for what seemed like the one-millionth time to stop being neurotic and learn to enjoy life. Like with her own grandmother, Rita told Camille that the less Carole knew the better. Besides, as long as she kept her grades up there was nothing to worry about. And getting a 75 on a mid-term was not the end of the world.

It always amazed Camille how versatile her friend was. Even though Rita often hid her intelligence behind her brassy behavior, she could rock with the best of them and out test the brainiest student in the class without breaking a sweat. Camille loved it, but she never understood how Rita maintained the balance. Over the next four years Rita continued to party hard. She went from just smoking weed to eventually popping whatever pill she found in her hand. Camille, on the other hand, liked to drink. She preferred to drown her worries in a bottle of white liquor and only got high on the weekends she spent at

Rita's.

Through it all, the pair remained thicker than molasses, pushing each other along when one slacked and even escorting each other to the senior prom. After both being accepted into Rutgers University, the two decided to attend the northern campus of New Jersey in order to escape Camden's city life. Before they knew it, they were celebrating graduation night at The Inkwell off the boardwalk in Atlantic City and vowing to the other an undying allegiance fueled by Seagram's Gin, peach flavored White Owls and Vicatin.

Camille blossomed into a headstrong young woman in college finally out from under Carole's watchful eye. She loved the freedom college life offered. The party animal in her found its niche with the 'wild-but-not-too-wild' clique that liked to drink and occasionally get high, while jamming to some serious underground hip hop. It was there, at a Saturday night Suarez in her junior year, that Camille met Trevor. His thuggish appearance and heavy Brooklyn accent quickly swept Camille into a whirlwind. The words that came out of his smooth black lips had her totally smitten and Camille fell head-over-heels for the six-two, one hundred and ninety pound senior. After playing cat-and-mouse for almost two years, he succeeded in talking Camille out of much more than her sanity.

As he taught her about love and more about men, Trevor showed Camille a side of herself she knew existed, but never experienced. He protected her from a lot as he also schooled Camille on how to take care of things when need be. And, although they fought like all young couples, Camille was like a lioness about her prey when it came to Trevor. She was determined to battle anything or anyone that came in the way of the two of them, and that also included him. While they went through the motions, Rita just stood back only giving her opinion when asked. She was there to calm Camille down when the two got into it, but it often seemed Trevor was the one calling for help. In the meantime, Rita was busy trying to get Hassan to notice her. Back then she had little time to be Camille's 'therapist' as she put it. But nowadays, it seemed she'd become a regular Iyanla when it came to her friend's love life.

"Well?" She urged as Camille placed her pocketbook on the desk. "What? Huh?" Camille was lost in thought.

"You heard me. Did you call Sean?" Rita repeated.

"No, he actually called me."

Rita huffed, chewing on the end of a coffee stirrer. "Unh-hun, after he dropped his jawn off."

"Whatever. And anyway, why are *you* so hostile? I'm the one sleeping with the man."

"Porque elles un chingada."

Camille turned her back on Rita who was eying her intently.

"He's not a bastard, Ree."

"Shit girl, you sound like you're still gonna see him."

Camille was silent. Rita turned her around slowly staring her friend directly in the eyes. Camille laughed at how different she and Rita were both physically and in personality. After Trevor died Rita, coaxed Camille into cropping her shoulder-length, auburn-tinted hair to be just below the ears. She hated it; but, it did draw attention to her soft face giving her an appearance much younger than her twenty-eight years. Camille had a lot of appeal because of her height alone. Surprisingly, at five feet ten inches, she was able to keep her figure up even after having Jelani. Her robust hips, full thighs, small waist and flat stomach allotted her the nickname, 'Stallion'. Camille always received compliments on her deep brown almond shaped eyes, even though she had wished since they were young that they were the color of her friend's. She kept her caramel-colored skin free of anything other than the occasional gloss to accent her pouty lips.

On the other hand, Rita's pregnancy had her spreading fast. Camille hoped she would be able to go back to her petite frame, even though motherhood complimented the already beautiful Puerto Rican woman. At six months pregnant, Rita's ginger-toned face literally glowed. Her green eyes glimmered as if her rotund belly held a secret only she knew. And, her thick light brown hair, which already cascaded down her back, seemed to grow more and more every day.

"Camille. You're not still going to see him, are you?" Silence still. "That's alright. Ignore me. I'm gonna get Hassan to kick his ass."

"You know Hassan is not kicking anybody's ass. He wouldn't hurt a fly," she laughed at the thought of Rita's meek husband.

"I swear. I still don't know how you two even hooked up, let alone got married with your rowdy ass." Camille chuckled.

"Man, I don't know either. You know they say opposites attract. And, don't act like since you're all corporate now that you're not still hood deep down inside." Rita joked wagging her finger and neck at the same time. "I remember having to pull you off of Trevor plenty of times. So, who's really the rowdy one?"

"Yeah, whatever. Come on, we need to get to work. The waiting room is almost full. Give me the patient list and take these samples to the lab. Just have them run the normal." Under her breath she added with a smirk, "Who would've ever thought the sight of blood would make Ree squeamish?"

"I heard that! I'm not squeamish, I'm pregnant." Rita retorted. "And, don't worry sweetheart, as soon as this nausea fades, I'll be back to sticking and sending them on their way with a pat, before you even get the tourniquet off!"

Camille chuckled watching Rita wobble away. Sliding into her lab coat, she looked over the patient list mentally preparing herself for the day.

Camille's career was one area in her life that currently needed no adjusting. Although it took a while for her to do so, once she accepted the position at Eastern Laboratories, Camille fell right into place. With Hassan's father as the C.E.O., she felt completely at home and was able to fully support her household. To her, taking care of Jelani was all that mattered. She would work on herself in time.

Chapter 2

Sean

The afternoon sun, warm on his face, reminded Sean how much he loved this time of year. The feeling of the autumn air right before the cold of winter set in and gave him a rush totally opposite the draining heat and humidity of the islands. Sean stopped at the drugstore for some peppermints and Lisa Frank stickers on his way to surprise the love of his life. Looking at his watch, he knew this was going to have to be a brief visit. He could feel the mountain of paperwork on his desk growing with each passing minute.

As he strolled through the park, mothers momentarily turned their attention from their children. His captivating, tall, lean, two hundred and thirty pound physique had them all on stuck. Paying no attention to the stares and whispers, Sean's eye was focused on trying to find the only female in the crowd that mattered to him.

He spotted her among the group of girls jumping hopscotch. With her pigtails bouncing on the bright yellow jacket, Morgan was too busy watching the rock land and calling orders to see Sean sneak up behind her. She bursts into giggles as he scooped her into his arms kissing her forehead.

"Hey, Daddy!" Morgan squealed grabbing his wide nose and giving it a familiar pinch.

"I didn't know you were coming."

As soon as he placed her feet on the concrete, she took off running towards her mother with her hair waving in the wind.

"Mommie, why didn't you tell me Daddy was coming?"

Looking at his nine-year-old twin's head cocked, hand on her hip, Sean couldn't help but laugh. She looked so much like him that Nicole could not deny it if she wanted to. Morgan had it all. Deep brown skin, broad nose, wide set eyes and the same lone set dimple. The only thing she had gotten from Nicole was her hair, which her mother kept braided even though Morgan hated it. She always told Nicole that when she got older she was going to let her 'Mum-Mum' give her locks like her daddy.

There she sat with a striking jawbone, thin nose, flawless skin and a body made to kill. "'Ello, Nicole." Sean bent down, kissing his ex on the cheek. It amazed Sean how much he still loved the woman even after a ten-year relationship and the ugly break up a year ago. Ironically it seemed he was more in love with her now than when they were together.

Camille popped into his mind stinging Sean with a twinge of guilt that he quickly dismissed. Although he had grown to care deeply for Camille in the past three months, he still loved the mother of his only child very much. Nicole had, however, made it painfully clear that she had gotten tired of waiting for Sean to come around and take the next step. She wanted to be single.

Sean was a good man. He had always taken care of her like he should. He bought them a house as soon as he found out Nicole was pregnant. And, even with the added expense of a baby on top of a mortgage, Sean never pressured Nicole about the finances. Anything she wanted he supplied.

It wasn't like she didn't know what she was getting into after all. Sean met Nicole in a pool hall. They were both tipsy that night and truth be told he was on the rebound from another relationship when they hooked up. He didn't know why she made such a big ordeal out of something she could not control.

Sean remembered the night Nicole was standing in the middle of the garden tub stark naked yelling at the top of her lungs. Sean never understood what possessed her to stay up all night waiting for him.

"Why don't you just take ya' worrisome ass to sleep? I don't remember ya' complain' 'bout me being out 'til 3 and 4 a.m. when I was creepin' wit' you!"

Sean thought he was making a valid point, but quickly realized he was adding fuel to an already blazing bonfire.

"Exactly, Sean! You want to be out all night long then come home like nothing is wrong!"

There were plenty of these occasions during their relationship. Usually Sean was able to make up for the wrongs. But, in the end Nicole was beyond tired of the deceit and the lies. She wanted to go on with her life without him.

The night it all came crashing down, she was waiting up for him in the den. He'd been gone for two days after promising her he'd be away for no more than one.

"I just need to be on my own for a while." Her words slivered through his soul like a searing knife. After all, it wasn't like she didn't know what he was doing. He had to handle business in order to provide her with the lifestyle to which she was accustomed.

Sean took it hard begging her to stay, but eventually Nicole moved out. She laughed when Sean found out she had purchased a condo and told her she had deceived him.

"Behind your back? See Sean, that's the problem. You have your secrets, but when I have one I'm being deceitful?! You want me to share everything with you, yet you leave Morgan and me for days at a time doing who-knows-what with who-knows-who. Hell, Sean if something happened to you, I wouldn't even know where to begin looking for Christ's sake."

"Oh, gwan Nicole. Ya' know wat' I do. Ya've known since ya' met me. Why is tis' such a problem now?"

"Because Sean, my daughter is almost eight and I can't take the thought of having to tell her that her Daddy is never going to come home again because some dope deal went bad or because he drank himself to death. Or, better yet, because some whore got mad and shot him!"

Sean stood there with disbelief in his eyes. "It is not tat' serious, woman!" He yelled.

"Well, maybe not to you!" She yelled back. "But, this is my life, too and I'm not going to keep exposing my daughter to this!"

He took the blows to his ego like an amateur on the ropes against a champ. There was no way Sean could tell her he'd stopped selling dope a long time ago. What he'd ventured off into, although less of an immediate risk, was still illegal. Nicole would never understand.

Sean fought hard trying to get her to come back. He called and she wouldn't come to the phone. He wrote letters and she would send them back without even opening them. He had flowers and jewelry delivered to her job weekly for more than two months. All to no avail.

Eventually, Sean decided that if space was what she needed, that's what he would give her. But, after almost a year, when Nicole still had not come around, he buckled down and sold their house. It held too many memories and was too much to deal with, so Sean ended up leasing a condo uptown closer to his office and started living the life of a full-fledged bachelor.

Sean and Nicole were now on speaking terms and were even able to be alone together without going at each other's throat. Taking a seat beside her, Sean placed his arm on the back of the park bench.

"Sean, how are you?" She asked without looking in his direction.

The scent of her hair had him in a daze. "Oh, I'm well. Just wanted ta' surprise my princess. I know Friday is 'park day', so I decided ta' come by. So 'ow's your boyfriend? Was he waiting for you last night after I dropped you off?"

"Ha-ha, very funny. Why must you always assume I'm involved? When do I have the time as much as we're together? And, with Morgan? You know me better than that, Sean."

"Together? Us? Woman the only reason I was able ta' get you over yesterday is because of the 'oliday. If it twasn't for Christmas shopping I'd 'ardly see you." He gave her one of those 'I'm serious' stares.

Nicole exhaled loudly, "Don't start, Sean. You could have spent the rest of your life with me. You chose otherwise. And, today I don't have the energy or the desire to discuss this."

"I'm just saying," he replied sleeplessly, "my daughter needs ta' see me more often tan' every other weekend."

Nicole sighed, "Look, if this is really about you spending more time with Morgan as opposed to you checking up on me, then why don't we alternate by the week instead."

"Really?"

He had been trying to get Nicole to agree to that arrangement for months. It was just like her to hold out until she was ready. But, Sean took no offense. That was actually one of the things that attracted him.

"We can start after Christmas. This way you can get your shit in order."

Sean ignored the implication and just shook his head.

"Nicole, ya'ar too much," he chuckled. "My father tol' me red women were a 'andful. I should'a listened."

She shot him a warning look making him throw up his hands as if to surrender. Morgan ran back toward them and plopped exhaustedly in the middle.

"Hey, little girl, how would ya' like it if you stayed with me for a week and ten' Mommie for a week? Tis' way we can both get ta' spend time with you." He pulled her onto his lap resting his chin on the top of her head lovingly.

"For real, Mommie?" She piped. "I get to stay all week with Daddy and go to school from his house? Who's gonna do my spelling words with me? Who's gonna pick out my clothes? Oh, and Mommie, since Daddy doesn't know how to braid, I'm going to need to get locks!"

Nicole looked at Sean and they burst out laughing. There at that moment Sean was in his glory. He wished they could be like this forever.

Sean said his goodbyes and made his way back to the office. Born a hustler, he'd worked for years at one of the largest contracting companies in Bensalem as a cover. All the while, he was transporting heroine back-and-forth between the islands and the states. By the time Morgan was born, Ecstasy had just hit the streets. Everyone from Asian kids to old white men were into popping X. The game, it seemed, grew more uncertain and less profitable. He decided that it was time to secure a future for his family and start his own company.

In the years he'd spent contracting, Sean ended up becoming an expert in the field. He figured since he had the money, why not embark on something new.

His former boss was devastated when he turned in his notice, though he tried to portray otherwise. Sean gave his word that he would not solicit to any of the company's existing clients, although he'd brought the majority of them on board. As expected, things were slow at first. But, Sean kept his word and started literally from rock bottom. Though it took some time, eight years later, Morgan Contracting, was amongst the top ten in the North East industry. Sean's business was the big payoff for years spent hustling.

Throughout this time, he made a few connections on the 'Wall Street' side of the game. As a result, four years in, he took on a new hustle that was more lucrative than any amount of dope he'd ever touched. Laundering money, Sean found, was not only extremely lucrative, but also elevating. Rolling up to posh affairs in his 'Big Boy' toy and turning heads as he sauntered in gave him a rush like no other. Shaking hands with white people who normally wouldn't look his way, let alone speak, empowered Sean. The icing on the cake was how easy it all turned out to be. Once he got the gist of how things operated, he was able to sit back and let the cash flow. Sean's clientele were among the elite in the Metropolitan area. This secured not only his bank account, but also the financial success of the only fully black owned and operated contracting corporation in Pennsylvania.

Sean was just about through tying up all of the loose ends of his plan to be out of the game for good. Within the next sixteen months, he intended to remove himself from all illegalities and walk the straight and narrow. He would've been clean sooner had it not been for a few times when his 'extracurricular activities' came back around biting him in the balls. Nonetheless, Sean regretted nothing he'd done in his life. Well, almost nothing.

"Mr. Jeffers. I have seven messages for you. And, Mr. Grimaldi's office called to confirm Monday's 10 o'clock."

"Tank' you, June. Did ya' send off the Fed Ex I left?" He walked past the secretary into his office pulling a tie from the slim mahogany armoire flanking the matching desk.

"Yes. The shipment will be in no later than Wednesday."

June appeared in front of him, placing a bottle of water between her legs to free her hands. Swiftly maneuvering the material into a perfect knot, she pulled the silk tie against his neck then sat the bottle on his desk and turned to leave.
"Great," he smiled as she walked out.

On top of being attractive, June was very dependable for her age. Sean was pleased with her thus far and that spoke volumes for June. Sure, having something nice to look at was a plus, but Sean easily got tired of the ditzy girls the agency started sending his way. Half of them were not able to separate business from pleasure and the other half couldn't send an email, let alone prepare an audit. The irritating part was that they had the mindset that batting their eyes would make Sean overlook their shortcomings.

June, on the other hand, was the total package. She not only possessed the looks, but was meticulous and bright. She had great attendance and showed no signs of personal interest in Sean or any of his customers. Though she was a little high strung at times, she had no problems fitting right in at Morgan Contracting.

What Sean liked most of all was the fact that he could trust her. On a number of occasions June would turn her head and remain silent, where as the others he'd employed would snoop around trying to pry their way into his affairs.

"Mr. Jeffers, Ms. Massey on line one," June buzzed.

"Voicemail please, June." Sean had a feeling Camille was going to call, but didn't have time to talk to her right now. Spending all afternoon at the park had put him behind schedule. I'll call her later he thought. I'm sure if it's important, she'll leave me a message.

After sitting in front of his computer for what felt like forever, Sean pushed back from his desk and spun around in his chair. Looking down at his watch he noticed it was almost 7:30 p.m. Sean was so busy he vaguely remembered June poking her head in to say goodnight. Sean pulled his cell phone out of his blazer. Checking his missed call log first, Sean scrolled down highlighting an unfamiliar number and hit send.

"Hello?" A sweet sounding voice picked up.
"Yes, who's tis?"
"Hello, handsome."

"Why do females always play this game?" Sean thought. *"If I said 'who's tis', isn't it obvious I don't know who's calling? They want you ta' recognize the voice and then get mad, if ya' can't. Women!"*

Sean tried to play it safe, "What's up?"
"You don't know who I am?" She actually sounded hurt.

This was a waste of time and Sean was too tired to play the game tonight. He decided to keep quiet. If the girl was dense enough to keep talking, that meant she was desperate and Sean liked them desperate. Those were usually the ones that would give him exactly what he wanted with a third of the hassle.

"Sean," she whined, "this is Lisa."
"Oh, 'ow ya doin' Lisa?"

They met at Dave and Buster's last weekend. Lisa was slim and tight in all the right places. She was all over him at the bar and by the end of the night Sean had her in a hall near the bathroom with his hand down her pants. He knew by the way she creamed all over his fingers she'd soon be calling soon.

"So, you have that many women calling that you don't know my voice?"
"No, not a'tall. Tis' is ya' first time callin'."
"Oh, yeah," she giggled densely. "Anyways, what are

you doing?"

"I'm still at the office. It's just been a long dey."

"Oh, I'm sorry to hear that. Well, I just finished cooking and I'm not doing anything special," she paused. "Are you about to go home?"

"I really do need to eat, I'm starvin'." Sean was pulling her strings. If a woman felt like you wanted to taste her cooking, in her mind she had you. He had no intentions of eating anything Lisa prepared. He was just testing the waters. "What did ya' cook?"

"Oh, I made a little something," she tried to sound nonchalant. "It would be nice to see you."

After getting directions, he straightened his desk and headed out of the door. The plan was to stop by to see Lisa and still make it to Camille's by 9 o'clock at the latest. He knew he was pushing it, but if his game was as tight as he thought it was, there would be no problems. *"I'm just gonna blow off some of tis' built up pressure before I see Camille,"* he thought heading down the connector. As usual he was trying to rationalize his upcoming indiscretion.

Nicole and Camille were so similar spiritually that Sean often wondered if he wasn't trying to recreate his previous relationship. They varied physically, but mentally they were both super sensitive and nurturing. Camille was a great mother and he knew that if they did ever try to take things a step further, she would be good to Morgan. Hell, she was good to him. He told her that he was in no way looking to commit and she took it like it was nothing. He called when he wanted and she asked no questions. She was just happy to see him.

Sean always tried to be as relaxed as possible when dealing with Camille. She liked to play 'hard', but Sean knew she wanted more. Surprisingly, she'd come to mean a lot to him and he knew she was fragile. He could tell she was still mourning the death of her son's father. For some reason she'd still never told him much about what happened except that he'd died. After shutting down once for about three days when he asked her how, Sean decided to let it go.

He loved Camille's spontaneous nature and wanted nothing more than to see her at ease. Though a lot of people would consider her standoffish, to him Camille was one of the most easygoing women Sean had ever met. She was the kind of person that once she felt comfortable with you, she'd show a side of herself rarely seen.

Physically, Camille gave Sean a run for his money. She was what's known as the perfect 'eye candy'. Unlike Nicole, Camille was 'thick' and received a lot of attention when they were out together. Sean loved every bit of it and took pleasure in wrapping his hands around her oversized thighs while onlookers peered on. Her skin was soft like plush carpet and her mouth sweet and warm. She enjoyed all the things Sean liked sexually and never complained about him being unromantic. Camille was fully capable of self-arousal by satisfying him and actually preferred it that way. For the two of them passion was the objective. Camille didn't nag him about trite details in the bedroom.

In the beginning she was hesitant and tried to hold back, but after a couple of months she started jumping all over him every chance she got. He could tell she was into him deep by the intense way her body responded when they made love. He loved being with her because she was so responsive to his every touch. It seemed the more they were together, the more she let go. Now that Sean had her playful side in full bloom, he took pleasure in deflowering her at every given moment.

Sean laughed aloud remembering one of their first adventures. While in the city shopping one weekend, they stopped at Ray's for some pizza. Sean was in the restroom washing his hands when Camille slipped in cunningly for a little risqué behavior. Her sneaky smirk was the last thing he saw before she hit the lights. The next thing he knew his hands were being guided to Camille's topless body while she nibbled on his ear. Her wet tongue flicked circles around his neck as her hands slid down to his waiting zipper. Continuing to massage her soft mounds, Sean leaned back on the cold ceramic sink as he felt cold air hit the tip of his manhood followed immediately by the warm sensation of Camille's mouth. Saliva trickled down his shaft as she pulled vigorously with her dripping lips. The vibrations of her loud moans coupled with the sounds of people outside the thin door drove Sean wild. Unable to hold it any longer he tried to pull out of her mouth, but she held on greedily. Legs jerking in excitement, Sean exploded straight down the back of her throat. Although it was far from the last, Sean never forgot the first time Camille made him lose total control.

Twenty minutes later Sean pulled up to Lisa's complex, rock hard. Life was crazy. There he was fantasizing about Camille and at the same time he was about to try and sleep with a woman he'd only met once.

"You'd tink I'd have learned my lesson," he thought to himself.

Still, he straightened his tie and plastered a smile on his face as he knocked heavily on the door.

Chapter 3
The Meeting

It was a little over three months ago that Sean and Camille met. Rita was finally beginning to spread and Camille had to drag her to the mall for some long overdue maternity wear. Since Hassan's mother was going to midwife her underwater birth, they paid Barnes and Nobles a visit in search for answers to the millions of questions Rita had. After leaving the bookstore, the two spent the rest of the morning in front of the dressing room mirror at Motherhood with Camille trying to convince her that she was pregnant, not fat.

After what seemed like forever, the two finally settled into a table at the far end of the food court. This was their favorite spot because they could see anyone who entered either from the shopping area or from the outside.

Rita plopped down in a chair, opening her wrap sandwich from the Bistro. The strong combination of ranch dressing, jalapeno peppers and vinegar burned Camille's nose.

"I don't see how in the world you're going to eat that."

"Shiiit, this sandwich is on point. You need to go ahead and take a bite."

"Watch. Baby Hassan is going to keep you up all night for feeding him that mess. You know all those spicy foods aren't good for you right now."

As soon as the words left Camille's mouth Rita winced in pain. "Sssss-ahhh," she grabbed her belly, grimacing, sending Camille across the table in alarm.

"What, what is it?"

"Nothing girl. Just a cramp," Rita shooed her away.

"Ree, that was more than a cramp. Quit playing."

"Shiiit!" Another pain shot up her side. "I didn't want to tell you."

"What do you mean? What are you talking about?" Camille rushed to her friend's side.

"See, look at you panicking!" Rita sat back breathing deeply, the pain subsiding. "It's nothing really. I had to have some tests done and I'm supposed to be on bed rest for six weeks."

"What?!" Camille yelled. "What are you doing out, Ree? Why didn't you tell me? I would have never had you walking up and down this mall all day if I knew that."

"Exactly! I don't want you treating me like I'm some sort of invalid. It's bad enough I had to lie to Hassan to get him off of my back about where I was going."

"Well, what's going on? Is the baby ok?"

"I still don't know. They're saying there could be some cell abnormalities and all," she shook her head wearily. "I'm so ready for this pregnancy to be over, you just don't know."

Camille grabbed her friend's hand. "Don't say that. It's gonna be ok."

"Look, I have six more months of this torture and nothing I love to do is 'good for me' anymore. No smoking, no drinking, no Jacuzzi's, no jalapenos. I can't even wear my own clothes. Now, they think I'm gonna sit up in the bed for six weeks! Yeah-right!"

Camille knew Rita never wanted children and had not gotten pregnant on purpose. Hassan, on the other hand wanted plenty. Rita would not have been surprised if she found out he planned the whole thing. She tried not to show her discontent with the whole situation and joked to ease the air around them.

"You lied to me Camille. You told me the only thing I would miss being pregnant was lying on my stomach and taking it from the…"

"Rita, shhh!" Camille interrupted "Somebody might hear you. And, anyway," she whispered "lying on your stomach is how you got pregnant in the first place, remember?"

Laughing, Camille's eyes traveled around the food court of the mall which was unusually busy. There were more people shopping than on any other typical weekday. Summer was at its end and everyone was trying to get a head start on school shopping.

Looking up at Camille, Rita noticed her eyes were fixed on something or someone behind her. She followed her friend's gaze to a man standing at the Mac machine with his back toward them. As soon as she spotted what caught Camille's attention, she sucked her teeth.

"I don't even know why you're bothering to look. It's not like you're gonna say anything to him."

"I just like his hair, Ree," Camille lied. "Why do you have to make such a big deal out of everything? For all I know he's a 'Butta' Face' anyway." Trying to take the spotlight off of herself she joked, "Everything looks good..."

"But, his face!" Rita finished, chuckling.

Their laughter turned to simultaneous gasps of surprise as the head of immaculately tamed, shoulder-length locks turned around. "I'm in love," Camille sighed.

Standing every inch of six foot three and weighing at least two hundred and twenty pounds was the most gorgeous specimen of a man she had ever seen. With a broad nose symbolic of his native land, the island prince noticed the pair staring and grinned humbly, revealing one lone dimple along with a set of stunningly perfect pearly whites. His smile sent a tingle to a place Camille had long forgotten.

He nodded politely to the women and no sooner than Camille dropped her head did Rita motion for him to come over.

"What are you doing?" Camille whispered forcefully.

"That man is fine as hell. Stop trippin'."

"So what?! I don't want him to come over here. I can't believe you're putting me on the spot!"

"I'm trying to get you something to put *on* your spot. That's really what you need in your life," Rita smirked. Camille rolled her eyes hard.

"Afternoon, ladies." His thick West Indian accent made

Camille's knees buckle even though she was already sitting.

"Hello, handsome, I'm Rita," reaching out to shake his hand, "and this is Camille."

"Nice ta' meet ya' Rita." He shook her hand and turned, "Camille."

Trembling, she placed her petite hand into his. The moment they touched, a warm surge shot through Camille's body. Squeezing lightly he bent down bringing his lips to her hand, "Sean. Sean Jeffers."

Rita interjected, "Well Sean, Sean Jeffers, my friend is sort of shy, but she thinks you are beautiful."

Camille glared piercingly. Rita's blunt nature was testing her patience.

"Is that right? Ya' tink I'm beautiful?" Though he was blushing, Sean tried to appear modest. "That is definitely a first."

Camille lowered her eyes. "Please excuse her. She can be somewhat forward. And, all too honest at times."

"No 'arm done. I'm actually flattered." Pointing to the maternity shop bags flooding the floor, he asked, "So, who's expecting?"

Rita sat back to reveal her small round belly. "Due in February."

"Congratulations, darling. What are you praying for?"

Rita tilted her head and thought for a second, "I guess a girl, but as long as it's healthy, that's the most I can ask."

"Yes. I understand," he looked back to Camille, "so are

you two on a lunch break or just out enjoying tis lovely dey?" Finally keeping silent, Rita forced Camille to speak up.

"We're out enjoying the day." Camille said no more. She felt Rita kick her under the table, but acted as if she hadn't gotten the cue to keep going.

After an awkward silence, Sean spoke up, "Well ladies, 'twas certainly a pleasure and I do appreciate the compliment, but I need to be on my'wey." Both Sean and Rita looked to Camille expectantly. Again pretending not to notice, she replied, "It was nice to meet you as well."

"Well, good dey." Sean turned and walked off.

"Bendeho ¿Qué es eso?" Rita snapped. "What the hell was that? The man was obviously waiting for you to give him some play. You didn't even offer him your card."

Camille sat up clearing her throat. "We were in no way discussing business Rita and he didn't ask for my number either. Besides, a man is the last thing on my mind right now."

Rita twisted her lips, "Shit, judging by the size of that vibrator in your drawer, it's the only thing on your mind!"

"Stay out of my shit, Rita!" Camille defended. "I don't even use that thing, while you're so worried about it. Trevor bought that a year ago." She brought her hand to her neck thumbing the charm unconsciously.

Rita sucked her teeth. "I wasn't going through your drawer, number one. I was looking for a pen. And, number two, that's what this is all about anyway. Trevor."

"Here we go!" Camille threw her hands up, "Why does everything have to be about Trevor? Why can't you just accept the fact that I'm not dating right now?"

"Because you haven't 'been dating' since he passed. You

haven't even attempted to give anyone half a chance. It's been over a year Camille. You have to..."

"Go on with my life," Camille sighed. "I know, Ree, I just don't want to feel like I'm betraying him. I miss him so much," Camille's eyes welled up. Rita reached across the table, taking her friend's hand.

"Excuse me," the voice caught both of them off guard. There in front of them, once again, was Sean.

He looked worriedly at Camille who was on the brink of tears, "I'm sorry ta' interrupt. I just couldn't miss out on possibly gettin' ta' know a beautiful woman because of apprehension." Camille's mouth fell open in total shock. Her grief subsided as Sean continued, "So, if ya' don't mind, 'ere is my number. Give me a call and allow me the chance to place a permanent shine 'pon that pretty face," he smiled, "I promise I don't bite."

Chapter 4
Rita

Rita pulled into the driveway circling her two-story brick home. The chandelier in the foyer shone through the tapestry, illuminating the paved cement below. She was surprised to see the white Lincoln parked next to Hassan's hunter green Q45.

"Why didn't he tell me they were going to be here?" She thought pulling in back of her in-laws.

Rita loved Linda. She was truly the mother Rita never had. From the first time she went home with Hassan, they hit it off. Ahmed, on the other hand was another story altogether. Hassan's dad was of Arabic decent and held a way of life too restricting for Rita to accept. She explained to Hassan early in their relationship that she was raised Catholic and worshiping another deity was out of the question. Hassan, who was passive at the time, easily dismissed this issue so it never presented a problem. But, his father made it very clear how he felt about Hassan bringing home an untamed girl.

Ahmed Abdullah was five feet seven inches, two hundred and forty-five pounds of pure intimidation. He was stern, rigid and customary in all his ways of thinking and living. From the very moment she shook Ahmed's hand, the vibe that emanated from him was one of irritation. Rita could tell from the look he gave her that the evening would not go well at all.

She remembered it like it was yesterday. As the young couple removed their snow-dusted parkas in the dimly lit atrium, Ahmed boldly asked her if she was not 'shameful of exposing herself so?'

"I'm sorry?" Rita asked looking down at her navy blazer, cream cashmere sweater, DKNY jeans, and Nine West boots.

The portly man shook his head, clucking his tongue in disapproval as Hassan's mother stepped out from behind him. With a smile as wide as the horizon, Rita saw immediately from whom Hassan got his good looks. Linda Abdullah stood all of five feet nine inches, with caramel brown eyes that mirrored the ones into which Rita spent plenty of nights gazing. Her face, the color of smooth milk chocolate, was warm and accepting. It was hard for Rita to determine her actual frame size because she was in, what Hassan had often referred to as 'three-fourths'. Linda was draped from head-to-toe in a beautiful ocean blue garb with stitches of gold throughout.

She stepped forward lifting her dress slightly. Rita noticed her flat moccasin-like shoes were made of the same enchanting color and design. Linda wore no rings or bracelets; she didn't even have on a pair of earrings. Rita immediately felt the pull of her gold 'bamboos' with her name in one Hassan's in the other. She was glad that she had to take off the chains that kept snagging her collar. Although she was never shameful of her own eccentric nature, Hassan's mother made Rita feel humbled, at best, by her unadorned natural beauty.

"Mi quierda La'Rita. It's so nice to finally meet you. Hassan has told us so much about you." The words touched Rita's coarse heart. Not only did she call her by her birth-given name, but Linda also spoke in Rita's native tongue. Hassan told her of his parents' worldly excursions and mentioned that his mother spoke six languages. But, hearing Linda speak in her dialect swayed Rita not to curse Ahmed out for his condescending attitude.

"Hola senora. ¿Cómo estás?" Rita allowed Linda to embrace her as if they were long time friends. Ahmed huffed walking into the formal living room. Hassan followed while Linda took Rita's hand leading her up a short flight of stairs to the colonial style kitchen.

Linda's home was everything Rita expected from the verbal pictures Hassan painted. The stained marble counters lining the walls were sprinkled with fresh fruits and breads. In the glass covered cabinets, spices galore along with boxes of organic foods Rita had never seen before caught her eye. Two of the four comers held baking racks filled with cookbooks from around the world. The third corner housed an oak rocking chair, perfectly positioned in front of a rectangular window set low on the wall.

Adorning the quaint refrigerator in the fourth corner were photos of Hassan's niece and nephews. Hassan told Rita his older brother, Mansoor, was more like Ahmed than he was. Looking at the pictures, Rita noticed Masoor's wife Noni also wore hijab as did their little girl. The older of the two boys looked a lot like Hassan and Linda. He had a stern look on his face in most of the photos. The younger was obviously the busy one, striking silly poses and crossing his eyes while his twin sister peered on disapprovingly.

"Those babies are my pride and joy. It gives my heart so much joy to see my grandchildren growing. I call my refrigerator my wall of love." Linda smiled walking over to Rita, "Would you like something to drink, dear?"

"Yes, please," Rita stepped back from studying the pictures.

As Linda opened the refrigerator, Rita saw it was packed with more vegetables and gallons of soymilk.

"I see where Hassan gets his healthy diet from," she smiled.

"Yes, well you know we're vegetarians."

"I know," Rita laughed, nodding. "Hassan has turned his nose every time I get a meatball sub from WaWa."

"Dear, your body is your temple after all. It's a gift from Allah. You should honor your body and do your best to keep it pure." Offering Rita a seat, Linda slid a glass of carrot juice in front of her. "It's so hard to find natural foods in the States, with everything being so tainted. Thankfully, I have friends in the East. A lot of our foods are shipped from overseas."

Rita eyed the drink then took a sip hesitantly. She was surprised to find the taste sweet, "This is not bad." Linda laughed at her son's friend. As they sat apart from the men for the remainder of the evening and conversed, Rita and Linda sealed a bond that would last for years.

"As'salamu alaykum, Auntie Ree!" The little hands smacked up against the driver side window jolting Rita out of the daydream.

"Salim. ¿Cómo estás papi?" Her nephew threw his arms around her neck hugging her tightly before Rita could open the door all the way.

"Whoa, Salim. Be careful of the baby," Hassan huffed walking over toward the car.

As Rita looked up at her husband, immediate worry fell over her. "What's wrong?" Hassan raised his hand to silence her.

"Salim, go get your brother and you two take these groceries into the house."

Once the little one was out of ear range, Hassan turned to Rita and began helping her out of the car. "It's dad. He's in the hospital. They think he suffered a mild heart attack."

Rita gasped in shock. "Oh my goodness!" Tears welled up in her eyes, falling rapidly down her cheeks. Hassan wrapped his arms around her and stroked her back.

"He's going to be fine, Ree. The doctor said he's stable. They just want to keep him for observation and run more tests." He pulled back, looking at his wife. Even with puffy eyes and a red nose, she was still the most beautiful woman he'd ever seen. He prayed at that very moment that they too would be blessed enough to experience over forty years of marriage.

"What hospital is he in?"

"He's at Virtua. Mansoor and Noni are still there and

Mom is in the house with the kids." Rita dried her eyes just in time for Salim to come running back down the driveway with his older brother, Elijah, trailing reluctantly.

After watching them unload the trunk, Rita followed the boys into the kitchen where Linda was standing over the sink with her granddaughter at her side.

"As'salamu alaykum, Auntie Ree." Rukayah walked up hugging Rita around the knees. "How's my cousin feeling today?" Placing her small palm on Rita's full belly she pressed her ear to her navel as if she expected an answer from inside.

"Wa' alaykum salaam. She's fine, Rukayah." It amazed Rita that Rukayah and Salim were twins, yet so different. Rukayah was reserved and far ahead of her six years while Salim was 'all boy' in nature.

"What makes you so sure it's a girl?" As Linda turned around, her worn face told it all. Rita could tell she'd stayed up half of the night. The pain in her eyes made Rita want to cry all over again, but she kept her composure, forcing a smile.

"For Hassan's sake it better be a boy." Rita kissed her mother-in-law on the cheek. "As'salamu alaykum, Ma, how are you?" It had taken no time for Rita to start calling Linda 'Mom'. They bonded as if she were actually Linda's child. Seeing her hurt sent a twinge of guilt through Rita's heart. She secretly wished Ahmed was in the family room lecturing Hassan and couldn't help feeling bad for not wanting to see him earlier.

"Wa' alaykum salaam. Alhamdu lillah. I'm just getting these babies something to eat. They've been at the hospital all day."

"Ma, you should be resting." Rita moved to her side. "Let me finish that for you. Rukayah, go upstairs with Geema and turn the bed down for her. Ma, I'll make you some tea and have Hassan bring it up."

"Jazakallah kheir. I knew from the day I met you that you were a good woman," she patted Rita softly on the cheek. "I knew you would be a blessing to my son." Linda headed toward the staircase with Rukayah following quietly.

Rita walked into the den where the boys were playing X-Box with Hassan.

"Baby, take this upstairs to Ma for me."

All three of them looked up simultaneously.

"I was talking to your uncle," Rita laughed. "But, if you guys want something to do, you can always come in the kitchen and help peel these potatoes."

"Kitchen?"

Elijah looked disgustedly.

"That's a woman's place, not a man's." He turned back to the television without a second thought.

"Who told you that?"

Rita knew very well where it came from, but wanted to hear what the twelve-year-old had to say. Without looking up, he replied smugly, "My dad, he says…"

"E, I'm sure we know what your daddy has told you." Hassan quickly interjected.

"Ree was just poking fun at you guys. Go ahead and keep playing. I'm going to take Geema this tea. Don't cheat and try to re-set the game." He looked at Salim, who fell on his side bursting into giggles.

As she walked out of the den, she prayed Hassan would talk to Elijah and help him realize that not all of the things

43

Mansoor tells him are right. She wondered what it was about the first-borns in that family. They were always uptight and rigid. Now, for her sake, she prayed the baby she was carrying was a girl.

Hassan came up behind Rita, rubbing her belly that now blocked more than the view of her feet. Rita's face was serious.

"Regardless of what goes on at their house, Elijah will respect me here," she scorned Hassan

"E's not disrespectful, Rita. You know this. He looks at you the same way he does his mother, Rukayah and Ma. He expects a woman to fulfill her role." As soon as he said it, Hassan immediately regretted his last statement.

"What in the hell do you mean 'my role'?" She hissed. "Oh, so I suppose you think I belong in the kitchen as well? What, you want me bare foot and pregnant?"

"That's not what I meant, Ree. I'm sorry…look, why are we arguing about Elijah? We're about to have eighteen plus years of fussing over our own. What did the doctor say?"

"He said he still wants to run some more tests. But, everything looks fine." Rita couldn't bring herself to tell him. Not now, not today, not like this.

"Did he take you off of bed rest?" Rita lied, "Yeah, but he said I should still take it easy until my next appointment."

"Well, we just have to keep making due, that's all."
She tried to change the subject. "You'd better pray that when my daughter gets here they don't make her feel like the oddball."

"What are you talking about?"

"She's not gonna be running around here like Rukayah,

with her head all covered up. She's gonna wear barrettes and ballies and bows like little girls are supposed to."

Hassan laughed, walking back toward the den. Rita hated being tense when Linda was over. But, her day had already been spoiled even before she came home. The truth was her doctor told her the pregnancy was extremely high risk. The baby had a small hole in its heart and if she made it to term, they would have to perform surgery immediately following the delivery. Rita felt guilty for not wanting the baby at first and she knew she was being punished. She had been instructed to stay off her feet until she reached thirty-six weeks and had not done so.

It was like she was the host of a fight between self and her maternal instincts. Hell, half the time she felt like she had no motherly instinct. After all, her own mother abandoned her and sought after the streets shortly after Rita was born.

Rita always feared what would happen to her if she ever had a child of her own. She often wondered what mother went through after she had her. Growing up, Rita comforted the pain of her mother's absence by getting high. On top of that she downplayed getting high by saying that other than the occasional joint here-and-there, the most she'd do was pop a couple of 'trips' and that was no biggie. It wasn't like she smoked crack like her parents and so many others she'd seen. Rita always wondered if getting pregnant sent her mom over the edge. Secretly she feared it would do the same to her.

Wishing she could pour herself a shot of Patron or spark a doobie to calm her nerves, Rita headed back into her kitchen. "I guess grape juice will have to do." She looked around cautiously to make sure no one saw as she slid the pink pill under her tongue and sighed.

Chapter 5
Hassan

Hassan sat alongside the hospital bed sobbing quietly as he stared at his father. Doctor Nakir assured him all of Ahmed's vital signs were stable and he was sure to have a speedy recovery. But, Hassan was having a hard time convincing himself everything would be fine. His mind wandered to the last conversation he had with his father, just three days ago, concerning Rita.

Hassan granted her as much liberty as possible when they first met. He understood Rita was raised in a totally different world and he didn't force her to comply with a lot of things his religion required. Truth-be-told, he himself didn't always agree with everything. But, even after they got married, Rita still kept her ways. She didn't cover her head; she still wore makeup, smoked and drank like a fish. Hassan rarely said much. She used to pop pills, but when they got serious, he made her agree to stop. So, at least he didn't have to worry about that anymore. Every now and then if an issue came up that really bothered him, he would tell Linda. She had a way of addressing Rita subtly that

47

worked like a charm. Because his mother and Rita were so tight, she took heed to mostly everything Linda said.

Still, within the past few months, Hassan found himself developing a different outlook on life. He wasn't sure if it was because he was getting older or because of the baby, but his heart was slowly changing.

He'd stopped to see Ahmed on his way home from work that night. He needed his father's counsel.

"Dad, I know while I was growing up I gave you a lot of grief on things, but I'm starting to wish I hadn't."

As usual, Ahmed didn't respond. He had a way of saying '*I told you so*' without opening his mouth.

He merely sat back knitting his pudgy fingertips through his beard. Hassan continued, "I don't know what to do about my wife. Don't get me wrong, I love her. I just wish she was more… disciplined. Especially now that she's carrying my child." A part of Hassan felt bad saying these things. But, it was weighing on him. Now that they were going to be parents, his child was going to be raised Muslim.

"Hassan, you are the man. She is the woman. You know your deen. You have known since birth. Your wife, sadly, has not been taught hers. It was your responsibility to guide her. But, you chose not to do so. As a result, your work will now be twice as hard. You must set your expectations immediately and make no exceptions. You must take control of your home, your marriage and your wife. Teach her with love, but do not use force to instill the truths. Otherwise, she may submit out of fear of you and not out of love for Allah."

Hassan shook his head, "You make it sound so easy, dad. But, Rita is nothing like mom. She has a temper like you wouldn't believe. And, she's stubborn," he sighed throwing both arms over the back of the loveseat.

"Son, I know more than you think I do. Your mother was no angel."

"What do you mean?" Hassan leaned forward with curiosity. "You telling me you had problems with mom?"

"Your mother was similar to Rita when I met her. It took a lot of patience. She was so stuck on her 'independence'; there were plenty of days I wondered if I was not 'beating a dead horse'. But, when you make the decision to marry a woman who isn't Muslim, this is what you are faced with. My father explained that to me in a conversation he and I had once, kind of like this one." Ahmed crossed his legs at the knee and piqued a smirk. "See, I was engaged to a girl whose father was close to my family for many years. I was to marry this girl on her twentieth birthday, but Allah had it that I was to meet your mother eight months before."

Ahmed's dark eyes seemed to lighten as he stared up at the ceiling recalling the past. "I was in Cambodia on business. The group I was with decided to go down to the marketplace to shop. There were people everywhere. I stopped at a stand that was selling beautiful hand woven rugs; your mother was standing next to me looking at jewelry. I noticed her glancing over, but I paid her little attention. Within no time, she stuck her hand out to shake mine and stared me straight in the eye. I was so shocked by her audacity, it left me speechless. She was wearing a green tank top with a brown skirt, full of laces and frills, and it seemed she had holes everywhere on her face." Ahmed chuckled softly. "Her nose was pierced and in each ear she had at least five sets of earrings. On both wrists, bracelets- up to her elbow- all of them gold." He waived his hand frivolously in the air. "On her leg she wore a charm filled anklet that jingled with every step. Her hair held no grey at all. It was pulled into a single brownish-red braid that fell to the middle of her back. But, it was her eyes that struck me." Hassan smiled assuredly as his father continued, "Although she was obviously worldly, her eyes were those of a queen. I had never seen anyone so captivating in my life." Hassan's imagination danced trying to picture his parents young and in love.

"We walked together that day. Talking until the sunset. She told me she would be back in the states in two months and demanded my contact information. She vowed that I would hear from her in America. Once I was back in the States, I thought a lot of our meeting, but nothing of her promise, until I found myself face-to-face with her again. She kept her word and located me a week after her return. The more time I spent with her the more I fell in love. I knew soon that I had to tell my father I wanted to marry Linda instead of Endola."

Ahmed tried to hide his grin. "He was livid. At first he told me there was no way I was going to marry your mother. In less than six months, I would wed Endola and his word was final! After listening to me pour my heart out, he finally agreed that once Endola and I were married for a year, I could take your mother as my second wife. But, there was no way to justify that to neither Linda nor my heart."

"Mom would never have it," Hassan interjected.

"You're right. She wouldn't have had it back then. Today, she would accept my decision without question. That comes from her deen and maturity. Maturity in self and in righteousness. I made it clear what I was looking for in my wife and she graciously adhered. As she opened her heart to let Allah in, we became one. See, even though your mother was this outgoing, headstrong, temperamental girl, her spirit was one chosen by Allah to be guided to the straight path. Once my father met your mother, he saw she was the opposite of everything he'd expected. It was then that he accepted my decision."

"That, my son, is what both frustrates and impresses me about you. You have a strong will yourself and I admire that you stand firm on your determination. However, in certain things you tend to be lackadaisical, until your back is up against the wall. I would have never presented anyone to my father of which he disapproved, until I was sure there were no flaws that he could point out. You, on the other hand, go against my will and then flaunt your disobedience."

Hassan lowered his head. His father's words, although harsh, were true.

Spending the day at Ahmed's bedside gave him a lot of time to reflect. He began to see many of the things Ahmed instilled in him coming to pass. Before talking to his father, he was at a loss as how to deal with Rita. Ahmed made him feel somewhat better. After all, he was sure of his love for Rita and sure she loved him just as much.

As he lay in the bed later that night, Hassan popped up with the sudden urge to pray. All day he'd been overwhelmed by the feeling he'd felt. Hassan knew it was Allah talking to his heart.

Hassan moved silently into the guest bedroom, assuming the prostrate position. Moments later he felt her presence, but did not acknowledge Rita standing in the doorway.

When he went back to their bedroom, she was in bed facing the window, as if asleep. "What's on your mind, Ree?" He asked, certain she was awake.

"Nothing. I've just never seen you do that before, unless your Dad was here."

"Well, you know prayer is better than sleep..."

Rita flipped over smiling, but immediately stopped when she saw the seriousness in Hassan's face. "You're not joking, are you?"

"No, Rita, I'm not. We need to talk. Rather, you need to listen."

Hassan's words surprised even him. He didn't know where this burst of testosterone was coming from, but for the first time in their relationship he had something to say and didn't bother to get an approval from Rita.

"I am a Muslim. You are my wife. You are carrying my first child and when he or she enters this world, there will be many evils plotting against his or her soul. Evils sent by the enemy to seek and destroy. It's up to us to prepare him or her for life. We can't do that if our lives are not in order. We can't do that if *we* have no unity."

Rita opened her mouth to speak, but Hassan raised his hand placing his fingers on her lips. "Listen," he repeated, "I know when we met you were you and I was me. I know we come from two totally opposite ends of the spectrum when it comes to upbringing, but that's no longer the case. I'm not using that as an excuse either. I've decided to completely dedicate my life to my deen one hundred percent. I love you with all I have in me to love. I always have and I always will. That is why this is so important to me. Our existence, our eternity and our child's life depends on what we do from this day forward. Every second from here on out counts, regardless of what we did in the past. No matter how hard we may want to, there is no way to change things that have already been done. Our only option is to move forward. I haven't had a chance to talk to mom about this, with everything going on with dad and all, but as soon as things get settled, I want you to talk to her and she can answer a lot of questions you have about Islam. You can also talk to Noni. You may not believe me, but she is very down to earth and easy to get along with, once you get to know who she really is."

Rita looked both annoyed and confused at the same time. She was in no way trying to get to know Noni any more than necessary. To her, Noni was weak and submissive with Mansoor governing her every move. Rita was too strong a person to let Hassan run her life. And, where did all of this come from out of the blue? It was like Hassan woke up today and decided to change her life for her. Without her input, permission or even finding out if she wanted to change in the first place.

As if he could feel the fury radiating from her pores, Hassan reached over to hug his wife. She pulled away turning over and burying her face in the cover. The bull in her began to emerge. Rita felt her temperature rising, her mind raced with feelings of treachery. Hassan scooted up to wrap his wife in his arms. At first Rita resisted, but as he began kissing softly the tender area on the back of her neck, she slowly gave way. Rubbing her thighs together she relaxed letting her husband caress her. Hassan knew just where to touch, making Rita more and more excited with each stroke of her skin. She turned to face him as he kissed her tasting salt from the tears on her cheeks. Pulling back Hassan stared deep into her sea green eyes whispering, "Baby, I love you."

That was all it took. The mesmerizing sound of his voice sent chills up her vertebrae. Goose bumps ran up and down her arms. She reached out pulling his warm body close. Hassan rolled over on his back guiding his wife gently into a straddle atop him. Looking up at her belly in the shadows of night, he placed both hands on her stomach, trailing his palms slowly down her inner thighs. With his thumbs Hassan pressed lightly on the moist cotton panty covering her heat.

Rita moaned softly as she grinded, tantalized by his erection beneath her. His large hands slowly maneuvered up her sides finding her full warm breasts with nipples extended in excitement. She rolled her head back in intoxication. He placed his fingers on her erect nipples, manipulating her curvaceous soft figure. Rita arched her back in pleasure as he lifted her nightgown and the rush of cold air blew over her skin like a breeze off of the water's edge.

Hassan placed his lips on her breasts, feeling the heat of her exude. Her scent made its way to his nose making it almost impossible for him to maintain his composure. Knowing what sweet moist treasure lay inside her made the anticipation unbearable. Rita smiled down at him while lifting up slightly, guiding herself onto his waiting ecstasy. Her moan of fulfillment was followed by a gush of release as she climaxed immediately. Hassan paced himself and continued to passionately make love to his wife.

Thirty minutes later Hassan lay snoring heavily under the light of the moon that crept between the cracks of the blinds. Rita eased out of bed, tip-toeing down two flights of carpeted steps to the fully furnished basement. Turning on the four-foot lava lamp, she sank heavily into the cushions of the sofa; the blank TV in front of her glowing from the peach reflection.

Rita sat back, listening to the sounds of the house as it settled, wishing she could do the same for her mind. *"What the hell is going on?"* She thought. *"It seemed like months ago my life was perfect. Now, I'm pregnant and my husband is turning into his jackass of a father. I swear I need a joint."* She looked over at the empty ashtray on the coffee table. The night Rita told him her period was late, Hassan had raided the basement throwing out every ounce of weed she had stashed away. *"This shit is ridiculous."*

Suddenly, Rita felt the urge to call Camille. She picked up the cell phone, glancing at the clock on the wall. *"12:46... I know she's up. Sean's been on some bullshit, too. Camille's like me... can't sleep when she's stressed."*

The phone rang through until the recording hit. Rita sucked her teeth in disappointment, disconnecting the line. She reached for the oak cigar box and pulled out the blue and white NagChampa packet. Lighting the end of the incense, she watched the smoke twirl lazily around her eyes.

Rita sifted through the box picking up a stack of pictures. Thumbing through the flicks, she processed each image. The memories from various times in her life seemed to make her more and more depressed.

Below the snapshots at the bottom of the cigar box, a bottle of pills rolled from the side, coming into view. She tried to act like she didn't notice them, but within seconds, she heard it whispering her name.

Rita threw the box on the table and pulled her legs up. Wrapping the blanket tight around her shoulders, she turned her back to the voices.

Like a Ping-Pong ball, her thoughts began to bounce back-and-forth. "*12:55... I gotta go sleep... I just need one... just to help relax... I'm sure it won't hurt anything... If I wasn't pregnant, I wouldn't be going through this shit in the first place.*" The longer her mind battled her flesh, the more she craved the grit of the capsule dissolving between her teeth. She ached to feel the weight of her eyes under the effects of the medication. The voices became louder, '*Go ahead... taste it...*' Eager murmurs now echoed around her like bat wings flapping in the dark.

She grabbed the bottle frantically tossing a capsule onto

her waiting tongue. Pushing tightly against the roof of her mouth, Rita seeped helplessly into satisfaction like water soaking into fresh soil. Within minutes, the lethargy consumed her sending her off into a deep tranquil sleep.

Rita was totally out of it when Hassan came downstairs. She didn't feel the brush of his hand against her brow as he pushed the fallen hairs from her damp cheeks. Noticing something tucked under her left arm Hassan pulled the box out from under her.

He placed it naively on the table before turning the light off and returning to his room. He never had any idea of what secretly lulled his wife to sleep and never once thought to look inside the clasped container held tightly in her sweaty palm.

Chapter 6
Camille

"I'm sorry, Ms. Massey, Mr. Jeffers is not available. Would you like his voicemail?" Camille hung up with no response. *"Not available? What the hell does she mean not available? I just spoke to him a few hours ago and I told him I would call him back. I swear that man gets on my last nerve."*

Later that evening as she ate dinner, Camille ignored the tune of Marvin Gaye's *Sexual Healing* repeatedly ringing her phone.

About an hour later, she stood at the kitchen sink finishing up the last set of cups. The sound of rumbling across the rocks in her driveway came just seconds before Jelani ran out of the den heading straight for the bay windows in the living room. Pulling back the curtain he yelled, "Mommie, Sean here!"

"How dare he pop up at my house unannounced? What if I had company? I wish I had company!"

Camille flung open the front door, fuming with mixed emotion. Sean strolled into the well-lit living room all smiles, bearing gifts. "'Ey, man," he bent down handing Jelani a Toys'R'Us bag.

"Thank you," Jelani skipped down the hall to the den to inspect his surprise in privacy.

"What are you doing here?" Camille demanded wiping water from her hands with a dishtowel.

"It's nice ta' see you, too," Sean leaned in to kiss Camille who turned her head coldly.

"What's the problem?" He looked at her puzzled by her reaction.

Throwing her hand on her waist, "I thought you weren't available."

Sean was dumfounded for a second, then, "Oh, so that's what ya're upset far, huh? Darling, I had a busy dey-that tis all. I told June to 'old all of my calls. Why didn't'cha leave a message?"

Camille was not hearing it. She was tired of being put on the back burner and sick of being placed on hold for the rest of Sean's life while he acted like her world revolved around him. She stood there refusing to move, hands planted firmly on her full hips. Her long legs glistened in a pair of grey, high cut track shorts. Sean could feel himself getting turned on as his eyes traveled up her bare stomach to the black sports bra that hugged her chest.

He tried handing her the African violet. "I 'ave something for you." Although the flower was beautiful, Camille refused to budge. Pulling the dishtowel from her shoulder, she turned. "No thank you, Sean. I'm busy right now and I don't have time to entertain guests."

Her words sent Sean's ego crashing to the ground. "Oh, so now I'm a guest, huh?" His warm eyes turned to ice.

"Y-y-yes," Camille stuttered seeing the frost creep up in his pupils. "You don't live here so… you're a guest and I'm in no mood for company." She shrugged her shoulders trying to hide her nervousness.

"Company?" He repeated. "Does all of yar' company 'ave a toothbrush, washcloth and cologne in yar' bathroom? Does all of yar' company sleep in yar' bed for deys at a time? Does all of yar' company 'ave a drawer in yar' armoire?" Sean whispered angrily, so as not to alert Jelani.

Watching the wrinkles in his forehead deepen, Camille knew she crossed the line. She could see there was no turning back; she'd gone too far. Sean shoved the potted plant into her folded arms, spilling traces of soil on the floor. Without looking back, he stomped back through the foyer and out the front door.

Gunning the ignition, Sean sped out of the driveway, rocks popping up from beneath the whirling tires in a million different directions. Camille stood regretfully watching, door ajar with tears running down her cheeks.

That was the last time they spoke. And to Camille it seemed like the last time she'd gotten a night's sleep. Unable to bear the pain, she walked around in a haze all the following week. In the mornings, she was like a mummy leaving the house. Depression clouded her mind, making the days seem three times longer than they actually were. By the time she got home in the evenings, it was all she could do to feed Jelani before retreating to her bedroom with her Unisom tabs and bottle of Cab Sav to wash them down.

Today the November air flushed Camille's face as she sat for a moment in her deep windowsill with the sun streaming through the blinds. Camille walked down the hall into Jelani's bedroom reflecting on the past seven days. The glare of the Saturday morning light made her wince as she viewed the damage he'd done while she was out of it all week.

"Jelani!" Camille called out. "Come clean your room."

"Mommie, it's cold." Her tyke dragged into the doorway wrapped in a Spider-Man comforter. She pulled the wood trimmed paned glass window shut locking the latch. "Now, who told you to open this? Good morning, Jelani."

"Good-morning. Are you gonna help me clean my room?"

"No. I didn't pull all of these toys out. You did. So, you are going to have to put them away on your own. Besides, I have to get started on the rest of the house. This place looks a mess."

"I know Mommie, but you didn't wanna wake up. Member?"

"Yes, Jelani I *re*member, but Mommie feels all better today. I'm gonna scrub this place from top to bottom. Then I'm gonna make us something good to eat." She pulled lovingly on her son's earlobe on her way out the room.

"Well, can I help you?"

"First, clean up this room and then we'll see."

Camille bounded downstairs, heading straight for her

stereo. Selecting disc twenty, she hit play as she rounded the corner out of the den. She strolled into the living room, adjacent to the kitchen and opened all of the curtains, cracking slightly each window. *Reasonable Doubt* blasting out of her Bose sound system seemed to make the sun shine even brighter. It was just what she needed to get her mind right.

On her way to the other side of the house, something caught the corner of her eye. Bending down Camille carefully picked up the small trail of soil still left on her snow-white rug. She rubbed the dirt between her fingers and then blew on her hand. The residue scattered under the weight of her breath. At the same time Camille made a promise to herself. *"I'm cleaning my house...my mind...and my heart... I swear I'm getting rid of all the bullshit I got lingering around here."*

Camille was an hour into her housework when Jelani came running into the laundry room with the cordless phone.

"Mommie, mommie, gramma' on the jack," he bounced up and down in excitement.

"Grandma's on the *phone*," Camille corrected, laughing at her son. "Hey, Ma," she lowered the volume on her remote.

Her mother's nagging voice echoed through the receiver.

"Why is my grandson referring to the telephone as a 'jack'?"

"Ma, why are you always so serious? You know Jelani thinks he's a 'little Trevor'. He's just coming into his personality, testing his boundaries. That's all."

"Well, if he knew what I knew he would want to be as little like Trevor as possible."

The comment struck Camille in the heart. As usual, her mother succeeded in bringing pain to what little bit of peace she was able to grasp.

"Ma, I'm in the middle of cleaning, did you need something?"

"I've been calling you all week. Your voicemail keeps picking up on the first ring when I call your cell phone, and your home answering machine says the mailbox is full. What's going on? Do I need to come out there?" Carole was in rare form today.

"No, Ma, we're fine." Camille knew her mother had already given Jelani the third degree and was in no mood for an interrogation. Today was her day to regroup. "I'll call you back." Camille hung up abruptly. As soon as she sat the phone on the charger, it rang again.

"Ma, I told you..."

He broke in before she could finish. "No, Camille, it's Hassan. I'm sorry to call so early, but..." Hassan hesitated for a moment, "Have you talked to Ree?" The worry in his voice sent Camille's heart into marathon mode.

"No why, what's wrong? Where is she?"

"I don't know. When I woke up this morning she wasn't in bed, so I assumed she was in the basement. She was down there last night when I dozed off and she'd been falling asleep down there lately. I figured she did it again, so I didn't think anything of it and just left for my run. But, when I got back she was still not upstairs. I went downstairs to check on her..."

Hassan rambled on while Camille's mind raced trying to piece together what he was saying. "...car isn't in the driveway and she left her phone on the counter."

"Hassan, calm down. I'm sure she's ok." Camille tried to comfort him while silently praying. She instantly felt guilty for not holding a real conversation with her friend all week. What type of 'sister' was she? She was so caught up in her own problems she managed to totally ignore Rita. "Hassan, let me call you right back."

Camille picked up her cell phone, which had been powered off since last Friday night. Twelve new messages were in her mailbox. Camille skipped over each message until the recording identified Rita's number as the sender:

"Camille, I don't know what's wrong with your ass, but you need to call me. I have to talk to you. Hassan is trippin' about this shit. He's acting like his damn dad, all of a sudden talking about devoting our lives to Allah. I don't know. I love him and all, but damn. Look you need to holler at me. Fuck Sean! I know he's the reason you been trippin' this week. Now you turn your phone off. You need to get your mind right! Call me back!"

Camille skipped over two more messages:

"Trick, I'm not your man and I'm not gonna keep calling you like I am! I've been doin' some thinking and I can't live my life as some slave, I don't care if I am having his baby. I'm not beat. But, you need to hit me 'cause I'm going to get a room in A.C. tomorrow night. I want you to go with me. We need some 'us' time to just get away, seriously."

Camille dialed 411 on her house phone. "Verbal business listing, please."

When the operator came on, "Atlantic City, New Jersey,

Trump Plaza."

"Miss, I show multiple listings. Would you like the main number?"

"No, front desk please."

"Here you are Ma'am...please hold for your listing."

"Thank you," Camille clicked over and dialed the hotel as soon as the recording ended.

"Yes, La'Rita Abdullah. I'm not sure the suite number."

The clerk placed her on hold, then promptly returned, "I'm sorry, I show no listing for Abdullah, La'Rita."

She thought for a quick second, "Try La'Rita Vasquez." Another moment and the clerk returned, "Yes, room 8818. I'll transfer you now."

After a short pause, Rita picked up as if she knew Camille was on the other end. "It's about time your miserable ass called me. It's a good thing I wasn't going into labor."

"You're not due for another fourteen weeks."

"Well," Rita sucked her teeth "haven't you ever heard of premature labor?"

"Look, what are you doing? Don't you know Hassan is going crazy looking for you? He called me about twenty minutes ago frantic as hell."

"Well, that's what he gets. Thinking he can tell me how to live my life. Camille he got me twisted. I'm not the one. He better go find him some young girl to have his kids if he thinks I'm gonna walk around all wrapped up all hot and shit."

"What are you talking about, Ree?"

"I'm talking about your brother-in-law trippin'!" Last week he came home like his name was Mahatma Gandhi."

Camille laughed, "Gandhi is Hindu."

65

"Don't mince words with me, bitch. You know what I mean. He started talking all this bullshit. Talking about, I need to get with Noni so she can show me the 'proper way' to live. Who in the hell does he think she is? Who in the hell does he think *he* is?!?!"

"Ree, I know you're pissed, but listen to yourself. You're almost eight months pregnant. You need to be easy. You've got to remember Hassan is going through some life changes right now. You're about to deliver any day plus his dad just had a heart attack. His birthday is coming up, right? He's gonna be what, thirty this year?"

"Thirty-two."

"Damn! See, he's having a pre-mid-life crisis. Don't divorce the man, support him. You 'ought to be happy he's not out tryna' buy a Aston Martin and chasing after some 'young girl'."

"Yeah, that's easy for you to say. Your man ain't tryna' have you walk around like a nun." Camille had to laugh at her friend.

"I'm serious, why are you laughing? I'm already hot as hell in the middle of winter, carrying this heavy ass belly. Can you imagine me in garb?"

"Ree, call your husband." Camille tried to be serious.

"Nope. I'ma let him sweat. He needs to know how it feels to be hot for a change. Besides, I have a massage scheduled later. I know him. He's gonna try to make his way out here and I don't want to see him. Anyway, this was supposed to be *our* weekend get-away."

"Ok, fine. Well I'm going to call him to let him know

you're okay."

"Camille, don't you tell him where I am! If you do, I'll leave. I swear!"

"Okay! Damn, I won't. I'll be there as soon as I can," Camille promised.

Camille called Hassan immediately. "Did you find her?"

"Yes, she's fine. The baby is fine. She said she just needed some time to herself."

"Well, why didn't she call me? Where is she?"

"Listen, I promised her I wasn't gettin' in the middle of this or telling you where she is. But I *am* going to spend the rest of the weekend with her. Don't worry, she'll be fine."

"Ok." Camille could hear the disappointment in his voice.

"Why don't you bring Jelani over here? I'll go pick up my nephews. They can keep me company until the two of you get back."

"Alright, great." Although it was on the way to A.C., Camille definitely didn't feel like stopping in Camden to drop Jelani off with her mother. Hassan was a lifesaver.

"I'll be to you by eleven."

Hassan was waiting in the driveway when Camille pulled up. His reddened eyes told the tale of his worry. He opened the passenger door to let Jelani out and slid in.

"Can you give her this, please?" Hassan held out a long slender box Camille was certain contained jewelry.

"Hassan, I gave my word to stay out of this," she shook her head.

"I know. I just want her to have it," shrugging his

shoulders.

"How about, you hold on to it until Sunday and when she comes home so you can give it to her. I'm sure she'll receive it much better then." Hassan hung his head, sighing heavily in agreement as he got out of the truck.

The ride to the shore took exactly fifty-five minutes; all of which Camille spent thinking about the fun she was about to have over the next twenty-four hours. She convinced herself that this was just what she needed to rid her space of Sean's cloud looming over her.

When she turned on to Mississippi Avenue, the season showed itself. The blocks normally crowded with tourists and churchgoers were nearly vacant. *"Only Rita would come to the shore in the middle of winter,"* she thought, *"and only I would follow her."* Laughing, she pulled up to the hotel's valet handing her keys to the attendant.

As she got out, Camille's short hair whipped along the sides of her face. The brutal air cut icily around the corners of the Casino buildings. She could still smell the mixture of salt water through the cold.

Camille hoped Rita had ordered room service. With all the maylay this morning, she hadn't eaten a thing. By the time she reached the suite, her empty stomach was rumbling.

"Who?" Rita joked from behind the hotel room door.
"Open the door girl. I hope you have something good to

eat 'cause I'm hungry as...," Camille's hunger vanished as the extravagant view struck her, "...hell-lo...." Camille finished in awe. "Wow, this is nice as hell!" She squealed, stepping into the threshold.

The suite was laid. In the living room was a sixty-two inch flat screen HDTV, mounted perfectly between a six-foot glass mantelpiece and a seven tier spherical DVD case, complete with a generous collection. Adjacent to the entertainment center were wall-length windows with dual sea spray stained glass doors lead out to the patio. Dead center in the room, the fully stocked round bar with four, thirty-two inch chrome stools surrounded the marble counter. To the left was what Camille assumed was the master bedroom and to the right was a post-modern mahogany kitchen complete with stainless steel appliances. The refrigerator, wine cooler and freezer were stacked modishly atop each other in a diamond display. The dark red granite counter top partitioned off the area from the rest of the living room, which held a full cream-white leather sectional and sand-stained coffee table atop wall-to-wall three inch plush scarlet carpet.

Behind the sofa, two bamboo massage tables were set up, equipped with two of the most beautiful black men Camille had ever seen. Their chiseled bodies gleamed in the noon sun that, in the winter sky, shone deceivingly through the elongated panes of glass.

Camille looked puckishly at Rita. "Damn, what is this," pointing to the men, "entertainment?"

Rita stepped back to get a good look at her usually stiff counterpart. "Why you so loose today? You been drinking?"

Camille blushed "Nah, I'm just ready to forget PA altogether and get my mind right. So, what's up, are you gonna introduce me?"

Throwing her hands up, she motioned toward the two studs who were nude except for their white linen pants. "Well, this is Drake and this is Thaddeus." Rita placed her palm on Drake's rock hard pecks. "They're physiatrists," she rubbed, "here to help relieve your mind."

Camille tilted her head, twirling a strand of hair jokingly. "Um, don't they know it's November?"

"Ya'll cold?" Rita asked, wobbling up to the massage table. The two smiled, but remained silent. Camille bit her lip in temptation before heading into the bedroom to undress.

"You better hurry up, Camille, before I start without you," Rita called from the living room. "It would be nice to have both of them to myself."

Chapter 7

Sean

It was almost 2 o'clock in the afternoon before Sean rolled out of bed. He could hear the stereo in the living room from where he left it on last night. *Last night. Damn. Tell me I didn't, please.* Sean sat up to the pounding feeling of a football game being played inside his head. Thankfully all the curtains in the room were drawn and with three of the four walls painted pitch black it was not only cool, but dark.

Moaning, he walked toward the bathroom with head in one hand, jock in the other. Paying no attention to the pink panties and matching bra beneath his feet, he stumbled into his walkthrough closet. It wasn't until he reached the doorway on the other end that he realized his hunch was right.

Behind the glass shower door was his late night excursion. All one hundred and twenty-five pounds of it. Sean turned to the deep grey countertop. The gleam of two empty Magnum wrappers caught his eye. In that instant his fear solidified and the pounding in his head doubled.

71

As if she belonged there, the girl peeked out from the fully steaming shower, "Hey babe," she called innocently.

"What?" Sean stuttered rubbing the bridge of his nose with his index finger and thumb. "Why are ya still 'ere?"

The girl turned off the water and stepped out. Already erect, Sean's penis jumped at the sight of her cherry colored titties and dark pink nipples. His eyes followed the water trail dripping down her tiny waist, bare pussy and slender thighs. It fell in a small puddle around two pale feet.

With a confused look, she began rambling. "Well, you were 'sleep and, like, I didn't want to just leave without, like, saying goodbye."

Sean turned around without saying a word, leaving her standing there along with the irritating drone of her voice. This was the last thing he needed right now. He could've kicked himself for bringing her to his house. But the combination of the Remy Martin and frustration made him throw all his common sense out the window.

Sean walked into his kitchen, trying to remember the events that led to his screw up, but hell, he couldn't even remember her name, let alone what happened. After turning on the cappuccino machine, he sat at the dining room table rocking his head back-and-forth on the cool marble. The chill soaked away the pain and flashbacks started popping into his head.

"Oh, 'ell no!" Sean jetted back into the bedroom. His eyes searched frantically in the shadows until he found it. Dumping the girl's gold Gucci bag upside down, he tore open the matching wallet. "Fuck me!" Holding the New Jersey state drivers license in his hand, Sean gathered the strewn dress, heels, panties and bra before marching back into the bathroom. The girl stood, still naked, in front of his full-length mirror towel drying her long stringy hair. She glanced at Sean, then at her clothes and wallet. A grin crept across her thin lips.

"At least I told you," she remarked, nonchalantly.

Sean grabbed her by the arm, thrusting the garments in her face. "Yeah, sure after you were in the front seat of my car with my dick 'pon your mouth."

The girl protested as Sean dragged her from the room by her elbow. "Well, you didn't stop me, did you? You drove me all the way here and then fucked this sweet young pussy all night."

By this time Sean was headed to the door with the girl trailing, hair dripping as she scurried to pull on her dress.

"What? Are you like married or something?" She just wouldn't stop yapping. "I thought so by the looks of this place. I wonder how your wife would feel knowing we made love all over her house?"

Trying to remain calm, Sean reminded himself that the focus was to get rid of her. Taking a deep breath he turned around. "Look, here's cab fare." Opening the table drawer, he pulled out three twenties. "My doorman will 'ail one for you." Stuffing the bills into her palm, Sean pushed her into the empty hallway.

Slamming it swiftly, he pressed his back against the door and slid down until his scantily covered buns hit the floor. After a second, something out of the left side of his eye caught his attention. Jumping up, he flung the heavy door back open.

"Here!" He yelled. The girl, now waiting for the elevator, turned around a second too late as her thick coat came to rest atop her damp head.

Sean walked through his condo and proceeded to clean up the remains of his fiasco. On his way to discard the condom wrappers, an earring pierced the sole of his bare foot. He hollered in aggravation, "Shit!" *I've got to stop drinking. Every time I drink I end up fucking up. I swear.* Looking around for the condoms themselves, Sean hoped the girl had enough common sense not to flush them down the toilet. The last thing he needed was a rubber resurfacing at the wrong time.

Spotting one at the foot of his bed and the other on the floor in the closet, he bent down to pick them up as the girl's words echoed in his memory, "I wonder how your wife would feel knowing we made love all over her house?"

"Made love my ass, you little smut." He laughed. *"I fucked the shit out of you and Camille would kill me if she ever found out."* The thought of Camille led his mind back to the blow up at her house. *"You know what? Fuck Camille, too. If she wasn't acting so shitty all week this would've never happened."* Getting up, he turned the shower back on, grabbed his coffee mug and began to start what was left of his day.

"It's not funny dawg." Sean was on the phone with his 'partner in crime', Tony. "She's fuckin' seventeen. She can't even buy cigarettes. What I look like bangin' tat girl? She ain't 'ave no business in the spot in the first place."

74

"You act like you ain't neva' hit off a young jawn before." Sean could hear the rasp as Tony took a heavy drag of the Newport.

"Man, she didn't even look seventeen. Those hoes she was with, now tey' looked young as hell, but I coulda' swore she was a'least twenty. Hell, it's not like I'm still twenty-four my damn self. I'm thirty-fucking-four. And, top 'pon of it, she a white jawn!"

"Yeah, I know. Her friends were mad as hell when you didn't let them ride with ya'll. So, you know I had to make sure the young ladies got home safe. Yah'a'mean?"

Tony laughed, coughing heavily. "Man them drunk ass hoes was all over me, yo'. I took them to a room and after I tore each one of 'em down, I left they silly asses passed out in the Jacuzzi."

"You ain't shit dawg."

"Man, my girl would'a killed my ass if I stayed out all night again. I already had to hear her beef all morning 'cause I ain't get in until after 2:30. Yah'a'mean? And I know you ain't talkin' about *I ain't shit*? Man you kicked the bitch out butt ass naked in the middle of the winter."

"Nah, she 'ad her clothes on. Sart'of." Sean heard his phone beep, "'Old on."

"Man, just call me back. I gotta go suck this girls toes or something, so she shut the fuck'up!"

"'Ello."

Sean's voice was still groggy from the liquor and long

night.

"You sound horrible." Nicole's voice triggered his memory.

"Shit! Nicole, I'm sorry."

"No Sean, don't worry about it. It sounds as if you need a few hours to sober up. I can imagine how your night went. I'll take Morgan myself and don't worry, I'll tell your mom you had a business dinner to plan for or something." Sean knew by her tone Nicole was upset, but was trying to play it cool.

Sean's headache returned in full force accompanied by the all too familiar feeling of regret. It had been over a year since he had a drink and the argument with Camille made him relapse. They'd never fallen out like that before. Hell, he couldn't remember arguing with her previously at all. Sean didn't like letting anyone close enough to directly alter his state of mind. He hadn't felt that type of irritation in over a year.

Sean vowed he would never drink again after the accident and then losing Nicole. It was after a series of ill-fated events that he realized alcohol stripped his conscious of clarity. The downward spiral caused destruction in not only his life, but he was sure the life of that man's family, as well.

He could still smell the same stench of booze, blood and antifreeze he smelled the night he burned his coat, shirt and tie in the fireplace of the pool house. Nicole was up, sitting at her vanity table with her back to him when he walked in wearing only his slacks and tank top. He could tell from her shoulder's heaving that she was crying, but he was too shook up to tend to her.

When he headed into the bathroom, she never even turned around to look at him. If she had, she probably would've seen the scratches on his chest and arms from where he reached into the overturned vehicle trying to pull the man out.

In the shower, Sean tried to make sense of the whole scene, but his head was whirling like a merry-go-round. There was no way he could go to the police. He'd already left the scene of the accident. From the looks of it, if the man he ran into wasn't dead, he undoubtedly had some serious injuries.

Sean just couldn't see himself going through the motions of a trial. They would dig into every aspect of his life. He was sure they'd find out about the laundering. Even if he were acquitted, he would undeniably lose his business. Then Nicole would leave for sure. He feared she'd even stop him from seeing his daughter. On top of that, what would his mother think of him? More than likely he would have to end up leaving the states.

Standing against the wall, water streaming down his back, Sean felt a presence and looked up. Nicole was sitting on the end of the garden tub, his boxers in hand. He turned off the now cold shower, stepped out and sat next to her.

"How dare you disrespect me like this? It's bad enough I have women prank calling my house, but to have the audacity to walk in here half naked."

Sean had never seen the look Nicole had on her face that night. He wanted badly to tell her the truth, but she wouldn't understand. The fact remained that if he were not out drinking and flirting, none of this would have happened. He should've been home with his woman and his daughter. No matter how he sliced it, in his mind he knew he was going to lose her. After getting no response, Nicole, with tears in her eyes, left him sitting there. She ended up spending the night in the guest room.

Over the next two weeks Sean heard broadcasts headlining the deadly hit-and-run. The press never released the name of the victim and there were no leads. Eventually, he stopped hearing about the story in the media altogether. He still, however, suffered from nightmares; his dreams replaying the dreadful events.

It was Thursday and Sean was on his way home from a motorcycle club in North Philly. The streets were dark at ten minutes past midnight; patches of black ice lay in the shadows on the ground from an early March snowstorm. Sean was tipsy, as usual, off of Remy and Heinekens. The *Elephant Man* blared out of his speakers as his phone lit up, signaling an incoming call.

Smiling as the caller id read Sade, Sean hit mute on the steering wheel flipping open the cell. "Damn ma, I just left ya' tirty minutes ago."

The girl on the other end giggled devilishly, "I wanna see you tonight. I can't wait until tomorrow."

"Nah, love, I work in the marning." His phone lit up again and the screen read 'New Media Message'. Sean hit view and a picture of one hundred and forty pound Sade displayed across his phone. Her hair cascaded down her bare front covering only her nipples, exposing the rest of her body.

"Damn girl!"

"Oh, so like that? Huh?" She giggled again.

"Uh-huh." Sean was speechless; his mind racing in and out of sexual fantasies.

"Then why don't you come ova' and help me wash off all this sweat from the club."

Grabbing his erection, Sean bit down on his lip. "I'll tell ya what…"

Those were the last words Sean spoke as he looked up to see the red traffic light. The white Acura Legend in front of him was at a complete stop.

When he came to, the icy barren street was smoking from the heat of the collision. His truck was plastered between the metal subway partition and the driver side door of the Acura that was now turned on its left side. Sean forcefully pried his door open and hobbled around to the other side of the mangled Acura. The smell of antifreeze was strong as he reached down into the broken window, cutting his arms in the process.

The man was between the door and the seat itself. From the looks of it, he was leaning slightly to the left and had tried to turn around to see what was going on behind him upon impact. Sean couldn't tell if he was breathing or not as he fought to yank the seat free. After about a minute of the base not budging, he reached back toward the rear of the car to try and get a better grip. Sean gawked at the car seat. He backed quickly out of the car, banging his head and cutting his chest on the windowpane. *Not a baby.*

He hopped back into his truck threw the gear stick in reverse, praying when he hit the four-wheel drive it would activate. Saying a silent 'thank you' he peeled off into the night leaving a permanent skid mark on the pavement that mirrored the permanent vision in his memory. He never even realized that the car seat was empty.

The next day, Sean was surprised when he went to the garage to check out his car. The only real damage was the driver side rear mirror that was dislodged and hanged by a few exposed wires. Both doors were dented in slightly with more paint missing on one side than the other. Since he had the hook up at a body shop in Pennsauken, Sean knew he could get everything fixed without causing a lot of suspicion. He'd spent the rest of his weekend getting his truck repaired and trying, to no avail, to make amends with Nicole. Eventually, he began staying at the pool house full time and within a few months Nicole moved out.

Chapter 8
The Meeting

"No he didn't. How is he just gonna show up at your house?" Rita popped another crab cake in her mouth, followed by a banana pepper. "Who the hell does he think he is?"

"And then he had the nerve to get mad 'cause I told him he was a guest."

Rita squealed, "Oooo! No you didn't!"

"He got me twisted," Camille jerked her neck back and forth. "I can only take so much. This is why I didn't want to get involved in the first place. It's like men ain't shit by nature or something."

"Oh, I know you're heated. I haven't heard you curse this much since you found out Trevor was messing with that Italian chick." Rita was trying to hide her smile behind her hand.

Camille shook her head, rolling onto her back, and stared up at the glitter-speckled ceiling. "Italian," she repeated half to herself. "To me a white girl is a white girl. Brothas just try to justify that shit by saying, 'She's Italian' or 'She's Puerto Rican.'" Rita, who was nodding in agreement, shot up chucking a pepper at her friend. "Hey, fuck you! I'm as black as you are trick!"

"In your dreams," Camille stood throwing a pillow at Rita and headed to the radio. Music was Camille's solace. Whenever her mind was heavy, she would turn to her radio. She liked all types of music, but listened mostly to underground hip hop. Turning the volume up, she allowed the music to wash over her in a wave while Rita went on stuffing her face, bopping her head to the hard base line of The Roots *Clock With No Hands*.

It was Saturday night. After spending all day ordering room service, griping about the men in their lives, the time had come for the two to hit the casino floor. They giggled like teenagers while getting dressed and then became critically silent as they stood side-by-side, nose distance from the bathroom mirror, painting their faces. After each customary ritual was complete, they gave each other a once-over and left the room.

"I'm not stuntin' this belly. I'm gonna wobble my fat behind right up to the craps table. I dare somebody to say something." Rita smoothed out her black pants suit as if there was actually any room for wrinkles. "Hell, at least they don't have to worry about me drinking up all of their cheap ass cocktails."

"Do I look ok?" Camille interrupted, brushing down the front of her dress for the hundredth time. "I hope it's some fine men down there." The two were standing in the hall, primping in the massive gold trimmed mirror.

"If not, we'll just have to schedule a late night therapy session." They both laughed as the elevator doors opened.

Inside was a woman in her early to mid twenties. The first thing Camille noticed were the piercing green eyes that caught her own as soon as the doors parted. They seemed to be fixed on Camille as she and Rita entered.

Wearing a black evening gown with a neckline that plunged all the way down to her belly button, her ginger colored skin glittered under the elevator lights. She had on no make-up, only gloss, which made her full lips glisten seductively. Her jet-black hair was swept up flawlessly in a tight French bun. Teardrop indigo earrings matched a bracelet that wrapped high around her arm well above her elbow. A pair of six-inch stiletto's revealed a tattoo on the top of her right foot that looked like a mix between a budding sunflower and some sort of name.

Camille surveyed the dame from head to toe, stopping at the tattoo. The woman leaned forward whispering directly into her left ear, "It says Kismet." The three words rolled off of her tongue like moist sap down a damp leaf. She pulled back her lips slowly brushing against her jaw line. A chill shot through Camille's body.

Mystified, Camille could not find any words to respond. Her body was too busy going crazy. Beneath her own canary yellow satin dress, her bare breasts began to tingle, catching her totally off guard. She immediately became conscious of her nipples now fully erect.

From her cheeks to her neck, Camille flushed in shame while the woman remained straight-faced. Grabbing at her ears, she tried to relax her libido and conceal her obvious excitement.

The doors opened and Rita waited for Camille to exit walking out defensively behind her. In the mirror in front of them, Camille could have sworn she saw the woman wink as the doors shut.

"What did she say to you?" Rita asked suspiciously. "I hope I don't have to get ugly in this casino?"

Camille laughed, trying to pull herself together. "Look at you being ghetto again. She just told me what her tattoo said. I guess she saw me looking at it."

"Oh, 'cause I was about to say…"

"You were about to say what, Prego?" She was relieved Rita didn't notice the come-on and even more relieved she didn't see her reaction.

After spending what seemed like forever at the craps table with Rita, Camille decided that she needed a real drink. Her mind was racing with a million thoughts, and the watered down Vodka she'd been nursing for the past thirty minutes was not hitting the spot.

"I'll be back." Rita barely nodded, her focus remaining on the red dice hitting the high side of the table with a crump.

The night was young and Camille wanted to get nice and tipsy. She'd spent all week with Sean on the brain. Tonight was her release. She vowed to do whatever she needed in order to make sure of that.

The slim bartender nodded as Camille approached the far end.

"Let me get a double shot of Patron, straight up."

"What, no chaser?" The scent of Victoria's Secret *Sexy* hit Camille in a wave. She turned to see the beauty from the elevator staring her seductively in the face.

"That is my chaser."

"It can't be that bad, sweetheart?"

Camille shrugged and smiled lightly taking a seat. "Yeah, well it won't be after I holler at Pat & Ron," Camille joked. "What's your name?"

"Ebony."

"What are you drinking, Ebony?"

Leaning in, she whispered, "Your choice."

Camille signaled to the bartender throwing up two fingers, "Make that two."

Ebony leaned back in the bar chair, crossing her legs at the knee as Camille handed her the tequila. Her eyes could not help but travel up the spilt as Ebony's dress fell lightly to the side, making her thighs throb. *What am I doing?* Camille cleared her throat flexing her legs together while scooting back in the chair.

"Are you asking yourself what's going on?"

Camille nodded wondering how she knew.

"We're having a drink." Ebony smiled then fell silent, but continued to speak with her eyes.

After a few minutes Camille spoke up. "My name is Camille."

"Oh, I thought it might have been a secret or something." Ebony was smiling with her eyes still unchanging. "Nice to meet you, Camille."

"Do you want another drink?" Camille asked looking down at her own empty glass.

"No, I'm fine, thanks," She raised her eyebrows. "I would, however, like a smoke."

"Ok," Camille turned back to the bar. "Let me grab another shot and then we can step outside." Camille downed her second shot like a pro and carried a glass of Merlot with her toward the door. Just before they reached the exit leading to the boardwalk, a pasty looking man in uniform approached them.

"Miss, you can't leave the floor with alcohol." The stern look on the attendant's face told them he was not letting this one slide.

Ebony suggested they go upstairs, "I'll have them send you up a bottle. That way I can smoke without freezing to death and you can drink." Ebony turned to the pale-faced worker, "Off of the floor." Camille thought for a second, shoved her glass in the attendant's hand and headed toward the elevator.

On the way up, Camille again stood on the opposite side of the elevator. Under the tinted lighting of the half mirrors on each side, Ebony examined the three hundred and sixty degree view of Camille's make-up. Her mocha colored skin was so even in tone it looked brushed on. Her eyes trailed Camille's neckline down to her wrists. Offering rest to her crossed arms, Ebony was captured by Camille's robust hips that led her eyes down the sides of her thighs, which were also full. Her well-sculpted legs towered her petite interlaced ankles.

The intensity Camille felt from Ebony's gaze was in no way like the feeling she got when a man stared at her body. Normally, she'd come up with an idea of what a dude was thinking just by the way he looked at her. If he was staring into her titties, Camille knew he was probably picturing her topless, pressed up against his wet mouth. Stares to her hips were usually signs of 'cow-girl' fantasies, while eyes stuck to her ass automatically meant 'back shots'. But, with Ebony it was different. Just knowing there was an attraction kindled a flame foreign to her. The heat bounced off the walls of the elevator as they ascended.

Once inside the room Ebony stepped out of her heels, turning the lights on over the bar. Lighting a clove, Ebony turned on the stereo then walked over and stood before Camille who had taken a seat on a black leather chaise.

Not knowing what to say, Camille mumbled, "What?"

Ebony remained straight-faced, eyes fixed, "You're beautiful."

"Thank you. You're very pretty as well. But, I'm sure men tell you that all of the time." She fiddled with a strand of hair, unsure if she was comfortable with Ebony being so close.

"Am I invading your space?" Again it was like she read her mind.

"No. Sort of." Ebony turned and walked over to the refrigerator when someone knocked, "Room service." The muffled voice freed Camille of her apprehension.

"Will you get that?"

As Camille closed the door, Ebony pulled two wine glasses out of the cabinet, "Sit."

Camille complied taking a chair opposite her hostess.

"So, what do you want to know about me?" Ebony asked.

Camille had a million questions, but didn't want to be

invasive or offensive. "I'm very open and I don't offend easily. If I didn't want you to cross, I wouldn't have lowered the bridge." For the first time, Ebony directed her attention elsewhere as she searched for the corkscrew.

Camille paused for a moment before accepting the invitation, "Where are you from?"

"Atlanta. I just got here about a month ago."

"You don't sound like you're from the south."

"Well, I was born in Trinidad. My family came to The States when I was eighteen. My parents still live in New York, but I moved to Atlanta when I turned twenty-one. "

"Where do you stay now?"

"Boring-ass Pleasantville. I had cabin fever this weekend. I didn't care how cold it was I was getting out of that house. Besides, the people out here are so dead. What, ya'll banned from partying or something? I don't see how you deal with it."

"It is not that bad. You didn't grow up here, so you wouldn't understand. But, all that is nothing to me. Besides, I live in PA. I mean, I come out here to chill or whatever every now and then, but I pretty much do my own thing. But, I heard Atlanta was like the 'Black Mecca'. Why did you leave?"

"My cousin. She just had a baby. There were some complications during her delivery, so I came to help her out. My aunt is old and stuck in her ways. She was driving her up the wall."

"Do you have any children?"

"No." Ebony laughed, "No. I want to, but the opportunity hasn't presented itself." Camille acted as if she hadn't caught the glib tone.

"So, are you going to move back any time soon?"

"I don't know, am I?" This time, Camille blushed.

"Hey, if you don't mind," Ebony moved out from behind the bar, "I'm gonna change. I only wore this dress because Rihana was performing tonight."

"Oh, how was it?"

Ebony shrugged, "I didn't go. I'm not a fan. I just couldn't have her walking around here looking better than me."

Again Camille laughed. "That dress is hot. I thought I was doing something," she leaned back, opening her arms, "but when I saw you in that, I must admit, I was taken aback."

"Yeah, I noticed." Ebony glanced down at Camille's nipples, bit her lip and walked coolly toward the bedroom.

The sound of the phone startled Camille. Knocking her purse off the counter, she fumbled to catch the incoming call.

"Where are you?" Rita didn't wait for her to say 'hello'.

"I... uh..." Camille stuttered, "came to a bar upstairs to get another drink." Her mind was racing. She wanted to tell Rita what was going on, but Ebony was in the other room.

She wasn't ready to leave, but her best friend was downstairs. If the tables were turned, and a little shaken, she knew Rita would make sure she was ok before she left to be with anybody.

"You still on the floor?" Camille asked gathering her things.

"Yeah, I'm about to cash out now while I'm up."

"I'll be there in five minutes."

Ebony came out of the room looking like a totally

different person. Her hair fell down in shiny ringlets past her shoulders cropping her well-sculpted jaw line. She had on a navy blue tank top, baggy dark sweat-pants and black ankle socks. Although the look was a total one-eighty, her beauty still stunned Camille.

"My friend is waiting for me." She got up. "I have to go."
"I'm sorry, did I offend you?"
"What? Oh, no my friend is really waiting."

"Ok." Ebony stood there with her green eyes shining as if she knew what Camille was about to say.

"Let me give you my phone number. We're leaving tomorrow. I live near Philly so…" rambling, she shuffled through her purse looking for something that would write. Ebony handed her the cell smiling calmly.

"Thanks. This is my cell number, so…call me whenever."

Leaving the room, Camille had to remind herself to breathe. Her watch read that she'd been gone for less than an hour, but the memory seemed like an eternity. As the elevator descended, she laughed aloud at the likelihood of tonight ever happening. She wasn't sure if it was the tequila or the stress of dealing with Sean, but she was certain the attraction found was like no other she'd known.

Rita was standing at the cashier's counter when Camille walked up.

"What's up?" She asked, unsuspectingly.

"I have to tell you something," Camille whispered.

"What?" Her tone was anxious as they waited for the

dawdling teller.

"I can't tell you here."

"Well, come on," Rita pulled her through the lobby. "Did you go sneak off and get you some?!" The couple in front of them turned around in shock.

"Shhh!!" Camille's copper face tinged as the white guy smirked looking her up and down. His wife tugged at his arm to speed up his pace. "See, why do you always think about sex?"

"Aww, come on. You know my hormones are going crazy."

"Lies!" Camille sang, "You've always been a freak." Taking her best friend's arm, Camille laid her head on Rita's shoulder as they walked. In a serious tone she asked, "Would you love me no matter what?"

"Of course."

"No matter what?"

"No matter what, Camille, now tell me!"

"Okay, okay. Remember that girl that was in the elevator?"

"Yeah. Why?" Rita still had no idea where the conversation was headed.

"Well, I saw her at the bar earlier and she invited me to have a drink with her," Camille continued, "in her room."

Rita stepped back, her eyes widened. "You're the freak! Ya'll had some men up there and you didn't call me! You ain't shit! I know you got your flirt on. What did they look like? Did you get their numbers?"

"No, Rita! It was just her and me. Her name is Ebony and I gave her my number."

Rita's eyes widened. "Oh…"

Chapter 9
Rita

When Rita got back home, she was pleased to see her house in perfect condition. Her weekend escapade with Camille left her drained and she was in no mood to clean up after the boys. It seemed Hassan had taken care of everything, which led the way for her to tell him her plan to spend all week in bed.

"I'm going to take some time off of work," she announced, certain her husband wouldn't mind.

"Well, Rita. Are you asking me or telling me?" He chose his words carefully. "Because if you're asking me, that's fine. We have plenty of coverage."

Rita glared at him out of the corner of her eye. Seeing no sign of joking in his face, she threw herself on the chaise and began sobbing uncontrollably. Hassan stood there for a moment, ready to reach down and console her. Giving it a second thought, he grabbed the duffle bag at her feet, turned and headed up the steps. Rita sat up looking around the empty living room. She was stunned. For the first time ever, her tears were futile. Her husband didn't come running to her side, but instead, he left her to her tantrum.

Unsure what to do or say, Rita crept into the master bedroom suspiciously. Hassan was nowhere in sight. Moving to the makeshift office at the far end of the hall, she heard him talking on the phone softly.

"Na'am. Yes. Uh-huh. I understand and I will, wa' alaykum salaam." He hung up the phone, but didn't move. Rita peeked around the corner.

"Can I come in?"

"Sure. You've been standing there haven't you?" Her patience was already thin and the attitude Hassan was giving off was starting to dissolve it.

"What's your problem? You got something you need to say to me?"

Hassan shook his head. "The last time I told you what was on my mind, you up and ran off like it was the end of the world. I don't know when you're going to learn that the earth doesn't revolve around you, Ree. I mean, I do everything I can to try and make you happy."

"What are you talking about, Hassan? I am happy."

"Then why don't you start acting like it? Why don't you respect the fact that I'm a man and you're..."

"A woman," she cut him off. "And, the sun and the moon and the stars. Yeah, I know. And you want me to obey your orders and live like a fucking nun."

"Watch your mouth!" Although Hassan's voice did not raise, his words struck Rita like a father would his child. "Why do you give me such a hard time? Huh? Why is it because *I'm* trying to change you think I'm trying to control you? I mean, don't you see this is important to me? It has nothing to do with me wanting to control you. *I'm* changing, Ree. I can feel it in my bones and I don't know what that means for us, but…" He rubbed his head wearily. "Look, I would never treat you a way that I wouldn't treat my own mother."

Rita's eyes gleamed devilishly, "You sure about that?" She joked.

Hassan didn't smile, "I'm serious. All I'm trying to tell you is that I'm starting to feel some type of way. I'm not saying I want us to forget who we are. I'm just saying, it's about time we do something different." Hassan reached into the light oak desk drawer beside his right hand removing a slender grey felt box. He held it out to Rita. "I saw this in The Gallery the other day. I…uh…I thought you would like it."

Rita pulled the box apprehensively from his fingers flipping open the hinged lid. On the ivory cushion lay a platinum plated linked anklet. It was small enough to hug her ankle femininely, yet fly enough to show her 'back home' taste in jewelry. She raised her gaze to Hassan and saw something in his eyes, something that she had never seen before. Unable to figure it out, a small thought inched into her mind. He was truly the love of her life and always had been. She was amazed that Hassan never forgot, nor overlooked anything she said; no matter how small. He had been listening when Rita had been complaining about her swelling ankles being unattractive. The diamond chipped anklet cracked the hard shell into which she'd drawn herself.

Hassan was the first constant in her world. Her mother

was long gone. Her father may as well have been. He was too out of touch to even come back and try to make amends. Her grandmother was like all the other tired Nanas. Still she loved Rita with what little she had. Since Rita was an only child, until she met Hassan she was in the world alone. A world that never explained-- only showed. And, like most, Rita built up a defense that Hassan had been chipping away at for years. She cried as he knelt down to fasten the clasp that held a diamond studded plate reading *Mother~ Wife~ Love*.

By Thursday Rita decided to begin preparations for the Friday night dinner she'd planned. She figured it was the least she could do to show Hassan she was trying. Rita called Noni to set a meeting time.

At 10 o'clock sharp Rita was outside of Mansoor and Noni's house. She rang the doorbell of the sand colored, two-story stucco home. Through the stained glass front door, she heard Noni call out for her to come in. She made her way straight to the living room meeting Noni as she came through the kitchen.

"I'll be ready in a minute," Noni breezed past her, heading for the main level master bedroom. For the first time, Rita saw her uncovered in a short-sleeve shirt. Catching the look of shock, Noni smiled.

"I am a woman you know. I do look like one underneath it all."

"I'm sorry, I just…"

"No, I understand," she called out the doorway. "A lot of people have questions, but don't ask. They think I'll get offended, but it doesn't bother me at all. I love talking about

Islam. I have no qualms with how I live."

"But, I thought you had to be covered all of the time."

"When I'm at home with Mansoor and the kids, I wear whatever I want."

"Don't you get tired of having to dress and undress all day?"

"It's not really like that. Plus, I'm used to it, I guess." She came out fully clothed like Rita was used to seeing.

"Don't you get hot in the summer?"

"Yeah, but just like you do. Think of it like this, if it was cold outside and you put on a coat, but sat in the warm house for 30 minutes before going out, by the time you went out you'd still be cold. Even though you have on a coat."

"Your body temperature adjusts."

"Right. And, let me ask you something. Have you ever seen a pair of shoes you wanted, but the only sizes they had were either too small or too big?"

"Sure."

"Have you ever bought them anyway 'cause you wanted them so bad?"

Rita laughed, "Sacrifice, huh?"

"Exactly."

As they walked through the farmers market, Noni was candid in all of her responses to Rita's endless questions. Rita found out more about her sister-in-law than she ever imagined. Noni also verified what Rita already knew to be true. She was a devout Muslim woman; everything Rita had problems with, Noni accepted. All of it instilled in her, she said, since birth. She explained to Rita that by there being rights in place, she and Mansoor had very few disagreements. As long as each one of them gave the other their due rights, things went smoothly.

"Yeah, that's because you have to do whatever he says. It's like you have no voice."

"No, that's not true. We make all decisions together that need to be made together. Those that he needs to make, he makes and vice versa." Rita still wasn't swayed.

"Ok, look," Noni asked, "if during your delivery, there were two doctors in the room, one surgeon and one anesthesiologist, would you feel comfortable if the anesthesiologist asked the surgeon his opinion on how much sedation you need?"

Rita thought, "Not really."

"Why not?" Noni challenged, "They're both doctors."

"But, that's what he's trained to do. What's the need for the anesthesiologist, if he's asking the surgeon's opinion?"

"Exactly. It's the same thing. Yes, we are both adults, but a man is created to be a man and a woman is created to be a woman. So, it doesn't discredit who I am in any way to let my husband make the decisions a man should make. A lot of the women today don't realize how much freedom Islam gives women and how much protection it gives us from the stress of this upside down society. See to me all of that pride and wanting to be like a man is a disgrace."

"Well, what about the women like me, who grew up with no father or mother? My abuela and aunties raised me. My mother was weak. She got strung out on heroine at sixteen and she let all of the men she knew, my father included, to use her until she died. She sold herself to man after man to support her and my dad's habit. Still he beat the life out of her over and over again until there was nothing left. She was only twenty-four when she died. I was nine. So for me, 100% obedience to a man is not gonna get it."

"See, you're not against being a woman. You're against where drugs lead. Inhumanity. I'm not gonna go into a long spiel, but you can't allow their mistakes to stagnate your growth. Knowledge is the key to understanding. So you were taught what, Christianity?"

With tears in her eyes, Rita shook her head.

"See, it's the same thing there. A lot of Christians don't admit it, or they don't know, but the Bible states in Corinthians I that man is the head of woman. It also says that a woman is to cover her head. In Leviticus it says the flesh of a swine is an abomination. Yet, people all over who call themselves Christians live and eat as they please. They criticize without even knowing and don't even follow their own book. But, read it for yourself when you get a chance. It won't do you any good hearing it from me. You have to get your own understanding, you know what I mean?"

Rita was speechless trying to process what Noni just said. It was so logical once she thought of it in that light.

"You 'um... You said you were born Muslim?"

"Yeah, my dad has known Ahmed for a long time. Ahmed actually introduced him to Islam when they were young. My mother used to tell me so many stories about my dad. A lot of them were hard to believe."

"Used to?"

"Yeah. She died after E was born."

"I'm sorry." Hearing Noni call Elijah 'E' and sharing the loss of her mother warmed Rita's heart to her.

"It's ok. From Allah we come and to Him we return. Alhamdulillah she saw her first grandbaby. "Anyway," pointing to Rita's Belly, "how's everything going with you?"

"Well, you know. Ok I guess."

Rita didn't feel like talking about the baby. The more she thought about what her doctor had told her, the more depressed she became. The more depressed she became, the harder it was to fight the urge for the pills at night. She knew she had to tell Hassan. He would be furious if he found out. But, what difference did it make? It was not like she could have an abortion now. If she'd only found out sooner. But, then what? Hassan would never agree to terminate the pregnancy.

The rest of the evening was surprisingly successful. Dinner turned out well and the kids had a ball. Even Elijah, who was usually in a sour mood, was upbeat in good spirits. Rita silently observed the way Noni was with Mansoor. Even though his rough exterior reflected that of Ahmed's, his wife's eyes still sent a gleam through his each time they met. His tone when addressing her was one of compassion, not control. The humbleness she gave off, complimented their attraction. There was no resistance in her nature as she sat enjoying the company of her family. Rita was amazed at how calmly they flowed and in such a way that she longed to have a part of it for her own house.

After everyone said their goodbyes, Hassan and Rita settled in the den to watch a movie. "Babe," Rita rested her head in the small of Hassan's shoulder, "I never apologized for last week. I know you were worried sick. I just needed to get away to re-evaluate things."

"I know. It was unfair of me to just spring this up on you and expect you to feel like I do. But, what had me surprised was you actually spending the day with Noni."

"She's cool. I found out a lot about her today that I never knew."

"Like what?" He asked cynically.

"Nosey! None of your business."

"Well, as long as you were comfortable with it." Hassan massaged her stomach. "I can't wait to see my boy. He's gonna be so awesome. I already know."

"Babe…" Rita started to go on, but stopped dead in her tracks. Seeing the joy on her husband's face, she lost all nerve to tell him about the baby. *I'll tell him soon,* she promised herself for what seemed like the millionth time. Rita had a long day and still had to get up early for her meeting in the morning. She let her head fall limply on Hassan hoping he would fall asleep first.

The next morning Rita didn't feel like being out the house let alone talking to anyone. The alarm had pierced the silence of her empty bedroom two hours earlier reminding her of the appointment she'd made weeks ago. As soon as she stepped foot through the threshold of the Philadelphia Marriott, her phone rang. Still groggy from a sleeping pill, she moaned annoyingly.

Not bothering to look at the caller id she brought the headset to her ear, "Yes?" Her attitude was in full flare.

"Hola' La' Rita." She dropped the receiver. Although it

had been almost ten years, Rita recognized the voice immediately.

One of the bellhops bent down, picking up her phone as he passed. "How did you get this number?"

"I called your grandmother's house. Raphael gave it to me."

Leave it to my stupid cousin, she thought, making a mental note to light his ass up as soon as she got Jose off her line.

"Look. I'm in the middle of something. I don't have time to talk right now."

"Aww, princess. You can never be too busy for your Papi. I heard I was going to be a grand..."

Rita hung up before he could finish whatever stream of apologies he was fishing up. It was just like him to disrupt her life and think she owed him the time, let alone the energy it took to confront him and all that came with it.

She hit call on her speed dial.

"Hello," her cousin answered on the first ring.

"Ralphie, why in the hell did you give my number out?" She tried to keep her voice low in the quiet lobby of the hotel, but her anger got the best of her.

"Man Rita, that's your father,"

She cut him off, "Medía, don't ever give anyone my number again. I don't care who it is!" Hitting 'End' Rita headed for the ladies room, followed by the suspicious stares of a few guests.

Looking at her face in the mirror, Rita began to cry. Her head whirled in a fog as discontented tears spilled from her eyes, staining her blue silk blouse with dark ill-shaped blotches. Rita felt like she was being pulled in a hundred different directions.

Why was he calling? What the hell was that about? The last time she heard from Jose she was heading off to college at nineteen. He had the nerve to show up at her house like it was nothing. As usual, he was stoned, smelling of Brute mixed with sweat. He ranted on about how sorry he was for missing her graduation and how much Rita looked like Jessica. Just hearing him speak her mother's name set off the bull in Rita's Taurean nature.

"How dare you? Who in the hell do think I am, some feign on the street? Don't come here tryna' beat me in the head wi'dat bullshit."

Rita's grandmother, who was silently sitting at the kitchen table, let out a gasp, crossing her chest, "Aye! ¡Dios mío!"

"No Nana, I'm for real. He thinks he can show up and I'm supposed to act like he didn't kill my mother. I'm supposed to forget the bruises and bloody noses." Rita's eyes bore into Jose's blood shot gaze. "What am I supposed to do-- forget you're the reason she gave me up?" Inching closer to her father, Rita's curled fists were now so tight her nails had begun to pierce the center of her palms. "Am I supposed to act like your daughter?! Well, let me tell you something Jose Luis, the day you held that pipe to my mother's lips and gave her that first hit was the day you murdered me and I wasn't even born yet. So, you have no daughter here!"

Jose tried to speak, but Rita lunged toward him wildly. "Get the fuck out!!"

Ralphie jumped in front of Rita, grabbing her arms as he pushed her down on the sofa. Jose turned, stumbling out leaving the screen door ajar. That was almost a decade ago. Still, his call today caused the memory to resurface as clearly as if it had been last night.

Rita held on to the side of the sink shaking her head. No one really knew what she was going through. No one even cared about what she wanted. Everyone thought she was living a fairy tale life with a husband, a house and a baby. Little did they know the 'gift' growing inside of her was far from perfect. And, the further along she got the more her gift seemed to turn into a bad joke. Down syndrome; how was she supposed to handle that? She barely knew anything about it. Sure, the doctor gave her literature and a list of websites to visit, but every time she looked at the information her head started hurting. All she could see were the faces of the children she had seen on T.V. The puffy cheeks and slanted eyes alone made her heart hurt. Having a child with a disability was just too much. Grabbing a few paper towels from the dispenser, Rita wiped her eyes then waived her hands in front of her face to dry her tears before she headed out the bathroom door to the front desk of the hotel.

"May I help you?" The receptionist did not bother to look up.

"Yes, my name is La'Rita Abdullah. I have an appointment with Mr. Bordeaux."

The unattractive woman ran her long fuchsia colored nail down the computer screen. "Your appointment was at 2:30."

Rita glanced at the grandfather clock behind the desk.

"Yeah, and it's 2:45."

The girl looked at her in silence as if waiting for an explanation. "I was in the Ladies room if you must know. Is he available or do I need to reschedule?"

The girl picked up the phone on the counter like the receiver weighed thirty pounds, "I'll let him know you're here." Rita rolled her eyes futilely before taking it upon herself to have a seat in the lobby.

"Mrs. Abdullah?" The manager had a warm face unlike his secretary.

Reaching out a well-manicured hand, he took hold of Rita's. "Guy. Guy Bordeaux." Rita concluded by the way he shook her hand that he was gay. He looked down at her belly, raising an eyebrow. "And, you want to rent the ballroom for a New Year's Eve party?" He clucked his tongue. "You better hope you don't pop before then."

Another baby joke. Rita faked a laugh. "Yes, it's my husband's birthday. I want the whole thing to be a surprise, so I'll also need a suite."

"Not a problem. If you'll follow me, we can take a look at what's available and you can tell me if it works for you."

Rita began to follow behind the manager. His switch was harder than the hookers on Broadway. Before she could let out a laugh, a sudden streak of heat flared up her lower abdomen so forcefully it sent her up against the wall.

"Are you alright? Oh, my goodness!"

"Yes, I'm fine," raising her hand to wave him off. "Just give me a second, I'm good." Rita pushed herself upright, took one step and collapsed. The last thing she heard was Mr.

Bordeaux's voice, high pitched and full of fear, yelling frantically. "Someone call the ambulance! Hurry!"

Chapter 10

Hasaan

Hassan sat in the waiting room beside his mother. He'd called her in hysterics after a nurse from the hospital contacted him on his way home from the masjid.

"I can't believe this! I should have kept my phone on me."

"Son, you had no way of predicting or avoiding this. Leaving your phone in the car had nothing to do with what happened." Linda held his head on her shoulder, stroking his back. Ahmed was strolling calmly up and down the short corridor of the waiting area.

Hassan felt like someone was holding a plastic bag over his head. No matter how hard he tried he couldn't catch his normal breathing rhythm.

"Mr. Abdullah?" Hassan looked up at the doctor. Even though he knew it was rude, he didn't have the strength to stand and greet her properly.

Her face, as soft as her voice, remained unchanged as the words rolled out of her mouth like boiling water on bare skin.

"We did all that we could for your wife. The fetus suffered loss of amniotic fluid oxygen due to the leak in the placenta. Without sufficient oxygen his heart rate dropped drastically. We performed an emergency caesarian and attempted to stabilize the condition, but we were unable to do so. I'm sorry."

Hassan's body slipped from his chair in devastation. Ahmed pulled him up, taking his son into his own weakened arms.

"Be strong. It's going to be fine son."

Linda was speechless and her complexion pale with disbelief. Her eyes welled up with tears that her mind could not catch in time for her reflexes to stifle.

"I truly am sorry. We did all that we could," the doctor continued. "Mrs. Abdullah is stable. You may want to go be with her now."

Hassan felt like he was watching himself from outside of his body as he followed the doctor down the hall.

"Rita took it hard when I told her about the condition. She was really concerned about the baby not having a normal life. Maybe this will somehow bring her comfort knowing that the suffering is over."

Hassan looked at the doctor confused. "What? What condition. What are you talking about?"

"Down's Syndrome. The triple screen came back positive for Down's Syndrome. That's why I placed her on complete bed rest. She didn't tell you?"

Like flames, Hassan's heart ignited as the doctor spoke. His grief rapidly evolved into sheer rage.

Hassan pushed the doctor out of the way and burst into the hospital room where his wife was sleeping with a look of exhaustion. He stood over her, panting heavily while his emotions battled with his common sense. He wanted to grab Rita, shake her and make her feel the pain he felt. How dare she betray him? How dare she hide the truth about something so vital? The life of his child was in her hands and she took it upon herself to gamble with it. At that very moment every modicum of love Hassan ever held for Rita evaporated with the tears that streamed down his face.

He stood there for what seemed like forever until he felt someone place a hand on his shoulder. Hassan turned around and was face-to-face with Linda. The look in his mother's eyes said, *'I know baby'*. Like a child he buckled, falling into her arms sobbing silently. He sobbed for himself, he sobbed for Rita, he sobbed for his marriage and he sobbed for his child. Swaying back and forth, Linda held Hassan tightly until he stopped.
"I want to go home."
Linda knew there was much that should have been said to her son, but as his mother, knowing what he needed, she turned with him and walked out of the room.

Hassan slept until 4 o'clock the next day. By the time he woke up, the orange haze of the afternoon sun burned his swollen eyes. He hadn't moved at all. He was fully dressed, laying in the same fetal position with the same pillow in between his legs that he had been holding on to when he cried himself to sleep the day before. He lay there looking up at the ceiling, trying to make the pain he felt go away. Before he knew it, a sour taste formed at the base of his throat. At the same time, the saliva in his cheeks tripled its normal content. Not having eaten anything in over twenty-four hours, the feeling was as febrile as it was unexpected. He barely made it to the toilet as the acidic taste of vomit shot up his esophagus and out of his mouth.

After brushing his teeth, Hassan took a hot shower. With his head directly under the water, he came to the conclusion that his marriage was over. Like a rubber band stretched too far, his desire to be with the one woman he'd loved for the last decade popped. The sound of her name in his mind now brought on intense anger instead of passion. *She's so damn selfish,* he thought. *She doesn't care about anyone but herself. All I've ever done was try to make her happy. This house, the baby, this life, all of it was for her.* Again, in the privacy of the empty bathroom, Hassan cried.

By the time Hassan dried himself off, threw on some clothes and knelt in the middle of his bedroom floor to pray, the rain had set in steadily. The sounds of the water pelted the roof, echoing through the seemingly empty house. Linda and Ahmed were both sitting at the dining room table eating in silence when he walked in slowly. Ahmed stood to hug his grieving son and gestured for him to sit, while Linda went back into the kitchen to make him a plate.

Linda placed the platter in front of Hassan. The aroma of tofu and freshly steamed vegetables triggered the suppressed hunger in his stomach. They finished their meal without a word being spoken. Linda got up and began clearing the table, "I went to the hospital this morning." Hassan remained quiet. "La'Rita was asleep. They have her on some heavy medication. We talked a little. She was in-and-out. All she kept saying was how horrible she felt. She wants to see you Hassan and there are matters to which you need to tend."

"What was it?" Ignoring his mother's statement.

"Excuse me?"

"My baby. Was it a boy or a girl?" The morose look on her son's face chilled Linda to the bone. She could tell by his eyes he would never be the same. There in front of her Linda watched a part of her child wither away from the death of his son.

"He was a boy."

Hassan dropped his head, taking a deep breath. He then looked at his father with watery eyes. "What? Do I need to do to divorce my wife?"

"Hassan this is not the time to have this discussion. First, you need to go downtown to sign some papers. There are arrangements that need to be made for the disposal of the body. You two need to decide if you want to have any type of memorial or a service. If so, we need to start making the necessary contacts, so you need to go see her. Son, do not forget that you are still responsible for taking care of Rita. She's coming home tomorrow. Now, if you want, your mother already said she'll stay here. We're going to need the extra set of keys so we can pick Rita's car up while you're at the hospital."

Hassan sat there for a second. He wanted badly to tell his

father, "No." He didn't want to see Rita, talk to her or make any plans with her. This was not the homecoming he'd spent months dreaming about confidently. The yellow and blue nursery across the hall from his own room would not be filled with the scent of his son. There would be no half asleep stumbles to quiet cries in the early morning hours. All that was left of his dream was bitterness. And to bring Rita back in his house, empty handed, was the last thing in the world Hassan planned on doing.

The twenty-minute ride to the hospital seemed to go in slow motion, with the rainfall adding to Hassan's anguish. He was glad Rita was in a single room. He didn't feel like being cordial nor did he want to talk in front of any strangers. When he walked in, Rita was in the bathroom with the door closed.

"Hello?"

"I'm coming." Rita came out slowly, shocking Hassan as she came into full view.

The woman standing in front of him was not his wife. The black rings circling her sunken dull eyes were as dismal as the rain filled clouds hanging low in the gray skies outside the window.

She looked at her husband then rushed toward him. His arms, usually welcoming, were cold and stiff as he feigned a hug. Rita drew back, feeling the detachment between them. "I don't know what to say. I really don't. My heart feels so heavy," she searched her husband's eyes as she spoke to him. Looking for forgiveness, she saw none. Instead, he looked at her like she was a total stranger.

There was no affection in his voice when he spoke.

"They're waiting for us to make a decision on my son's body," without giving her a chance to respond, Hassan continued, "so we are going to have a private service at the masjid. My parents will be there and if you'd like, Anna as well. But that's it - no one else. No friends, no cousins, no aunts. My son is gonna be buried as I see fit and that's going to be the end of it."

Rita figured it was in her best interest to keep quiet. Hassan stayed long enough to sign the papers the social worker left. By the time Camille arrived, he was on his way out.

She hugged him warmly, unable to hold back her tears. "I'm so sorry, honey."

Hassan was aggravated and in no mood to deal with Camille trying to console him. No one had any idea how he was feeling inside. No one felt the burning sensation in his chest that started at his throat and went all the way down to the pit of his stomach.

"Yeah," was all he could say. He brushed past Camille without saying goodbye or looking back at Rita.

Hassan decided to go to the masjid. He needed to feel some type of release and figured being in the company of his brothers was the best thing for him right now. As he socialized with Mansoor and the others, he noticed a woman toward the back of the room who looked like she was lost.

Hassan focused his gaze on her slender brown face. There was something about her striking features that had him drawn. She stood in the corner alone studying everyone, unaware that she too was being watched. Her head was partially covered and her hair pulled back in a ponytail. She wore a white turtleneck underneath an olive cardigan, with a matching kaki shirt falling to her ankles. Hassan had never seen her before. He figured she was visiting.

Hassan moved across the room to find Noni. He pulled her aside. "Who's that?" He asked, pointing to the far corner of the hall.

"Her name is Nicole. She's been coming on and off for about a month. Why?"

Hassan ignored her question, "Is she Muslim?"

"No, but I talked to her for a while the other night when she was here and she's showing a lot of interest. I don't know. I think she's just gotten divorced or something. I do know she has a daughter. That's her over there in the pink." Noni pointed to a group of girls sitting at a table giggling incessantly as they ate cupcakes and made faces at each other.

Looking at Hassan, Noni raised her eyebrows. "What's up with all the questions?"

"Come on, Sis." Hassan laughed for what seemed like the first time in forever.

"I'm just saying. I can talk to her if you want me to."

"No, no. I just wanted to make sure she wasn't married, you know?"

Noni knew she was about to overstep her boundaries, but she couldn't help it. "Are you sure you know what you're doing?"

Hassan was cool about it and took no offense. "I think so. I'm not sure, but there's something about her that's like, drawing me to her. I don't know..." To himself he finished his thought, *"We might just have something in common. From the looks of it, I'm about to be divorced, too."*

Chapter 11

Camille

After Hassan left, Camille helped Rita shower and started packing up her things. Seeing her best friend in so much pain made Camille's soul hurt in a way words failed to describe.

Once Rita was settled, Camille sat in the oversized chair beside the bed and stared blankly at the television in the corner. Rita dozed in and out, tossing and turning nonstop. She whimpered lightly, her closed eyes dripping tears from her disturbed slumber. After an hour or so, a nurse came in to check on her. She leaned over the metal frame waking Rita as she took her vitals.

"Your heart rate and temp are fine. Your blood pressure is a little low, but that's to be expected right now. Are you sore?"

"Yes. I'm a little tender here." Rita pointed to where the laceration had been made for the c-section.

"Okay. I'm going to give you something to ease the

115

discomfort. You know," the nurse hesitated looking at Camille then back to Rita who nodded her head, letting her know it was ok to go on, "we have a physiatrist on staff that's really helpful when dealing with the type of loss you've experienced. If you want, I can give you her card."

"Thank you. I think that would really help."

Camille could tell Rita was trying not to cry. She'd never seen her friend so vulnerable. She tried to imagine what Rita was going through, but it was too much to bear. The whole scene brought back haunting memories of when Trevor died. She started to remember the void that developed in her own heart along with the grief that seemed to steal her every breath.

"Camille... Camille..."
"Yes? I'm sorry, babe."
"My cell phone. Can you pass it to me?"

Camille gave her the phone and walked over to the window. The rain had subsided. Night was setting in the clouds, giving off a deeply bruised color. They seemed to eerily display the current state of affairs.

Camille was half tuned in to Rita's call. She assumed Anna was on the other end because Rita was speaking in Spanish. And, although Camille didn't understand everything, she could tell by Rita's tone along with a few choice words she knew, the conversation was not a pleasant one. By the time she hung up, Rita was in shambles.

"Why is this happening to me?" She started sobbing

heavily. Camille took her into her arms. "Camille, I never meant for this to happen."

"I know, baby. I know."

"Everybody is acting like this is my fault. I didn't have nothing to do with the baby being sick. How was I supposed to deal with all of that shit by myself?"

"Sick, what do you mean sick?" Camille didn't understand where Rita was coming from-- Rita pulled back, dropping her head in her hands.

"He had Down's Syndrome. They put me on bed rest and said he was gonna have to have surgery because of a hole in his heart. But Camille, I couldn't tell Hassan. He was too happy. I was gonna tell him I swear I was, but I waited too long."

Camille was struck with disbelief. Why hadn't Rita told her? Why did she keep such an important secret? How long had she known? Bed rest? With all of the ripping and running Rita was doing, it was no wonder she went into premature labor. What was she thinking? Camille's thoughts faded in and out, recalling the last couple of months when she caught the tail end of something Rita said that made her mind stop dead in its tracks. "...stopped taking those pills."

"What? What did you say?"

"The pills!" Rita screamed, with wild, tear-filled eyes. "I got hooked on those damn pills! I couldn't stop taking them! I killed him, Camille. I killed my baby!" Rita was in hysterics.

Hearing the commotion, two nurses rushed into the room pushing Camille aside roughly. One held Rita's shoulders, forcing her to lie back while the other injected something into the I.V. Within seconds, Rita's body collapsed under the weight of the narcotic. The nurses retreated, instructing Camille to leave the room. Rita's ashen face with low droopy eyes sent a chill down her spine as she backed out.

Camille drove down Mt. Ephraim Avenue on her way back from picking up Jelani. The older she got the dirtier the city seemed to become. *Is this what I spent my entire childhood trying to experience?* She thought. *Is this all Camden has to offer these kids? These people?* Her Range Rover bounced over several potholes in the street as she drove past rows of boarded up houses. The barred, screened-in porches displayed broken kitchen chairs, tables and even old loveseats. Although it was well past eleven at night, girls were out on the stoops. Teenage boys sat upright to eye each car that drove past intently. Once satisfied the passenger didn't pose any threat or need any 'work', they eased back puffing heavily on cigars stuffed with 'kush'. Children too young to be outside that late ran up and down cracked sidewalks draped in mini designer outfits. They affectionately spewed obscenities to each other while dodging passersby. Their little feet, covered in sneakers that cost as much as a week's worth of groceries, crunched heavily on broken glass. Grandmothers lay wearily on the other side of the open screen doors, while most of the mothers were out with the next man they'd soon bring home to be 'daddy'.

She rode past the corners sprinkled with guys in their mid-twenties strolling up and down the block scarfing down pints of LoMein to ease stomachs lined with shots of Ciroc. They spoke harshly to the young boys that, instead of being at home getting ready for school the next day, were outside trappin' for them until the early morning hours.

Proud of the knot growing in their pockets, the boys took the verbal lashings and stayed posted up. Like soldiers, they nodded in silence, swallowing whatever ounce of 'pussy' they had left in them and 'got their minds right'. They took every insult as love, vowing to play their position and lock shit down. Crack heads that needed 'just one more' followed like puppy dogs behind whomever didn't spit in their faces when they came up begging. The small city was humming when it should have been snoring. The never-ending night sounds of the streets echoed through the silent truck. Camille looked back at Jelani, who was fast asleep across the back seat, wrapped in his coat looking like a stuffed Eskimo. She was so glad Rita had talked her into leaving after high school. Had she stayed there, she probably would have ended up another lost wanderer never willing to venture out with no determination to alter the endless cycle of complacency.

Rita. Man, what was going on with her? The whole scene had Camille so shook up she didn't know what to think. All of this time she thought everything was ok. Yeah, she knew Rita really didn't want kids, but she was sure she was looking forward to becoming a mother. Camille thought they shared everything with each other. *Why hadn't she confided in her? What kind of pills had she been taking? How long was this going on?* She had so many questions and no one to answer them.

Her phone vibrated on the dashboard, startling her.
She hit the speaker button on the steering wheel, "Hello?"
"'Ello, stranger," Sean's voice sent Camille into flashback mode. She saw his face in front of her as if he were right there in the car. She was stuck in a stunned silence.

"'Ello?" He repeated.

"Yeah, what's up?" Her voice was full of Jersey Girl attitude.

"What's up wit' you? Long time no 'ear from. You sound a little out of it. You ok?"

"I'm alright, I guess. Ree lost the baby last night."

"Damn, ma. I'm sorry," she could hear the sincerity in his tone. "Where are ya'? Drivin'?"

"Yeah, I'm on my way home from my mom's. I had to pick up Jelani."

"Oh, is she gwan be ok?"

"I don't know Sean, this shit is heavy. It's just a lot going on right now, you know?"

"Yeah, I bet. Look I know now's not a good time, but I just wanted to 'ear your voice," he hesitated, "I wanted ta see you actually."

Camille felt a flutter in her aching heart. She was happy he called. She needed to be in his arms right now more than anything.

"I'm, um, just getting off the bridge. I have to stop at the supermarket real quick. Where are you?"

Another hesitation, "Don't be mad, I'm actually turning down your street. I know ya like to be infar'med of comp'ny n'all, but I was just 'oping you would see me."

Camille laughed at his attempt to sound bashful.

"Nah, I'm not mad. You can go ahead to the house and let yourself in the front. You know where the key is. There are some leftovers in the fridge, if you're hungry. I should be there in about thirty minutes."

When Camille pulled up, the sight of the silver truck in her driveway struck a calming sensation that washed over her like a wave. Sean met her at the door taking a sleeping Jelani into his arms. Camille walked into the den and fell wearily on the sectional while Sean carried Jelani upstairs. *He knows just how to soothe me*, she thought. The intoxicating scent of burning candles filled the air. The easy sounds of Afromentals floated around her allowing her to escape within them .

Before she knew it, Sean was kneeled in front of Camille unzipping her boots. She placed a hand in his dreads tugging at them softly. He massaged her feet first. Taking them eloquently in his large hands, Sean kneaded the tension out in slow circular strokes. He moved to her ankles with the same fluent movements making his way up to her calves. Through her jeans, Camille melted as he manipulated her muscles into releasing the harbored tension.

By the time he reached the top of her thighs, Camille was breathing heavily with excitement. Her body lunged forward as Sean rose up kissing her hungrily on the mouth. Sweet sounds of desire escaped her throat, fluttering lightly into the minute space between her lips and his. The familiar scent of Bulgari coming from Sean's skin drove her senses wild.

Camille pulled back, "Let's go upstairs." Camille hit the power button and the same melody that played downstairs filled her bedroom. Playfully, she started stripping to the music. Sean was mesmerized by her hips swaying to the beat. Peeling off her jeans Camille slowly revealed her smooth, long legs hidden underneath the denim. She turned around bending over, offering a complete view of the bright red g-string resting lightly in the small of her back. Sean's dick thumped at the sight. Camille continued with her back to him, unfastening her bra while she eased into the adjoined bathroom letting the lace straps fall to the floor. Once out of sight, she threw the panties in the room laughing.

She started the shower and Sean wasted no time joining her in the rapidly steaming bathroom. Seeing his chocolate body glisten under the water reminded Camille how much time had passed since they were together. She lathered her hands anxiously running them as slowly as she could stand across his chest. She forced herself to an even pace as she moved down to his stomach. Bending at the knees, she stroked his thighs firmly covering his dark mocha skin with creamy white suds. Sean stood under the streaming nozzle watching Camille in awe. She dipped her body, her fingers slipped in and out of the crevices of his chiseled upper body like snakes around a tree.

He couldn't hold back any longer. Reaching out Sean ran his fingers greedily through her soaking mane and face. With every stroke he got more and more excited. Before he knew it, he was pushing her head between his legs. Quickly, Camille washed away the suds from his rock hard muscle. Up and down she stroked, the warm water helping her to move with ease. Slipping him inside her mouth, Camille smiled to herself as she bobbed until she felt Sean jerk as his knees buckled.

Moaning in pure delight, Sean admired the view for as long as his senses would allow. Once he felt the pulsing sensation at the base of his nuts, Sean knew he'd reached his limit. He pulled Camille upright turning her around and running his hands down her sides. He was hard enough to enter her from behind in one swift move. Camille's body exploded instantly from the mind rushing force. She grabbed at the tiles helplessly as he stroked her, playfully tapping her on the ass.

"Gwan, get in bed," Sean ordered giving her one last smack. Sean stood in the doorway looking at her soaked body glistening atop the neatly made satin comforter. He took two steps toward her and was stopped dead in his tracks. Like an alarm disrupting a wet dream, the phone on the dresser started ringing.

Sean looked over at the clock on the nightstand, "Who the fuck is calling ya' at 12'clock in the mar'ning?" All traces of romance flew out of the window. Camille slid off the bed apprehensively and sucked her teeth.

"I don't know," she squealed, trying to slide past Sean to silence the ringer.
He held his arm out blocking her path.
"Nah, Camille who's calling you this time a'night?"
Throwing her hands up, Camille jumped on the defense.
"I don't know Sean." The damn cell kept singing.

Seeing his anger mount and his erection deflate, she tried desperately to pacify him. "You answer it then!"
Sean didn't delay. He snatched the phone boldly.
"Hello?" Furrowing his face he pulled the device away from his ear, looking at it like he could see the person on the other end. "Who is tis?" Nerve turned to irritation on Sean's

brow. "Yeah ok, 'old on," he held his arm out to Camille.

"Who's Ebony?"

The question threw her for a total 180. She tried not to show it, but her eyes gave her away. Seeing guilt written all over her face, Sean let the handset slip from his hands to the floor and walked out of the room.

"Hello?" Camille sounded dumbfounded.

"I'm sorry. Did I get you in trouble?"

"No," Camille tried to cover up with a laugh. "I was just about to lie down."

"Um, I see. But um'era, you don't sound sleepy."

"Very funny." Camille could tell Ebony knew what the deal was and was trying her. She peeked into the hall to be sure Sean was out of earshot. "Anyway, I hadn't heard from you in almost three weeks and you call me at midnight? What's up with that?"

Ebony's tongue was a pistol. "Do I detect a hint of frustration in your tone?"

"Nah, not at all. I'm just saying. I was waiting on your call," Camille said, playing mouse right along with the cat.

"What happened? You get tired of waiting?"

This time she was thrown. Stuttering, she tried to recover. "It's- it's not like that."

"Then what's it like? Is that your man?"

This chick is for real, Camille thought. "Something like that. We not official or anything but, you know, we been seeing each other for a minute."

"I see." Ebony was so cool Camille didn't know what to make of it. "Well, I didn't mean to disturb you while in the midst of your cut. Call me tomorrow, if you get a chance."

Before Camille could ask her what she meant by 'cut' Ebony hung up. *Ain't that some shit*, she thought. *I got this chick checkin' me like she my nigga' and my nigga' downstairs trippin like I straight violated. What's really going on?*

Sean was in the kitchen eating a sandwich when Camille came down robed, with a sheepish look on her face. She didn't feel like arguing. All she wanted to do was wrap herself in his warm arms, cum a few times, then fall asleep to the rhythm of him breathing close to her. Sean, on the other hand, was miles away from the romantic mood that lingered upstairs like incense smoke.

He got straight to it. "Who's Ebony? I never heard ya' mention her name."

"I met her in A.C. a few weeks ago."

"You met her? What's tat 'posed ta' mean? And, when did ya' go to da'shore? It's fuckin' November?"

"What are you talking about Sean? I went with Ree when you was on ya' shit. Remember?" She was getting frustrated.

"Ya' don't even 'ang with females like tat."

She tried to play it off, moving around the kitchen fidgeting at the already clean countertops. "What?" Camille knew full well what. She knew where Sean was going and what he was getting at passively. And he knew that she knew.

"Ya' know what I'm talking about Camille. Don't try and

'old me. What's up? Ya' like girls now?"

"Why would you say something like that?" She tried to sound surprised.

"Don't try ta' play games with me! Rita is the only woman I've ever known ya' to be wit let 'lone talk to on the phone."

Camille was squirming. She tapped her foot nervously on the linoleum unable to look at him. Seeing her reaction, Sean lowered his voice.

"Look, I'm just tellin' ya', I know that unless it's 'bout business ya' don't fuck wit' broads like tat. Now all'a sudden ya' meet tis girl and she's callin' here at 12:25 in the mar'nin'?"

Camille started to ask him if he forgot that *he* was in *her* house, but decided not to quickly. Sean was still beefing, "I could tell by the way she asked for you wha'the deal was Camille. Me'not slow to yar' game, ya'know."

Camille wanted to drop the whole thing. She tried to brush it off. "You're trippin.' She was in town and wanted to see what I was getting into tonight." Camille moved over to him rubbing his shoulders innocently. Sean turned back to his plate.

"Yeah, I'm sure she was."

Camille moved toward him, straddling his lap. She kissed him tenderly on the lips, "What are you jealous? Are you trying to act like my man now or something?" Taking his chin in her hands, "That's so sweet."

"Go 'head with all that, woman. Ya' know I 'ave no reason ta' be jealous 'specially over no female. You see tis here?" Sean reached under Camille robe placing his hand between her legs, "Tis has my name written all over it."

To prove his words true, Sean grabbed Camille catching her off guard. She nearly fell flipside, but Sean was quick. Wrapping one arm behind her like the back of a chair, he used his free hand to guide her waist. Sliding her on his lap in one swift move Sean found her moist and ready. Easing himself inside, he finished making love to Camille. The scent of anger replaced by aromatic airs of passion floated above their muffled sounds of excitement.

By the time Thursday rolled around Camille was so ready for the week to end she didn't know what to do with herself. Sean was still acting funny behind the whole Ebony incident. He'd only called her a few times this week and each time it seemed he merely wanted to find out where she was and what she was doing. Once he got the basics, each time he'd made up an excuse to have to call her back.

Work was also a bitch. All week long Hassan walked around the office, without saying more than two words to her. No matter how hard she tried to strike up a conversation, his wall was so thick all she ever got was a half-hearted reply. Camille eventually stopped trying. If Hassan wanted distance, that's what she'd give him. The other employees spent all day whispering amongst each other and becoming conspicuously silent when she walked in past them. Camille hated gossip. She could tell one of them had gotten wind of what was going on and succeeded in spreading the news like wildfire. A few times she had to bite her tongue in order to keep from cursing them out. She'd only spoken to Rita once. They discharged her after three days, but every time she called the phone just rang. Camille made up her mind to drive over there if she didn't get a hold of Rita by Friday.

"Jill Delano."

A young scantily dressed blonde approached the window.

"Do you have your insurance card?"

"Yeah," she handed Camille the card.

"Come on around." Once inside the room, Camille reviewed her chart. Unsurprisingly the girl was here for a pregnancy test. "You're seventeen, is that correct?"

"Yeah."

"Do you have a parent here with you?"

The girl went off at the question. "Look, I know you have, like, some kinda' doctor-patient code where you can't tell my business!"

"Whoa, sweetie, hold on. I was asking because I saw you sitting in the lobby with a woman I assumed was your mother. I was going to say she could come back if you wanted her to."

"Oh. Well yeah, that's my step-mom. My dad is gonna, like totally kill me if I'm pregnant."

"Ok, hon if you want to go at this alone that's fine. I need to ask you a few questions and then we'll get you squared away. When was your last period?"

"Um, November 2nd."

"Have you taken any kind of 'at home' test?"

"Yeah, twice. It came back positive" she started to fidget, "both times. I don't have a gynecologist 'cause my dad thinks I'm still a virgin. And, it's not like I could go to my pediatrician. I told Maryanne, my step-mom, and she bought me here."

"Well, I'm going to take some blood, run a pregnancy

test, and check for any STD's as well." Camille drew two vials of blood then walked out to have them run to the lab.

Cases like these made her stomach churn, young girls with no kind of direction having unprotected sex. The kicker was they always popped up pregnant. It was like they had the mindset that no matter how many times they'd seen it happen to their friends they thought they were invincible. *At least she's not black*, Camille thought. *If she was, there would be another notch in the belt of the statistics.* Camille walked into the back room looking for one of the PCT's. She found the girl huddled up at the copy machine along with another employee. When Camille rounded the corner, they looked like they'd been caught stealing. Ignoring the obvious, Camille bit her lip until she tasted blood and held out the vials.

"Paulette, run these for me please."

Without waiting for a response, she headed back the room. No sooner than her heel hit the opposite side of the wall, did she hear them exhale loudly, like someone pressed 'pause' releasing them from the frozen state.

Jill was talking so loud on her cell phone, Camille heard her before she even opened the door. "Yeah, I'm here now. I know it's his. Wait until my dad finds out he's black. He's gonna like, totally kill me!" Looking up at Camille she raised a finger. "Kris, I gotta go. The nurse is back. I'll call you later."

Camille shook her head as she sat down to complete the examination thinking, *With all that's going on in the world-- the last thing this baby needs is a dim-witted blonde for a mother and a naïve black daddy that has no idea what he's gotten himself or his child into.*

Camille drove straight to Rita's house that afternoon. She'd knocked for a good ten minutes before Rita came to the door, draped in an oversized nightgown. She pushed back her wet hair from her sullen eyes and seemed to look straight through her friend. Camille reached out to hug her, "Hey baby. How you feeling?" Rita pulled back, turning away. She walked silently to the family room, leaving Camille to close and re-lock the front door as she entered the gloomy house.

"Did you eat today?" Camille asked taking off her coat and laying it on the back of the couch. Rita perched on the edge of the sofa with her hands laced in her lap like a six year old who had been instructed to 'sit' by her teacher. Glancing up from the muted television in front of her, Rita nodded slowly and then turned back to the screen.

Camille moved through the rooms on the first floor surprised at how empty they seemed. Normally full of life, Rita's home looked like it had been stripped dry although everything was clean and in place. From the looks of it, neither one of them were doing anything above the bare minimums. The kitchen looked as if no one had used a single dish for days although Rita had said otherwise. Camille checked upstairs finding the master bed neatly made. The bathroom was still steaming from the shower Rita had obviously just finished.

Camille called out as she trotted down the hardwood

steps, "You need me to help you blow dry your hair?!" She poked her head around the corner. Nothing. Rita didn't budge. Camille settled herself next to her best friend. Sitting quietly she offered nothing other than her presence. *When she's ready to talk she will,* she thought. One thing Camille knew for a fact was that the bull in Ree made her stubborn as hell. There was no moving her until she wanted to be budged; so Camille just sat and waited. After about thirty minutes, she looked over to see Rita's head tilted to the side and her hands limp. She softly stretched her sleeping friend out and covered her with a blanket she found in the hall closet. Grateful she could lock it from the bottom, Camille again closed the door behind her, reversing the steps of her entrance.

It wasn't until she was back in the car that it hit Camille. The pictures were gone! Every time she got the chance, Rita was snapping shots or dragging Hassan to a studio. She made it a habit to get their pictures done professionally for every major holiday. Every room in their house was decorated with flicks that told the story of their life together. Someone had taken down every single picture. It was so odd that Camille had to push the thought from her mind due to worry. Whatever Hassan and Rita were going through, she was sure they'd come out of it soon enough. In the meantime, she decided to focus on getting ready for the upcoming holiday.

Camille made plans to see Ebony later on that week. Normally, she would never allow Jelani to meet anyone she was involved with unless she was certain the time was right. But, she told herself since Ebony was just a 'friend' it wouldn't mean anything for her to come through. She'd invited Ebony to spend the four days before Christmas Eve at her house. As a tradition, Rita had always spent that time with them. Camille figured it would be good to have someone there since her best friend was in no state to do so this year.

Jelani was still at aftercare when Ebony called lost. After giving her directions, Camille plugged in the lights on the huge evergreen looking around one last time to make sure everything was perfect. She was in the downstairs bathroom checking herself out in the mirror when the doorbell rang.

"Come on in!" She yelled. "Make yourself at home, I'll be right there." She took one last look and was satisfied with the reflection staring back. The velour pink and gray Victoria's Secret sweat suit hugged her curves just right. Camille blushed when she realized what she was doing and strutted out of the bathroom.

Ebony looked stylish in a soft gray blazer with double button cut and a baby blue halter underneath. Her Polo jeans were fashionably cut into a 'v' at the front of each leg bottom. They barely covered a pair of navy and powder blue Chuck Taylors laced neatly on her feet. She stood and smiled, seeing Camille's look of satisfaction.

"I swear, you have a style all your own. Where in the hell did you get those jeans?"

"I made these," she looked down at herself, pinching the seams of her pants. "I love to sew. And I seem to be getting pretty good at it."

"Let me find out you're a Martha Stewart chick," Camille

laughed, happy she was finally able to make Ebony turn red for a change. "Come on. Let's go in the kitchen. That couch is hard as hell."

"Yeah, tell me 'bout it."

Camille shot her a look that made Ebony grin. "I'm just joking. You have a beautiful home," she followed Camille down the short hall.

"Thank you. Are you hungry or do you want something to drink?"

"Sure, water is fine."

"Water? Oh, so now you're gonna act all shy on me? You weren't shy knocking back those shots of tequila at the casino. And you definitely weren't shy calling me, checking me last week. "

"No, I'm just fasting that's all."

Camille was surprised, "You're fasting?"

"Yeah, but only for a few more hours. It's how I keep my clarity. Mind, body and soul you know?"

Ebony smiled at Camille the same way she had in the elevator the day they met. "I like your outfit, too. You look hot, babe." Camille handed Ebony the bottle of water and tried to act like she didn't notice the 'come-on'. Ebony took it, but still held on to Camille's wrist. "Come here, let me check you out," She eyed her hostess from head to toe smiling at her pink footies with the gray cat on top. "Cute."

"Thanks. I have a thing for socks," Camille looked down at her feet.

"So what are we gonna do? Where is your son, anyway?"

"Jelani is still at daycare. I pick him up at six. We can do whatever. Oh, but first let me show you the house so you can put your stuff away."

Camille walked Ebony through each room. She was attentive to all of her descriptions and looked through each section with genuine interest.

"You know, most guys would hate this," Camille looked back at Ebony.

"Well, in case you haven't noticed, I'm not a guy."

"I know. I'm just saying?"

"What?"

"Well, you know. It's like, I'm tryna' act like we're friends, but then on the other hand it's like you're..." She couldn't find the word to describe what she meant, "Never mind. Forget it."

"No, tell me," Ebony whined. "Don't be like that. Always say what's on your mind. You never know when you'll get the chance to say it again."

The words buzzed around in Camille's head for a second before settling on the side of satisfaction. "Nah, what I was trying to say was, it's like there so much more between us than just you being my 'peoples', you know? I mean, I don't know how to describe it because for-real for-real, I've never been in this situation before. This is all new to me. That's all."

"Okay, ma," Ebony wagged her neck jokingly back and forth. "That's all you had to say, Miss Philly," she tried to mimic Camille's accent.

Bending over with laughter, Camille threw up her hand. Trying to catch her breath she blurted out, "Hold on 'Little

Country'. I'm from Jersey! Get it right!" They cracked up and headed to the second floor.

"And, this," Camille saved the best for last, "is my hideaway."

She led her through the closed doorway. Lavender paint covered the ceiling as well as all four walls. Thick white trim ran along the center, and the hardwood floors, deeply stained, gave off a gleam that reminded Ebony of new money. To her left, lace curtains covered the bay window above the broad sill that was as wide as a love seat. To her right a 32-inch, twelve-tier walnut bookcase sprouted out of the wall. The long shelves were stuffed from end to end with various series, novels, short stories and manuals; all arranged neatly. Each section separated by an assortment of thick glass angel figurines.

In front of her was a bed that looked like it came straight out of a 13th century castle. Like a kid Ebony ran over to the stool hopping onto the regal silk, down comforter. She slid around playfully before settling in on the plush mattress looking around at the fancy set up, "This is fire!"

The headboard was square with a wavy top that curved up and down. Plum colored sheer strips draped across the canopy and tied at the four ivory pillars with purple and gold trim. "I love it! This shit is fire as hell."

"Yeah. Jelani's dad tricked out one year for my birthday. He even had someone come in and build my bookshelf."

"Oh, so that's who answered your phone the other night?"

"No," Camille turned and began shuffling the perfume bottles on her dresser. "Trevor passed away almost two years ago."

"Oh, I'm sorry," Ebony felt bad.

Camille was ready to change the subject. "Well, you've got to see my bathroom, too. It matches, you know."

Ebony got the hint, "Oh yes, show me the bathroom."

After she was finished with the tour, Camille announced that it was time, for her at least, to eat. She was starving. Ebony decided to retreat to the den and relax while Camille cooked. Plopping down on the chaise she fumbled with the remote, tapping the screen. The television and stereo came on at the same time, both full blast scaring Ebony half to death.

"The volume is at the top right hand side!" Camille yelled from where she stood in the kitchen. She spread the mayonnaise across the wheat bread of her chicken patty. "*I can't believe she's here,*" she thought, shaking her head.

Camille walked into the den and settled down next to Ebony. Embarrassed from her mistake, Ebony was ready to change the focus to Camille. "Exactly what do you do?" Ebony asked pointing to the device. "I only seen this type of shit on Scarface."

"You're crazy." She laughed. "What do you mean what do I do? For a living?"

"For a living, for fun, for the hell of it. Anything."

"Well, I'm a lab tech for a living," she pointed to the high-tech remote. "I listen to music for fun and I write for the hell of it."

"That's what's up. But, you bought this decked out contraption to listen to the radio?" Ebony furrowed her eyebrows.

"Nah, I bought this decked out entertainment system to listen to my music. And, watch movies and control my computer. The remote, that just came with it."

"You know what?" Ebony squealed shaking her head. "So, you write, huh? And what is it that Miss Camille writes exactly?"

"Everything. Poetry, songs, short stories."

"For real?"

"Yeah."

"Let me hear something."

Camille placed her tray on the coffee table, thought for a second and closed her eyes.

"Like whispers in the wind you call me Not by name but by emotion Pulling me toward you Like the tides of the Atlantic Ocean I'm frantic as the waves crash inland Pulling sand out to sea I'm hesitant as I wonder Where it is you're trying to draw me I wonder what it is You're trying to achieve But still... I follow" When Camille looked up, Ebony was grinning from ear-to-ear. She snapped in applause, "Damn that was tight."

"Thanks."

"Nah, I'm serious. You're talented. That was deep." A serious look washed over her. "Was that for me?"

"Who else would it be for?"

"Oh come on, don't act like you've never dealt with a woman before. It could have been something you wrote for your ex-girlfriend."

Camille was taken back. "I never did this before," she

shook her head. "Trust me, this is a first. I told you I'm new to all of this," she waived her hand around.

"Well, well, well. I have a virgin on my hands. And, all this time I thought you were acting."

"What you mean acting?"

"You know, trying to play the shy role. But, let me ask you something Camille. Do you have any idea what it is you're getting into?"

The gravity in her voice made Camille a little weary. "Why you say it like that? What are you talking about?"

"Listen. Dealing with a woman is totally different from dealing with a man." Ebony noticed the worry clouding Camille's face. "Don't get all nervous or anything. I'm just saying it's much more... intense." Now, it was Ebony's turn to close her eyes and spit her flow. "It's like the kind of passion you read about in love stories. Like some ultra-magnetic, super sensuous, mind blowing, 'I can't seem to understand it' shit. It's a kind of bittersweet passion that you can't just forget once you've experienced it. It's sweet on those days when you don't have to utter a word and she understands. Even sweeter those nights you don't have to wish he would 'touch you there'. But, the bitter days. They come in full force. We always hear jokes about the wrath of a woman. The crazy thing is you know this, but you don't know until you the one receiving those flames how serious that shit can be," she laughed, but Camille was still teetering on the brink of her words. Just when she was about to fall face over in panic, Ebony changed the subject. "Anyway, tell me about you and what's his name?"

"Sean?" Camille perked up. The cloud over her wisped away like smoke being blown by a gust of wind.

Ebony nodded. "Right, Sean. You say he's not your man right?"

"Well, it's hard to explain. We met almost five months ago. He was the first guy I dealt with since Trevor died."

"And, Trevor is Jelani's dad?"

"Um-hm. I guess Sean was like my release. He pulled me away from all the drama I was going through. My depression, my solitude, my sex drought-- everything. And..." she shrugged, "I don't know. We've been spending a lot of time together lately, but we never really talked about any kind of commitment."

"So what? Ya'll just cuttin'?"

"What's that?"

"You know 'cuttin''. Fuckin'. He's your sex partner. Your cutty."

"What is that some down south term or something?"

"Yeah."

"Well, I guess so. But, it's like he's happy with things the way they are. And, I know I'm not the only chick dude deal with on a regular. I know for a fact he still fucks with his B.M."

Now it was Ebony's turn to have jokes, "What's a 'B.M.'? Is that some up north term?"

Camille had to laugh, "His baby's mother."

"How many kids does he have?"

"Just one. Morgan. She's adorable. I never met her, but I've seen pictures and I talked to her on the phone a few times."

"So, you said he still sleeping with his ex?"

"Yeah. He tries to play it off like he don't fuck with her like that, but a few months ago I saw them coming out of his house together. Plus, he's been actin' real funny lately. We've been arguing about a bunch of bull and we never fight. Plus, I'm finding myself getting jealous behind little things." Camille crossed her legs into a pretzel, scooting back on the sofa. "It's like when I was with Trevor. Man, I gave him so much hell. Whenever I thought he was stepping out on me, we'd fight like dogs one day and the next we were back in love. Sometimes I feel bad loving Sean the way I do 'cause I still miss Trevor so much."

"If you don't mind my asking, how did he die?"

Camille's face darkened, but she answered, "He was killed in a car accident. A hit-and-run. They never found the person that did it."

"Damn. That's terrible," Ebony rubbed her knee. For the first time Camille didn't mind the touch.

"Yeah, it's been hard. Shit, it still is. But, I know one day I'm gonna find out who did it."

"So what? The cops are still looking after all this time?"

"Nah, but like I told you I'm a lab tech. So, you know, I got a few connects. They found some of the driver's blood on a few shards of glass in the car, but because dude didn't have a record they didn't have any leads to follow. So after awhile, I made a few calls and got what I needed. I wasn't about to just let it go like that. I got the reports, DNA stats, blood type, all of that. It's all on my P.C. My connect hacked into the national link and set me up on alert. So, as soon as that muthafucka' so much as takes a piss test-- it's a wrap! I'ma have his ass."

"I hear that."

Camille looked from Ebony's hand in her lap to the green eyes watching her selflessly, "You're good for me. I can tell."

"What makes you say that?"

"Because, you are the only person I've talked to about

Trevor besides my family. And, you're the first person that didn't look at me like I was crazy when I told you my plan."

"Well," Ebony sighed, "that's because not everyone embraces inner self. See, as people get older it gets harder to accept emotions for what they are. A lot of people use logic as an excuse to harden their hearts. Now, I'm not in any way saying be irrational. But, at the same time, a lot of people won't nurture introspective. Me? I'm all about doing what makes you happy. I'm about living life the way you want. Shit, as long as you don't hurt nobody, to hell with what the world says. How ya'll say it up here? Do you?"

"Yeah," Camille nodded. "Do you. Anyway while we sitting here spilling our guts, how in the hell did you get blue eyes? Don't tell me you mixed or something. 'Cause for-real for-real, I don't dabble on the 'other side'." Reaching out, she ran her fingers down her leg and lightly rested them atop Ebony's soft hands, taking them in her own. She was happy she'd confided in Ebony and for a brief second, she felt a surge of something she couldn't understand. But, as quickly as it came, it left leaving Camille curious as to where it came from and what it meant. She could tell the next four days were going to be all peace, if nothing else.

Chapter 12

Sean

"What? Are you out of yar' mind? I don't know who ya' tink I am, but ya' got me fucked up. For-real for-real, yo! How did ya' get my number anyway?"

It was New Year's Eve. Sean was out shopping for the perfect outfit to wear to the lingerie party. Tony and his girl, Angela, were hanging in the Pocono's. So, there he was, walking down Market Street with seventeen-year-old Jill on his phone, telling him some bullshit about being pregnant. "Sean, you knocked me up. I know it was you. You're the only one I've been fucking."

Sean was livid. "Been fuckin'? Bitch, I fucked you one time and to tell ya' the trut', I don't even remember tat shit! Look, let me tell ya' someting. Me not one'a tese yun'bois ya' use'ta dealin' wit. Ya' 'erd? Me not gwan believe I'm the only man ya' screwed. So, ya' gwan have ta' find someone else ta' try'n play far ya' fool."

With that, he ended the call. Although he was fuming, Sean decided that Jill's little stunt was not going to ruin the rest of his day. He knew just the voice that would lift his spirits.

She picked up on the second ring, sounding sexy as hell. "Hello."

Sean's dick jumped in his pants. "What's up woman?"

"Hello, dear. How are you?" He was surprised not to hear any aggravation. It had been well over two weeks since he'd gone to see her. He'd called her on Christmas, but never left a message.

"Fine, 'ow are ya'? Merry Christmas and all dat. What'cha getting into ta'nite?"

"Well," Sean heard a female in the background.

"Who's that Ree? Tell her I said 'hi'."

"Nah, that's not Rita," she hesitated. "It's Ebony."

"What'cha mean? The Ebony that's just a friend? I see, that's why I 'aven't 'eard from ya', huh?"

Sean felt his jealousy bringing back the agitation that had begun to subside.

"Sean, don't start. I've just been chillin'."

"Well, listen 'ere. Tony and Angela are 'avin a party ta'nite up in the mountains. Why don't you and ya' girl come ride wit me so I can meet her. Plus, I wan' bring the New Year in wit' my woman." Sean knew he had just opened a floodgate with his last statement, but he wasn't about to lose Camille, especially to a female. If the two of them wanted to play, he had a trick for their asses.

"That's what's up." He could tell by the sound in her voice, he had her. "What time should we be ready?"

"Well, I wan'get there in enough time ta' get my pick of a'room and settle in. So, wit the drive I guess 'round six-tirty."

"Alright. I'll be to you by six-thirty then."

"Cool. Oh, Camille, it's a lingerie party so, ya' know. But, don't ya' come bringin' no scampy shit."

"Yes, Daddy," she joked.

"Nah, I'm serious. I'm not gwan 'ave ya' out looking like no smut on me arm."

"I said ok, Sean. Damn!" She paused. "How about you get me something to wear then you'll know it'll be appropriate."

That was the goose. But, Sean was far from a slouch. "Not a problem." His response bounced back at her like a brick off a basket ball rim. "Ya'wan' me pick ya' friend up something, too?" He was dead serious in his pursuit.

Shocked, Camille hesitated, "Um... yeah, ok."

"Alright, let me go then. Later."

Sean strolled into Victoria's Secret with total confidence. If it was one thing he knew better than the mind of a woman, it was the body. He prided himself on his ability to shop for his females who were 'deserving' of such.

"Can I help you with anything?" The salesgirl was jovial, but her voice was irritating hell. Sean hated high-pitched nagging voices. After hearing her, he didn't even want to turn for fear of her trying to assist him until he left the store. But still, so as not to be rude, he spun around. "No tanks..." Sean was stopped dead in mid sentence. The voice deceived him like Pandora and her box.

Sean's mouth hung low as his focus fell on the half-Asian, half-Black stunner in front of him. Right away Sean forgot how reluctant he was to acknowledge her. Smiling hard to show off his irresistible dimple, he went into mack-mode. "Ya' sure can, beautiful. What's yar'name?"

Blushing, the manager tilted her head to the side. Her long highlighted curls bounced off of her shoulder. "Hi. I'm Trish. Nice to meet you."

"Well, Trish, has anyone ever told'ya that ya' 'ave the most exquisite smile known ta' man?" The girl fell for the line. Like putty in his hands, she molded.

Sean told her he was looking for some sexy, but elegant eveningwear for his sister and cousin who were going to a lingerie party. They weren't able to shop for themselves because they were still at the hairdresser getting all 'dolled up'; but, of course Sean would do anything for those two. They meant the world to him.

Trish told him she found it sweet noble of him to spend his day helping them out. And since she was the General Manager, she offered him some special assistance. Proposing to model some pieces he was sure to like.

Sean was in heaven, as he sat back in the reserved dressing room with his own 'private dancer'. Trish was speedy, but detailed in her displays. With each selection, she pinned her hair differently giving a full overview of how the ensemble should look.

He took full advantage of her customer service, all the

while laughing at how good it felt to be so damn good looking.

"Turn 'round let me see the back."

Trish complied with his every order. Sean could tell she enjoyed putting on the show just as much as he enjoyed watching. After about twenty minutes, she came out in a white teddy with matching garter and sheer stockings that stood him straight up right where he sat. "Ahh, that's perfect," Sean visualized the curves of Camille's long voluptuous body filling out the nightie.

He motioned in front of him, "Come here-- let me feel the material."

Trish obliged parading over to Sean's lap. She moved up close on him, standing between his legs. From where he was sitting, Sean got a full view of paradise. The plum sized gap between her inner thighs exposed a sheer thong that covered two of the juiciest lips Sean had ever seen. He placed his hand, palm up in the space where her thighs were supposed to meet, but didn't. Pressing his thumb up against her mound he immediately felt the heat she was giving off. Like a professional, he began to massage her hot clit until her juices seeped through the lining of the panty. Trish exuded sweet smells of buttermilk from her point of arousal. She came so fast she didn't have time to brace herself when her knees gave way. Trembling lightly at first, the orgasm sped up throwing her off balance until she had to take hold of his shoulder to keep from falling.

After he made her climax, Sean knew it was time to stop. *"I know just what I'm doing,"* he thought. Sean made an art of giving women just enough to make them beg for more. He pulled his moist hand back smiling up at her pleasure-filled face that was red with embarrassment.

Trish hurried back to the dressing room, "Did you decide on which one you want?"

Sean took a handkerchief from his pocket, wiping her residue from his fingers. "Yeah, I'll take the white one and the greenish blue one."

"You mean teal," she came out adjusting her blouse.

"Yes, teal. What would I do wit'out you?"

She brushed past with her back to him, teasing her hair. "Let me go ring these up for you, Mr...." Trish didn't even know Sean's name. She had gotten caught up so fast that she never bothered to ask. Seeing her shame, Sean hurried to fill the awkward silence.

"Mr. Jeffers. Sean Jeffers."

It was too late. The girl left the room quickly, signaling her shut down, but Sean didn't sweat it. He stood and brushed his suit off. Popping his collar, he strolled out behind her as if nothing out of the ordinary ever went down.

He stood at the cash register waiting, while Trish carefully wrapped each item in the decorative tissue paper. Sean reached up to stroke his beard and caught a whiff of her scent. It reminded him that he needed one more thing. Reaching over he picked up two bottles of perfume- *Heavenly* for Camille and *Sexy* for Ebony, the friend.

"They get smell goods as well?" Trish teased, writing her number on the back of his receipt. "Lucky girls." Sean pocketed the slip of paper nonchalantly.

"No, lucky me," he thought, as he headed out of the galleria.

By six fifteen Sean had shopped, seduced, showered and shaved. The only thing he needed to do now was to pack his bag. He'd already pulled his gear out and was sure Camille would do the rest when she got there, like she always did.

He was standing in the kitchen, decked out in an all white silk, round-bottom shirt with matching silk slacks leading to white and cream custom loafers with alligator stripes going down the side. His dreads were pulled back in a ponytail and fell atop his neckline that was fresh with the scent of his favorite cologne.

The doorman called at approximately six-thirty informing Sean of his guest's arrival. "I love her punctuality," he thought, giving the 'ok' on the intercom.

When he opened the door, Sean was taken aback at the sight standing in his hallway. Camille was wearing satin. The auburn and black China Doll dress, clutched all the way down to her knees where it stopped, revealing her shapely legs. Meeting her hemline were a pair of reddish copper colored straps that laced from her calves to her ankles stemming from her seductive heel. *"Damn, this girl can rock a shoe,"* Sean thought. He looked over to the cutie at Camille's side. "Tis must be Miss Ebony." On the stranger's small feet, soft pink and gray five-inch stiletto's boosted her well above her true height of five-five. He hated to admit it, but she too looked amazing in a gray and salmon pin-striped Capri suit. The jacket had one lone button that casually held on to Ebony's full honey-colored breasts which were adorned by a pink lace bra. Midnight black tresses fell well into the cleavage she so openly shared. Sean pulled his gaze from her trail of temptation and honed in on the girl's soul windows.

Her huge eyes, clear and full, shimmered off of her baby powder like skin giving her the innocent look. And, though her face was youthful, Sean saw right through to the surface. He knew immediately that they were not going to mesh.

Camille walked in assertively, kissing him as she passed. "Sean this is Ebony. Ebony, Sean." She headed straight for his bedroom to get started on his overnight bag. Sean was glad he'd already folded and prepped everything he wanted packed.

"Nice to finally meet you." Sean extended his hand to Ebony, who reached up kissing him on the cheek also. Taken by surprise, Sean stuttered, "Um, did ya' leave your bags with Sal?" He was well aware his doorman had taken their luggage. Sal always did. But, Sean was searching for something to say because for the first time in his life, he felt on edge in the presence of a woman.

Ebony sensed his uneasiness, "I'm sorry. I didn't mean to invade your personal space. I guess you can call it southern hospitality. Plus, I've heard so much about you-- I feel like I know you."

Sean gestured for her to sit, "Ya' not from down sout'. Can't be?"

Ebony took a seat daringly on the arm of his chaise.

"No, I'm Trinidadian, but I've lived in Atlanta since I've been in the states."

"Ah! Ya' Trini, huh!?" Sean called over his shoulder to Camille, "Ya' know ya' in trouble woman? 'Ow dare ya' bring an island girl in me'ouse wit'out so much as a warnin'? She's gwan give you a run far'ya money ya' know? An' she's a red-bone?" Sean clucked his tongue.

"Oh, I know you're not talking?"

"Me?" he yelled. "I'm as 'armless as a field mouse."

Ebony cut in, "You're from the Virgin Islands, right?"

Sean nodded, "Yeah. Camille's got her hands full."

Ebony smirked, her accent rolling off of her tongue, "Tell me 'bout it."

"What are you two out here talking about?" Camille came from the room, with Sean's tote behind her.

Ebony got up, "Nothing important. You ready?"

Sean took a deep breath and followed the pair to the exit. *"I'm in for a hell of a ride,"* he thought, holding the door as the two pranced like thoroughbreds toward the elevator.

The forty-five minute ride through the snow-topped mountains was peaceful. Sean was in the company of two very beautiful women that kept him entertained the entire drive. Watching Ebony flirt with Camille turned him on. What got him even more excited were the fantasies creeping into his mind, outlining the possibilities that could very well take place on that eve of a new year. Sean had no idea what was in store for him or his ego.

He quickly found out when they encountered their first

dilemma at the check-in counter of the hotel.

"Will that be three separate suites?" The clerk looked at Sean, who for the second time today found himself speechless. He wanted to tell the clerk only one room was necessary, but he didn't want to jump the gun or offend Camille. He looked at her sheepishly for an answer.

"We're actually going to need two adjoining suites." She was so matter-of-fact the receptionist never caught on.

Once Camille instructed the bellhop, he took their luggage to the rooms and the three decided to check out the bar. Everyone was ready to take the edge off and start the celebration. After two shots of tequila, Sean told leaned over and whispered in Camille's ear, "Listen, I know ya' ready to party an'all, but don't go getting too buzzed too early. We got a long night ahead of us." Camille didn't respond. She knew that sometimes it was better to let Sean feel like he was in control, "I'm about to call Tony and see where they are."

The last time he checked, his friend was almost an hour behind schedule. This time Tony sounded more tired than frustrated when he picked up, "What's up, where ya'll at?"

"What up, dawg? We just checked in. That damn Angie couldn't make up her mind what she wanted to wear. I spent all fuckin' day tryna find her these damn shoes and when I get back to the house, she's crying about what outfit she's gonna wear! I'm so fuckin' beat I'm ready to take a gotdamn nap. Fuck this party shit."

"Yeah. You know that's how they do. But, come up to the bar and 'ave a drink wit' me. Fuck tat old man shit."

"Aight cool. We'll be there in a sec."

Minutes later Tony approached with Angela trailing. The two looked like Ricky and Lucy strolling in the place. Angie was all smiles and full of energy. Tony, on the other hand, was aggravated as hell and ready to collapse.

Sean gave him dap, handing him the double shot of Grey Goose.

"Good lookin' dawg. This damn girl is gonna make me kill her. Yah'a'mean?"

Angie ignored Tony's remark. Pushing him out the way, she hugged Sean warmly, "Hey, how ya'll doin?"

"'Appy New Year, Angie. You remember Camille, right?" Angela and Camille exchanged hellos. "And, tis is Ebony." Tony, who was too busy complaining, had not paid any attention earlier to the little 'brick-house' sitting next to Camille.

He blinked hard at Sean who gave him the 'I'll explain later' look.

"Nice to meet you. Thank you for inviting me."

Ebony stood to shake hands with her hostess, but Angie was a 'Southern Bell'. She nearly pulled Ebony off her feet as she embraced her.

"Oooo, you's a tiny litlle thang ain't ya?" She looked over to Camille. "You need to bring this chile on ova' the next time ya'll come for dinner. She could sure use some of my cooking." They all laughed while Ebony blushed under the spotlight.

"Look, me and Sean are gonna hit the pool table."

"Ya'll can go ahead. Do whatever it is ya'll need to do." Tony looked at Angela. "The party starts at 10:30, Angie, and you cannot be late."

"Boy, go'on ahead. I know what time my party starts," she waved him off and pulled up a stool.

Whap! Sean cracked the balls something lovely on his break shot.

"So, what'cha tink?"

"Nigga- you a pimp. That's what I think."

"Well, ya' know. I gotta bring the '07' in big boy style."

"Yeah, yeah, yeah. Just make sure you can handle all that ass 'Big Boi Style'! Yah'a'mean?!"

"Nigga, I got more 'andle than A.I. Ya' bes' respeck."

"Man, I'm tryna figure out how you go from *'I ain't fuckin' wit' Camille no more-- the bitch drove' me to drink'* to bringin' her to one of the hottest New Year's Eve parties in PA? Wit' another jawn!?!?" He leaned back on the cue. "Tell me how the fuck you pulled that one off?"

"Ya' know tese women can't resist da'kid. Ya' seen me in action, nigga."

"Man, I just hope Angie don't pick up on that shit. Then she gonna swear I be havin' big ass orgy's every time I'm out wit' you," Tony sucked his teeth. "And, you know she all dyke-a-phobic. I hope ya' girl play it cool, man."

"A 'omie, my girl ain't no dyke. And, some pussy'll probably do Angie some good wit'er 'igh-strung ass!" Sean knocked the six-ball into the middle pocket on an almost impossible shot.

"Yeah, fuck you. You wanna be rasta motherfucker," Tony laughed to himself chalking up the tip of his stick.

When the waitress came over to see if they needed refills, the brunette struck a flame in Sean's memory. "Yo! Let me tell ya' wha'appened! The white girl called me'phone talking 'bout she pregnant!"

"By who?! You nigga?" Sean nodded. "Get the fuck outta here!"

"The girl done lost what little bit brain she'ad. I tole' her she got me fucked up if she tink I'm fallin far the bullshit!"

"Well, what you gonna do?"

"Do? I'm not doin' a damn 'ting."

Tony leaned over the table positioning his body for his shot.

"Yeah, you just betta hope that shit don't come back and bite you in the ass. Yah'a'mean?"

"Whatever man, you gonna shoot or we gonna talk 'bout tis bullshit all night?" Sean was laughing, but Tony's words continued to echo through his mind.

By the time 9 o'clock rolled around, more of Tony and Angela's friends made their way down to the pool hall. By 10 it was packed with people they knew and even a few guests they'd acquainted themselves with over the last couple of hours.

Once 11 o'clock rolled around, Sean was ready to get his dance on. He left Tony and walked back up to the bar to find Camille. With no sign of her or Ebony, he made his way upstairs. He paused for a brief second in front of the room to the left of the one reserved for him and Camille. He then pressed his ear against the door, but heard nothing. Shrugging, he slipped the key into his door softly.

Sean wanted to sneak up on Camille for some fun and the sound of running water was the perfect welcome for what he had in mind. Sean had already begun to undress before he noticed the door adjoining the rooms was slightly ajar. He continued to the shower figuring Ebony came in for a look around before going back to her own room to get ready.

Pulling back the curtain, Sean stopped dead in his tracks. Ebony whirled around in surprise giving Sean a real life view of his daylong fantasy. She looked him squarely in the eye without turning and finished washing the suds from her hair.

Sean was stuck. His mind was telling him to apologize then leave, but his throbbing manhood was telling him something else all together.

"So, what do you think?" Sean jumped at the sound of Camille's voice.

"I um... uh...I ..."

"You what?" She asked seductively, wrapping her arms around him from behind.

He felt the warmth and firmness of her bare breasts against his unclothed back as she slipped her arms through his, caressing his six-pack. She slid her hands down to his zipper, inhaling deeply, before letting out a slow chuckle once she found what she was looking for.

Sean tried to turn and face her, but she stopped him, "No, you just watch."

With that, Sean relaxed letting Camille take control. She opened his zipper, pulling his slacks apart like she was unfolding a piece of wet paper. As usual, Sean was hard and ready. His dick throbbed heavily in her palm.

Ebony stood with her back against the linoleum. Looking past Sean, her gaze fixed on Camille as she massaged her own neck, throwing her head back. Ebony moved her hands to her breasts rubbing her long manicured nails in circles over each nipple. She hissed in pleasure loud enough to make Sean's erection jump in Camille's grasp as she jerked him softly forth and back.

With water dripping from her smooth skin, Ebony placed one of her legs on the side of the tub. Tantalizing her audience, she revealed the top of her finely shaved lips. Rocking her hips to her own beat Ebony's face oozed ecstasy, while she teased her spectators offering just enough to keep them on the edge.

Camille was beyond horny. Enjoying every second, her body responded with a flow of light twitches as she became more and more wet. Feeling her jerk, Sean reached back clutching her between the legs. Teasingly, Camille pushed his hand down before he was able to slide his index finger between her soaking lips.

Sean couldn't hold on any longer and was ready to climax. He bent slightly at the waist causing his dick to slip from Camille's fingers the moment he came. Ejaculating intensely without uttering a sound, he spun grabbed Camille by her hair and hungrily kissed her mouth with groans of satisfaction vibrating from his lips.

The two held each other in a passionate embrace, bare upper bodies sticking together from the steam. Sean whispered in her ear, "Damn, woman."

Pulling back he surveyed the scene and thought, *"Wow, that was a great nut."*

Ebony walked past them nonchalantly, wrapped in an oversized towel.

"We need to get ready," Camille pulled away, removing the rest of her clothing before stepping into the still-running shower. "I laid your clothes for you on the bed in your room."

Sean was sure he heard her wrong. *"Your room."* He strolled into the master suite to make sure. And, there on the king size comforter were two sets of neatly arranged clothes. Neither of which, belonged to him.

He looked over his shoulder confusingly. In the mirror Ebony shrugged her shoulders, smirking cunningly, while she blew her hair dry.

Sean stormed back into the bathroom, slamming the door. He reached in the curtain and turned off the water, "Camille what the hell is gwan'on?"

"What are you talking about? What is wrong with you?"

"Ya' put me'shit in the other room?"

"Yeah, Sean. What's the big deal?" She looked confusingly at him.

"The big deal? Are ya'crazy? Ya' tink I'm lettin' you sleep with her and I'm right'here? What kinda fool do ya' take me'far?"

Camille turned the water back on, "Sean, stop trippin'. It's not that serious. I need to get dressed." With that she closed the curtain.

Sean marched out and into his room. Pushing his clothes onto the floor, he plopped down on the bed like a kid having a full-blown tantrum, *"She's takin' tis too far."* He picked up the phone staring at the speckled ceiling. "Yes, room service please. Yes, I'd like a bottle of Remy Martin to room 1642."

"Me night isn't gwan be ruined by tat fucking cunt," he thought.

Room service arrived in less than ten minutes and Sean was on his second drink in less than fifteen. "She won't catch me again wit' me pants down," he vowed.

Sliding his silken-socked feet into the crimson Gators, Sean was ready to make his grand appearance. He left the room in full swagger, decked out in a cherry red and snow white Louis Viutton silk pajama set. His hair fell wildly around his freshly shaven face, augmenting his rude-boy appearance. From the lobby to the ballroom he turned heads. Women that were on the arms of the loves of their lives couldn't help but do a double take. Even a couple of the housekeepers stumbled over their feet trying to hold on to the picture perfect view. Sean smiled internally, assuring himself that he once again had the trump hand.

Chapter 13

Camille

Normally, Camille would be apprehensive exposing her body. But, the white teddy clinging to her every curve made her feel like a goddess on this night. Her hair was swept up into a soft bun with ringlets falling lightly down her temples; the gloss from her full lips shone dramatically against the hotel lighting. Her almond eyes accentuated with deep lining and sparkling shadow spoke volumes of the sensuality exuding from her every pore. Her long legs glimmered under the satin hosiery she wore, accented by the metallic gray heels covering her freshly pedicured feet.

Ebony too was astonishing in her teal lace camisole and boy shorts trimmed in black. Her bare legs, though not as long as Camille's, were shapely and well defined under the layers of rubbed on oils. With her eccentric nature on full display, her long tresses were corn rowed in z-shaped braids horizontally to the side, the end of each bearing tiny black conch shells and sliver beads. Around her waist, clipped to her navel piercing, a sliver belly chain matched the thigh high black leather 'hooker boots' she rocked with sliver buckles from top to bottom and open at the tip.

The music in the ballroom was jumping. Bun B was spitting his verse on Beyonce's *Check Up On It*, when in they walked. Feeling loose, Camille was ready to shake off whatever inhibitions she may have had left. This was the last day of the year and she was going to make the most of it no matter what.

Heading straight to the dance floor, she wasted no time and began to whine along with the baseline. Closing her eyes, she let the music move her like a cobra under the spell of a musician's clarinet.

Ebony followed, placing herself in front of Camille with her back toward her and fell in line with the rhythm. Soon the two were entranced by the melody. Grinding intensely against each other they were oblivious to anyone or anything around them. All of a sudden, Camille felt Ebony's hands clutch her hips and a surge of heat shoot straight to her erogenous zone making her body flinch lightly.

Ebony threw her head back and smiled up at Camille. "You like that?"
Camille nodded.
"Can I touch you?" She nodded again.

Ebony slowly slid her hands down to the inside of Camille's thighs. With her body still reeling from the effects of the liquor, her mind was in overload processing her libido's reaction. Ebony swayed her waist in sync with her hands, stroking Camille wildly beneath the flashes of the strobe. Surrendering to her touch and to the dance, they rocked—still oblivious.

After a while, the rising heat coupled with their energy pulled Ebony from the daze. "You want something to drink?" Camille was still feeling it from the shots she had earlier, but she was far from drunk.

"What the hell," she thought. "Yeah, you know what I like."

Ebony walked off, leaving Camille to the music. Within seconds she felt a pair of hands around her waist, followed by the scruff of a goatee brushing against her bare shoulder. "You're cheating on me," Sean's cologne seemed to bite her feverishly. *"Damn, I can't take all of this,"* she thought.

Her eyes met his, "Hey, baby."

"My, my, ya' look better than I imagined." He stepped back, holding her arms open to get a full view. Happy that the lighting was so dim, Camille blushed heavily.

"You look damn good yourself, handsome," She threw her arms up on Sean's neck, kissing him eagerly.

"Are we excited?" He asked wiping her gloss from around his mouth.

"Just a little. Besides, I thought you were still mad at me and I wanted to make sure my lips were the last you kiss this year."

He pulled her in close hugging her firmly, cupping her

ass. "No worries, I want your lips to be the first I kiss next year as well."

Sean's silk pajamas on her skin gave Camille a soft sense of security. Her mind was reeling into total bliss. She had Ebony, beautiful as could be, coming on strong and Sean was starting to act like he was ready for the relationship for which she'd yearned.

Ebony appeared out of nowhere with drinks in hand and an unlit clove dangling from her lips. Without a word, she stood smiling at the two until they saw her.

Sean turned, "Ya' tryin' ta' take my girl from me, eh?"

Ebony handed Camille her glass. Stepping directly in front of Sean, Camille was out of earshot as Ebony whispered. "Now honey, you know I would never do such a thing. She can be both of ours." Sean glanced at Camille, who was back to moving her hips to the rhythm.

Drawing Ebony close, as if they too were dancing, Sean bent down.

"Let me explain som'ting ta' you, Little Bit. That right tere is my pussy, ya 'erd?"

Ebony retorted cunningly, "Not after tonight." With that she flicked her lighter, sparking the end of the Djarum and walked off.

Sean was left with distress and embarrassment plastered across his face.

"What's wrong?" Camille looked behind him for Ebony,

who was nowhere in sight. "Nothing baby, come'ere."

Sean held her tight for the rest of the night. Grooving like there was no tomorrow, he counted down the little bit of time remaining in the year wishing with each second Ebony was wrong.

When the ball dropped in Times Square, Camille was still wrapped in Sean's embrace. He hadn't been able to take his eyes off her. Ebony was AWOL and Sean could care less.

They left the ballroom floating on the cloud of their love. No sooner than the elevator doors closed was Sean all over Camille, pinning her into the corner while he confessed his adoration. "Baby, ya' know I care 'bout ya' right?" He was poking anxiously through the silk of his pajamas. "I want ta' be with you."

The rounds of cognac he'd been knocking down all night had him loose. Grabbing her roughly by the chin, Sean extended his large hands up to her cheeks pulling her lips to his.

"I would do anyting for ya' girl, anyting. I need ya' ta' know that."

Camille just stared at him, his strength pulsating through her charged body. As if he could read her mind, Sean forcefully bit her nipples through the lace scantily covering her breasts sending her up the wall. She gripped the railing, rising to meet his hungry and waiting mouth. Grabbing his dreads with one hand she balanced herself with the other, sliding his head down to her flat stomach. He nibbled on her waist just below the garter, flicking his tongue rapidly. Pressed helplessly in the corner Camille shuddered as she climaxed under his thumb rubbing wildly across the tip of her clit.

The elevator dinged, forcing them apart just in time for the doors to open. Sheepishly Sean peeked out pulling Camille, who was in giggles, by the wrist and onto the floor.

Sean stopped in front the doors alongside each other. "So where are ya gwan? To be with her or me?" He hoped Camille couldn't see the anger clouding his question. Pulling the key from his hand she pushed her way into Sean's room, unlacing her negligee. Without another word, Sean followed closing the door softly behind him.

Chapter 14

Hassan

It had been almost two months since Hassan dropped Rita off with her grandmother and she finally stopped calling him all together. Not long after Rita came home, Hassan contacted Anna. He'd decided the best thing for both of them was to let her come back home for a while, until they decided what they were going to do.

"Anna, it's Hassan."

"Bueno, Papa. How is everything?"

"It's tough. On both of us. She's still not eating. All she does is sit in front of the T.V. all day like she's in some sort of trance. I mean, I'm trying to do what I can, but I can't sit here waiting for her to snap out of it." The agitation in his tone began to rise. "I still have to work and go on with my life. I don't know what makes her think she's the only one going through it." Anna sat on the other end in silence, knowing very well where the conversation was headed. "She acts like this wasn't her fault in the first place." No sooner than the words left his lips did Anna interrupt.

"Listen. I know you're still very angry. Bring La'Rita to me. You both need some time to yourselves. I will take care of it."

She needed to say no more. Later that evening Hassan pulled up in front of Anna's with Rita and her bags packed and ready to go.

Anna's eyes never met his as she held the screen door open, wrapping her arms around her granddaughter. It was just as well. The anger falling down Hassan's cheeks in the form of tears was a sight colder than the icy winds that ripped through the night air.

At first Rita's stay was supposed to be temporary. But, things took an unexpected turn when Hassan called about three weeks later to speak with Anna for an update on Rita. He wanted to find out if she needed anything or if she'd come around at all. When Rita's cousin answered, Hassan got much more than he'd bargained for.

"Yo, man, I'm glad you called. Ree is out here wildin'," his tone was thick with concern.

"What? What are you talking about, Ralph?"

"I'm talking about ya' wife, homes. She's out here all strung out and shit. She been runnin' behind this trick Marie."

"Wait, wait, wait. What? Strung out?" Disappointment flared through Hassan igniting his temper.

"Yeah, homes, she on that shit. It started out with just a little 'erb and some Ex. But now, she high every time I see her! And, I know she on some major shit. Half the time she don't even be here. And, when she do come in she look like she got ran over by a fuckin truck or somethin'!"

Hassan was boiling, "What is Anna saying about all of this?"

"Man you know Ree. She don't give a fuck what anybody say when she got her mind set on something. It's useless."

That was all Hassan needed to hear. He called the bank as soon as he got off of the phone and canceled her debit card. Washing his hands of Rita for good that day, he vowed never to let her back into his world. A woman so weak had no place in his life, his home or his heart.

No one but him and Anna knew that Hassan had sent her away like a child who'd shamed her parents. When Linda asked, he gave her the impression it was Rita who made the decision to go home. He went on with his life without missing a beat and actually began to finally come out of the shell where he'd buried himself.

Word of Hassan and Rita's tragedy spread throughout the masjid. But instead of gossip, it was out of love that the congregation spoke of their troubles. The Abdullah's were valued in the tight knit community and everyone held a genuine concern for the family. With Linda the head of a number of workshops for the women and Ahmed's long-standing reputation, the respect the family earned was well deserved. Hassan started to accept the condolences with an open heart and he'd been spending most of his free time around his spiritual family. Mainly to be in the company of the sister he'd come to favor. Nicole had him smitten. Hassan was determined to find out as much about her as he could. It turned out she was not involved, never married and now set on dedicating her time to learning about Islam. After going back-and-forth with himself Hassan decided today was the day he was going to make his move.

He walked up to the table where Nicole was sitting along with three other women, "As'salamu alaykum." They all replied in unison, "Wa' alaykum salaam."

"Excuse me, Sister Nicole, can I talk to you?"

She looked surprised, then rose silently following him to the courtyard. The January air was unusually tepid, blowing softly, as they walked.

"I've been noticing you a lot lately. My name is..."

"Hassan," she finished. "Noni told me."

He was embarrassed. "She did? What else did she say?"

"Now, don't go getting worked up. She cares for you a lot. I can tell she has your best interests at heart. She just wanted to know what I was all about," she smiled radiantly. "I guess it was sort of a prescreening."

"Oh," he relaxed, "I know you're new to Islam, right?" She nodded. "Well, what do you think?"

"Oh, goodness. It's all so overwhelming. I mean I've learned so much in such a little bit of time. I'm like a kid in every class, just soaking it all in."

"What made you want to learn about it?"

"Well," she paused, "life I guess. There was just so much turbulence going on, I needed something to ground me. Something solid I could trust and believe in. My friend back home, she's Muslim,"

Hassan interjected, "Where are you from?"

"Maryland, originally. But, I've lived in almost every state north of the Mason Dixon. Anyway, when my boyfriend and I broke up, I thought I was going to lose it. My best friend told me to find a masjid, just to visit, and see what I thought. The first time I came here I got this feeling. Like a peace came over me and I felt so..." she closed her eyes momentarily, "I don't know...free I guess. The men are so humble and the women have such beautiful natures. It's like, there's no gossip, no backbiting, no competition. They really live everything that it means to be a woman. It's amazing."

Nicole finally stopped to take a breath, looking up at Haasan's hazel eyes, "You're really listening to me." She was shocked.

He tilted his head to the side, "Of course I am. I wouldn't have asked you the question, if I didn't want an answer."

"You see? That's what I'm talking about. So many people these days are just shallow. They talk just to hear themselves, without any kind of substance behind what they're saying."

"I know exactly what you mean. I'm tired of just going through the motions. I'm ready for so much more out of life. I've kind of hit a point where I can't settle anymore." Hassan turned to face her. "What do you want Nicole?"

Without hesitation she answered. "I want to serve Allah with every breath I have. I want to be a good wife and mother. I want love, I want loyalty, and I want to believe in my husband and for my husband to believe in us."

Hassan felt the yearning in her eyes. He wanted to grab her up, hold her, and engulf himself in her innocence. He wanted to let her make all of the pain go away.

"What? Why are you looking at me like that?"

"Nothing. I'm just thinking. Let me take you out to eat tonight."

Nicole thought for a minute before answering.

Hassan was just about to apologize for coming on too strong when she spoke up. "Okay, that's fine."

Chapter 15
Rita

"La'Rita! La'Rita!" Her grandmother's voice rang violently inside Rita's severely hung over head. The sun glared in, stinging her swollen eyes as Anna pulled back the curtains.

Rita sat up looking around the bedroom. For a split second she was lost as to how she got there. Then in an instant, the memories of her ruined life came flooding back through the channels of her memory.

"I'm up Nana." she muttered. The foul odor of booze lingered in her pasty mouth. She turned to sit up, but immediately plopped back down under the weight of her inebriation. Rita looked up at the clock. It had been less than two hours ago that she stumbled into the house, up the stairs and into bed fully clothed.

"Nana, give me a minute please. I'll be right down after I wash up."

Mumbling under her breath, the elderly woman left without closing the door behind her. Rita rolled off of the mattress and trudged down the short hall to the tiny bathroom. The cold tile beneath her feet sent chills up her spine, as she stood in the mirror looking at her discolored reflection.

"Yo, you okay?" Ralphie poked his head in the open door.

"Nah, Pappi. I'm still fucked up," she turned. "You got anything?"

"It's some Alka-Seltzer downstairs."

She looked at him sucking her teeth, "I don't need any damn Alka-Seltzer. I need something to take this edge off."

Her cousin frowned. "Come on, Ree. You know I don't fuck wit' that shit, yo. Where you was at last night anyway?"

"I went to Night Train with Marie."

"Why you hanging with that bitch? She ain't nothing but trouble, homes."

"Whatever Ralphie," Rita closed the door in his face. She wasn't in the mood to hear a whole bunch of mouth. All she felt like doing was getting back in the bed and going back to sleep until the sun went down. But, from where she stood she could hear Anna clinking dishes loudly, which meant she was pissed off.

Rita rinsed her face in cold water, wiping the smeared make-up from her eyes. She brushed her rank mouth until her gums burned, then pulled her hair tight into a ponytail. Tears streamed down her eyes as the heaviness of mourning resumed its place in her heart. She stayed in the bathroom until she was all cried out. Feeling lower than low, she dragged herself into the kitchen to face her abuela.

Anna was standing over the hot stove with her back to the doorway. The smell of the fried eggs lingered heavily in the air, threatening to make Rita hurl at any moment.

"Ralphie said you was with that girl last night."

Rita didn't reply. Instead she silently stared down at the lukewarm Alka-Seltzer in front of her.

"I know you were out drinking. You smelled like a brewery when you came through the door." Rita tapped her foot nervously as her anger began to rise.

"These streets La'Rita, no mas problemas. They don't care that you've lost your baby. They don't care that you've lost your husband. All they care about is you losing your soul." Anna turned to face her. The sight staring back was beyond disturbing.

Rita's face had contorted into a malicious laugh. A chilling emptiness clouded her tone as she spoke, "Did you tell my mother that when she left and never came back for me? Did you tell my husband that when he dropped me off at your doorstep without looking back?" She stood, eyes wild, spittle running down the sides of her twisted lips. "I have no soul abuela! My soul died with my son!" Rita stormed out of the front door and took off running.

She made it three blocks oblivious to the debris beneath

her bare feet before pausing to catch her breath. Panting heavily, Rita took in the city around her. Although it was just reaching 10a.m., the early morning streets still offered poison to anyone searching and Rita was one of those in pursuit.

She walked up to a young boy sitting lazily on the stoop of an abandoned row house. Steadying her breathing, she tried to straighten her clothes as she approached him.

"You got any Hype?"

The boy looked past her up and down the vacant street. "Yeah, what you need?"

"Well," she began fidgeting with her hands in her empty pockets staring at the concrete. "I left my money at the house, but I live right up the block."

He sucked his teeth, finally focusing on her, "Yo, you Ralph's peoples, right?"

She nodded. "Damn, ma. I ain't know it was like that. Well look, since I know ya' peoples I know where to find you." He reached into a ceramic pot beside him.

"Thanks man, I'll be right back."

"Yeah, aight', ma."

Rita hurried back clutching the capsules in her sweaty hand. The anticipation of the high became more and more overwhelming as she neared her stoop. Before her foot hit the first step, her fingers were to her lips. *"Gotta go to sleep. Gotta relax. I'm alone. I killed him. It was my fault. My fault. Alone. Stop it! Shut up! Leave me alone!"* She ran up the stairs making a beeline to the bathroom, the voices in her head now screaming obscenities, while spewing vile thoughts through her psyche. Rita rushed to the faucet, cupping her hands. She gulped the hot water, sending the disintegrating tabs to the back of her throat.

Hobbling back to her old room with her hands pressed over her ears, she collapsed on the unmade bed wrapping her body in the pink crochet blanket trying to guard herself from the demons.

Within minutes the drugs took effect, quieting the voices-- replacing them with a dull hum that escaped Rita's throat. Her closed eyes reflected images in her clouded mind. Rita saw her silhouette standing in the middle of an empty hallway, surrounded by black shadows that pranced all around her. Red ringlets of blood swirled through the sodden air. Fear gripped her heart. Though her mouth appeared to be open as if shrieking, no sounds came out as she stood encircled by the jinn. Humming louder in alarm, Rita tried to muster a scream, but nothing came out. The nightmarish vision sent her body into convulsions.

Ralphie strolled past the room, then stepped back noticing something was wrong. He ran to the bed turning Rita's shaking body. "Ree? Reeee," he screamed. "La'Rita!"

After what seemed like forever, the sound of her name being called finally yanked Rita from her violent state. She came to chanting, "*Alone. I'm alone. Alone.*" Ralph stared in horror, not knowing what to do.

"Rita! Rita!" He placed his hands on her shoulders and began shaking his cousin. "Yo, what the fuck are you doing?"

Rita came to, defensively, pushing his hands away. "Get off of me boy!"

She turned, wiping saliva from the corners of her mouth, embarrassed and aggravated. Ralphie backed up to the edge of the bed.

"You was shaking and shit, like you were having some kind of seizure. I was just tryna help you, damn!"

"Well, I don't need your help?"

She lay back down and stared blankly at the wall. Rocking herself, she clutched onto her frozen arms as the high manipulated her mind.

By the time Rita woke up, the sun was gone. A brisk nightfall had set in over the city, giving off a glow of twilight. She stared out the tiny window at the orange lights lining the seemingly deserted street. From where she sat, Rita felt like she was the only person on the earth for miles. After hearing the tune for the sixth time, she reached into her coat pocket, grabbing the phone, "Hello." Her garbled words fell heavily from her mouth.

"La'Rita?" Linda sounded confused as if she'd misdialed.

"I can't talk now, Ma. I gotta call you back."

Before her mother-in-law could object, Rita closed the phone disconnecting the call. She turned on the lamp in the corner of the small room, pulling a duffle bag from underneath the twin frame. Shuffling through the contents, Rita pulled out a pair of jeans, a black wool sweater and her all-black Timberland boots.

She quickly dressed, then placed a call to Marie.

Sweeping her hair into a ponytail, she headed out the door zipping the North Face up to her chin.

"Donde vas?" Rita ignored Anna calling from the kitchen and trotted down the icy steps.

As she rounded the corner on her way to meet her friend, something yanked her violently by her right arm.

"What the fu..." Rita stopped face-to-face with the young boy from earlier. The hustler no longer looked empathetic, "A ma, where the fuck is my dough?"

"Aw, shit pappi, my bad!" She reached into her back pocket. "That shit you gave me was so good, I've been gone all day." Finding her jeans empty, her heart rate sped up. "All I have is my MAC card," she pulled out the blue piece of plastic.

"Do I *look* like a *fuckin'* ATM machine to you?!" He snarled.

Rita looked nervously down at the grip he had on her. "Chill the fuck out, aight?" She looked up the block. "Look, I'ma run up there to WaWa real quick and I promise I'll be right back."

"Nah, sweetheart. You only get to fuck me once in a day's time. You gonna give me mines." He jerked her toward the curb, opening the door to a steel gray Honda Accord with pitch black tinted windows, "Get in!"

For Rita the five-minute ride to the convenient store was nothing, but a blur. She was pissed at herself for falling asleep earlier. All she wanted to do was give this dude what she owed him, so she could go on with her night. Marie wasn't gonna wait for long.

Rita stood at the MAC in horror. The beeping screen flashed red: FUNDS NOT SUFFIENT FOR REQUESTED AMOUNT. Certain it was a mistake. She punched the keypad again very slowly: Four-Zero-Zero-Zero. Beeping, red flashing-- again.

Rita pulled her phone from her pocket, glancing anxiously out the window as she dialed the twenty-four hour customer service line for her bank.

"Yes. There seems to be a problem with my account." After giving her information, she was placed on a short hold.

The operator returned, "I'm sorry, Mrs. Abdullah. Your card has been deactivated. The message you're seeing is used to deter fraudulent card users."

"What do you mean, *de*activated? By who?"

"It looks here as if Mr. Abdullah requested the cancellation two weeks ago."

Rita's mind started whirling and she felt like she was going to vomit. She turned down the aisle, heading to the restroom, when he cut her off.

"Where in the hell do you think you're going?"

"I...uh." Pushing her around toward the door, he fiercely whispered, "Keep your mouth shut."

Back in the car, he held out his hand. "Well?"

Rita stuttered, "Th-th-ere... there....was something wrong with my card. My... my husband..." Before she could finish, the guy reached out seizing her neck. Squeezing down hard on her pressure points, he pinched his thumb and index finger until Rita blanked out.

When she came to, the car was parked on the barren riverfront. The driver was on her side of the car, with the seat pushed down as far as it would go. Rita was laid back with her shirt up to her chin. She looked down at her exposed breast as he chewed hungrily on her stiff nipples. She tried to sit up, but her body felt strange as if something other than his weight was bearing down on her.

"Yeah bitch, you like to get high, huh?" His hot breath smelled of weed and beer. "Well, let's see how much you like this trip."

Kissing her roughly in the mouth and holding her arms with one hand, he ripped her pants open with the other. Rita wanted to push him off, but the drugs he'd given her while unconscious rendered her lethargic. Although she knew she was being assaulted, her mind couldn't focus on gathering strength. He yanked her hand down to his small penis, forcing her to jerk it. "Tell J-Money you want it. Say my name, sweetness," he placed his hand futilely on her throat. Once fully erect, he climbed up on the seat forcing Rita's mouth open for his satisfaction, "Now don't you bite me." Inside of her head, she saw herself fighting back, gagging as he moved in and out. But, rolling from the high of liquid acid, her body was motionless until he came down the side of her face.

Riding back, Rita was unable to process what had just occurred. Whatever she was on was a feeling like no other she'd ever experienced. The car seemed to fly down the streets. The glaring lights danced before her eyes wildly. They looked so close, Rita was sure she could touch them. She stretched out her fingers trying to grasp the mirage, but reality would not let her close enough. She whispered to herself, while teetering on the edges of sanity. *Pretty colors. Yellow, orange, so pretty.*

J-Money reached over tapping her on the cheek shattering her stained glass delusions into a kaleidoscope. "So, how did you like making love while trippin'?" She stared at him blankly. His voice echoed in her ears like an old record being played in slow motion. "Oh, what? You not gonna talk to me?" He laughed turning back to the road. "Fuck it then. I'll just take you back to my crib and make your hot ass scream my name all night."

All Rita was able to do was shake her head.

"What? No? So, answer the fucking question. Did you like it?" Rita nodded, half out of desperation and half out of fear. J-Money chuckled again. "Good, 'cause see, I liked it, too. So, what I'm gonna do for you, sweetness, is keep you close. I'll give you what you need. Keep you geeked up and in return, you'll give me what I want. Understood?" She nodded again. "Good, now straighten yourself up."

Chapter 16

Camille

"Miss Delano," Camille watched as the girl sauntered through the door. This time her stepmother followed her into the consultation room.

Camille greeted them, gesturing for them to sit. "Well, you are definitely pregnant."

"Yeah, I knew it," Jill's tone was indifferent.

Camille continued, "You're about nine weeks, if we go on the date of your last cycle. There's an OB in this plaza with whom we're affiliated. The receptionist can schedule you an appointment, if you'd like."

Maryanne spoke up, "Jill knows who the father is, but he's denying it. Apparently he's married and as you can see, Jill is underage. My husband doesn't know about this yet. We didn't want a false alarm, but now that we know for sure we want a DNA test performed immediately."

Camille blinked trying to absorb what she had just heard. "Mrs. Delano, you can have a paternity test done after the baby is born," she replied.

"No!" She sat up staring Camille straight in the eye. "I want this bastard to know now that he is the father of this child! He will not leave me and Joey to take care of Jill and this baby. He's not going to escape nine months of obligation."

"Okay, look. I'm not a physician. You're going to need to, first of all, consult with her doctor." *"I can't believe this woman is serious,"* she thought.

Jill finally opened her mouth, which had been glued shut during her stepmother's outburst, "Well, like what are they gonna do?"

"One option is to perform an abdominal aspiration."

Maryanne nodded. "And, the results are 100% effective from an amnio."

"Right. If you insist, your doctor will perform the procedure. They pierce your abdomen around the navel into the placenta, and they extract fluids containing the baby's DNA."

"And, what about him. Doesn't he have to, like, get tested too?"

"He'll need to be sampled also, yes. But he has to agree voluntarily, since there is no order from a court."

Maryanne's tone was icy. Her eyes blank. "Oh, don't worry. There will be."

Camille left the two in the room, bumping into Hassan on her way to the front desk. "Camille," He didn't even look up, but seemed to peer harder at the chart in his hand.

"Hey, how's Ree?" Hassan had told her Rita decided to go back to Anna's to recuperate. She hadn't heard from her since. She had tried her phone a few days ago, but the number was disconnected. On top of that every time she called Anna's house, they said Rita wasn't there.

"She's fine I guess. I haven't really talked to her." Hassan still kept his eyes diverted.

Something shady is going on, Camille thought.

"Well, maybe I'll give her a call," she tried to find a way to catch his eye.

The detachment was unnerving. It seemed as if all love was lost between them, like they hadn't been a part of each other's extended family for nearly a decade.

"Hassan, if you need to talk you know I'm here, right?"

"Yeah, I'm ok. I mean, I'm fine." He stressed emphasis on the word, *I*. "Camille, I think…," before he could finish, one of the PCT's came around the corner.

"Mr. Abdullah, there's a Nicole on line three for you."

Hassan turned, "Ok, I'll be right there." He looked nervously back to Camille. "Um, I've got to take this call."

With that he walked off, leaving the name ringing in Camille's head, Nicole. *"Nicole, I know that name from somewhere."* Unable to place it, she headed back to the room, vowing to stop by and see Rita later that evening.

When she walked in, Jill was on the phone, apparently trying to reach the culprit of her impregnation. Maryanne was beside her like a hawk. "Well?"

"Shit, Maryanne, he's not answering. I told you he won't take my calls."

"Dammit Jill, hang up! Don't bother leaving a message. We'll call him from my phone later."

Camille cleared her throat, interrupting the performance. "Now, Jill, you realize that you're still in your first trimester. And, since this procedure is so invasive, there is no way Dr. Jordan is going to approve it until you are at least four to five months along. Even still, I don't see him giving the green light on something so dangerous to you and the baby without it being necessary."

Jill looked at Camille as if she were speaking Greek. "Whatever. As long as I can prove to him that this baby is his. That's all that matters to me."

Camille usually remained neutral in these types of situations, but something about this whole ordeal made her uneasy. She felt sorry for the unsuspecting father who had no idea of the plots of destruction being drawn against him. That's what happens when brothers mess with white girls. They always get caught up. More than anything, Camille felt sorry for all of the innocent parties involved. For one, the brother was married. This was surely going to uproot his home, whether he turned out to be the father or not. On top of that, this fetus's life was being put at risk in order to prove some infantile point. But, the truth of the matter was that this was not any of her business. All she could do was pray that everything would turn out for the best.

Camille stood, bundled up on Anna's front stoop, about to ring the doorbell a second time when the voice cut through the icy wind, "Hey, you." She recognized the voice and turned to see one of her old high school classmates.

"What's up, Marie. How've you been?"

"Me, I'm chillin'. Just came by to check Rita out."

"Yeah, me too." As Marie came closer, Camille got a better look at her from head to toe. The woman standing in front of her was a faded shell of the bright, outgoing, senior Camille remembered. She looked like twenty years had been added on to her life instead of ten. Her skin was dry, cracked and dull, like someone took a vacuum to her lips sucking the life from her and she was at least thirty pounds lighter than Camille remembered. Her hair was pulled way too tight into a matted ponytail that sat on the very top of her head. Camille couldn't hide her shock.

"Damn, Marie! What's going on? You look like shit." Camille knew the insult was obvious, but if her assumptions were right, it wouldn't even matter.

"Girl, you crazy," Marie laughed a hoarse laugh shaking her frail arms at her side.

By this time the front door opened and one of Rita's aunts stood, refusing to crack the screen. Lizvette was evil as hell. She never seemed to like any of Rita's friends. Camille and Ree used to joke that it was because she didn't have any friends of her own. Peering at them through the mesh, she sucked her teeth hissing out a loud sigh.

Camille spoke up, "Yo, Liz, where's Ree?" She sucked

her teeth again looking over her shoulder as she spoke, "She ain't here." Offering no more info she stepped back and began to close the door. Camille banged her palm against the pane of glass, "Yo, Liz! Ey!" Demanding her attention, "You know where she is?"

"Man, Camille where the hell you been? She probably out East Camden with that nigga J-Money she be trickin' for."

Camille's face contorted in disgust. "What you ain't know? Her 'Prince Charming' ain't been keeping it real with all ya'll 'cross da' bridge? It Figures," she chuckled, pushing the door shut with a thud.

Camille was stunned. She didn't know what to say. As she turned to leave, Marie stepped anxiously in her path. "Yo, Camille! You gonna ride out there?"

She moved past the crackhead toward her car. Pain gripped her heart like a crow's claw seizing a still wreathing carcass.

Marie trailed behind her pleading, "Come on man. Let me ride wit' you. I need to holla at her real quick." Camille's pain boiled over into anger, raising her temperature despite the frigid winds.

"Look, Marie, back the fuck up out my face." With that, she pushed past the girl and popped the rear hatch of the SUV. Removing a pair of lime green and white 95' Air Max's, Camille threw them on her feet. She felt like she was going to have to rock for what she was about to go and demand and the 'kicks' were a signature that some shit was getting ready to go down.

Throwing her truck in gear, she sped off toward Baird Street heading into East Camden. As she passed the high school, her eyes became like binoculars, zooming in on every female figure in her focus.

Less than three minutes later, Camille spotted her standing outside a liquor store. She was bent over the driver side of a Honda with windows like midnight, hiding the view inside. Pulling up wildly, Camille boxed the Accord in between the curb and her 'Range'.

Rita jumped back as Camille burst out the left side door embodying every ounce of 'Jersey' she had running through her veins. "Get the fuck in the truck!" She ordered, staring into her best friend's glossy eyes.

Rita's dry mouth cracked a smile, revealing tartar stained teeth. "Camille, what are you doing here?" She slurred. "Just leave me alone. I'm good."

The door of the Honda opened immediately. A short, black, ugly, raw looking dude barely over twenty stepped out. He was fresh to death in a pair of original Timberland boots and a smoke grey Meskine sweat suit. He strolled over to Camille, 'ice grilling' her under the wide hood of his leather bomber.

"Yeah, Ma. You heard my Sweetness. You ain't got no business here. Be out." He snapped his neck back like he was talking to his child.

Camille had grown up around 'wanna be' thugs all her life. She was in no way intimidated by the young hustler or the cold-blooded stare he held.

The truth of the matter was the blood in her veins ran just

as cold when it came down to certain shit. And, Rita was exactly the shit that could make her feminine frame create just as much adrenaline as any nigga on the street.

Camille knew enough not to cause a scene by disrespecting him directly, but there was no fear in her. She understood the code of the streets and rather than pop off at the mouth, she chose to simply ignore his presence.

"Rita, get the fuck in the fuckin' truck," she repeated, glancing for a split second at her friend then back.

The guy, who Camille assumed was J-Money, stepped in front of her grabbing Rita's arm. "Let's go bitch." He started dragging her toward the car by the elbow, but Camille was quick. She swept around the couple, placing herself between them and the passenger side. Her heart pumped like light bolts in her chest, but she refused to let her nerves get in the way of her judgment. "For-real for-real, I don't have no beef wit' you. But, that one right there is goin' wit' me."

J-Money laughed as Rita, obviously 'blowed' out of her mind, stammered forward, "Whoa, Camille. Move. Go home, I told you I'm good."

Agitated that she interrupted the flow of his day, J-Money'd had enough. Reaching around his waistline, he pulled a .357 from behind his back.

As he went to point the Magnum blatantly in her face, he realized that not only was he too late, but also how serious the female in front of him was. He stood eye-to-barrel with a matte black .45 Governor, cocked and ready to reel.

Eyes fixed on her target, Camille, for the third time, echoed through gritted teeth, "La'Rita, get your muthafuckin' ass in the car, right now."

Rita, who was now free from J-Money's hold, scurried to the passenger door of the Range Rover as Camille moved backwards keeping her arms up and clip extended. Once inside, she hit the button locking all four doors, threw the gearshift in reverse and peeled out, leaving the boy stunned beyond belief.

The normally thirty-minute drive seemed to take all of ten as Camille sped through the bumpy streets ignoring the 'sure to ruin any suspension' craters that sprinkled the broken asphalt's path leading to the Walt Whitman.

Camille's voice shook as she screamed at her friend, "What the fuck, Ree?!" Tears of fury and guilt streamed down her face. She was furious at Rita for violating all she stood for as a woman. At the same time, guilt seized her heart. She had been so overly engrossed in her own life that she wasn't there like she should have been.

Rita sat, making no eye contact. When she spoke, a foul odor exuded from her mouth, damn near choking Camille. "Man, why the hell you go and do that? J-Money gonna be mad as hell."

For the first time, Camille took a good look at Rita. She looked like shit on a stick. Her feet were barely covered in a pair of red slippers that looked like they came from the corner beauty supply store. With no socks covering, her ash from the cold ran up her heels and ankles meeting a pair of white footless tights that were supposed to keep her warm. The bright red "pleather" jacket she wore over a flimsy tee matched a mini skirt that barely reached past the bottom of her ass. But, worst of all was her head. Rita's beautiful thick mane was dyed midnight black and butchered into a horrific rendition of what some junkie told her was the 'latest style'.

"Muthafucka! What the hell did you do to your hair!?" Camille screeched.

Rita reached up patting her smelly, damp hair, "Oh, I cut it. You like it? I mean I was alone, but then J-Money came and I got a lot of friends and then I can make my own money without no nigga. 'Cause I don't need no nigga. I got the world in my pants!" Rita rambled on, twisting her hands around the frayed ends of her discolored hair. Camille realized it was useless to try and talk to her now. She was so lit nothing Camille said made any difference. They rode in silence the rest of the way home.

Camille took Rita straight upstairs to her bedroom. She was glad Jelani spent the night at her mother's. She was even more relieved he'd be there all weekend. Thank God he didn't see his Auntie like this.

"Take those clothes off. I'ma run you a bath."

Rita huffed and puffed as she flopped down on Camille's plush mattress, kicking off the dirty house shoes.

Heading into the bathroom, Camille decided Jill Scott was just the album to calm her nerves.

She filled the deep tub to the brim with scolding water and scented bath gel. Then she sprinkled some jasmine and rosemary across the bubbles before pouring the remainder in the oil burner sitting on the counter top. The calming, rejuvenating scents filled the spacious lavatory taking effect almost instantly. She inhaled the fragrance filling her lungs with the aroma.

"Rita, come get in the tub."

Her friend sat listless at the corner of the canopy, with her head leaned against a pillar.

"Look at me, Camille," her tone suggested sobriety was rounding the corner. "I'm just like my parents. A fuckin' junkie." Mascara ran coal swirls down her deflated cheeks. "Why didn't you just leave me there? It ain't even worth it no more."

Bending on her knees, Camille took Rita's bland face in her hands.

"Because I love you and I'm never gonna sit back and let you fall. You're my sister and I'd die without you. You hear me?" Rita nodded. "Now come on, let's get you cleaned up."

"It was horrible. She smelled like she hadn't bathed in days. And poor Anna, when I called her, she was so worried. She said it had been weeks since they saw her."

"I'm so sorry, Camille," Ebony stroked Camille's head tenderly looking down into her watery eyes. "Don't cry baby, she's ok now."

"I know. I'm just so pissed for letting this happen. I want to kill Hassan."

"Well, you have to realize that he's going through it, too. I mean look at what happened. The whole thing is just so devastating. You never really know how tragedy affects people."

"But, Ebony, we've known each other forever. He's Jelani's godfather. I mean he treated her like she was nothing to him. And, on top of that, I think he's seeing another woman."

"What?"

"Yeah, this chick named Nicole keeps calling the office and shit. It's just messy right now. That's why I took this leave. I need some time to get my mind right, so I can be here for her 'cause he obviously doesn't give a fuck."

"I've never seen you so mad." Ebony smiled trying to lighten the mood, "You doin' all that cussin'."

"I'm sorry, dear. I'm just vexed right now, that's all. But, anyway I've missed you."

"Yeah. Well, I've been doing a lot of running around myself trying to get Carla situated."

"Oh, yeah," Camille looked up. "How is your cousin?"

"She's doing great, actually. And, the baby's grown so much. She really doesn't need me here anymore." The distress reappeared in Camille's eyes and Ebony regretted her last statement.

"Are you leaving soon?"

Ebony bent down softly kissing Camille's lips as she lay in her lap. "Not before I get the chance to taste you," she whispered.

Camille sat up, ignoring Ebony's advance, "So you're

serious. You are leaving?"

"Camille, you knew that when I first met you."

"But, you said..." Camille shook her head. "Nevermind." She walked out of the den into the kitchen and poured herself a shot. Ebony trailed her walking out onto the patio for a smoke.

Camille leaned against the sink, glass in hand trying to decipher the emotions circling through her. *"Am I catching feelings for this girl? Like a real relationship? 'I wanna be with her' type feelings?"*

Her thoughts shifted to Sean. He'd been so distant; Camille wasn't sure where their relationship was going. Every time she called him he sounded paranoid, like someone was after him. But, when she asked what was going on, he brushed it off to stress at work. To Camille that meant he needed space, so she backed off. On top of that, Ebony was quickly becoming a constant in her & Jelani's life. And, even though she battled with the thought of being gay, Camille was more and more at ease each time Ebony stepped foot in her door.

"Hey, I'm going upstairs," Ebony walked past her, leaving a trail of spices and smoke from her cigarette. Camille placed the empty glass in the sink and headed to the room. Ebony was sitting on the bed arms folded across her chest. She was prepared for a debate. Camille was drained and just wanted to pass out for the night.

"What is it you want?" Ebony uncrossed her arms leaning back on her palms.

"What? What are you talking about? What do you *mean*, what do I want?"

"Just what I said. You've got me running around here on one leash with Sean on the other. You want to be in the middle of the street Camille and that's not good. Nor is it fair to either one of us. Even though you say ya'll aren't together, I'm sure he's feeling some kinda way about you seeing me like you do."

"This is not about him."

"Yes, it is Camille," she cut her off. "And, is that what you say about me when you're with him? It's about all of us and you making a decision."

Camille jumped on the defensive, "Why do *I* need to make a decision? What's wrong with things the way they are?"

"I'm gay, Camille. I like girls. I like you. I would love to be with you. But, you don't know what you want. I would love to kidnap you and Jelani and take ya'll to Atlanta with me. But, I know you're not ready for that. I lay beside you wanting to touch you and make love to you. I go to sleep every night horny as hell thinking about how sweet you must taste. But, I don't pressure you 'cause you are not ready," she sighed heavily. "This is me. This is my world, my life. And, I would love nothing more than to hold your hand and walk you through, so you can see how much I feel for you."

Camille was silent, eyes glued to the floor. Ebony held out her hand, "It's okay baby. Come here." Camille melted into her embrace, a wave of gentle peace flowing over her. Her body lay atop Ebony's, as it had many times before. Camille gazed into her eyes and began to tingle. Her thighs started to spasm in excitement. Unable to resist the flame burning intensely throughout every pore of her skin, Camille lowered her head bringing her lips to Ebony's neck.

"I'm not trying to make you do anything you don't want to do. I'm just letting you know where my heart is." The vibrations from Ebony's lips as she spoke sent electric chills up and down Camille's spine. She felt like she was ready to explode.

Camille pulled back, moving her hands down to the front of Ebony's waist. She slid her hands underneath her sweater, slowly stroking. She was in awe of how soft Ebony's body was. The warmth radiated through Camille's palms as she traveled back up, cupping her breasts with both hands. She gasped lightly in enchantment as her eyes locked on to the picture perfect view of Ebony underneath her. Camille couldn't help but explore every tangible part she could get her hands on. Ebony whimpered and squirmed. She reached out running her finger along the rim of Camille's mouth.

Camille sucked softly on each finger. In one swift move Ebony flipped her over straddling her waist.

"Tell me you want me."

The sultry sound of Ebony's voice intensified the kinetic energy flowing throughout the room.

"Tell me what you feel."

She grinded her body tenderly against Camille who was speechless, with her mind traveling one hundred miles per hour through a tunnel of pure bliss. "I…" she stuttered, "I…"

"Yes? You're what?" Ebony kissed from her neck to her mouth and back to her neck again. Unbuttoning her pants with one hand, she stroked Camille's hair lightly with the other.

Ebony's body jerked when she felt the wetness inside

Camille's panties. Camille's body exploded, bursting free the instant she felt Ebony's touch, "I'm coming!!!" Shaking ferociously, Ebony helped her along, rubbing circles in the juices that flowed down the palm of her hand.

Ebony moaned licking her dripping fingers, "You taste like buttermilk-- just like I imagined."

In an instant Camille seeped back into reality. Rolling onto her side, she buried her face in the pillows.

"Oh, my goodness."

Ebony collapsed beside her, running her hand through her hair. "What? You didn't think you would come for me?"

Camille's muffled voice was barely audible.

"Don't make jokes."

"I'm not joking," still Ebony laughed. "I'm just asking? Seriously, what is it?"

Camille popped up, "What is it? You just fingered me and I came all down your hand. That's what it is."

"Well, actually, you were hella wet before I even touched you, so um..."

"That's not funny, Eb."

She tried to keep a straight face, "I'm sorry, babe. You're right, it's not funny. It's absolutely beautiful."

Ebony stared at Camille buttoning her pants muttering to herself under her breath. "Camille."

"Huh?" She looked up, still red with uncertainty.

"Let me make love to you." Camille was silent. After what just happened she didn't know what to say. Shit, she barely had time to process her orgasm. Still her body was screaming for more.

"Go ahead, take those off."

Camille paused. Before she knew it, she was complying with Ebony's command. Dropping her pants to her ankles she stepped out of each side, slowly revealing her smooth brown legs. Reaching around, she unfastened her bra and removed her shirt at the same time. Her firm breasts fell softly on Ebony's passionate gaze.

Camille crept onto the bed and laid back. Opening up like a flower in bloom, she steadied herself as Ebony moved ever so gently and made love to her.

Chapter 17
Sean

Sean was beyond pissed. Out of nowhere it seemed, his life managed to fall into complete shambles over the last two months. First, there was Jill. As it turned out, she was pregnant. She called him day in and day out, hounding him about taking a blood test. Somehow she managed to convince her doctor to perform a pre-delivery DNA screening.

Jill and her step-mom, who Sean came to know very well via 'hate mail', were determined to make his life a living hell. After weeks of debate and daily threats of incarceration, Sean arranged for the test to be performed by his own personal physician. Setting it up, so the results would be forwarded online, Sean made sure there would be no chance of him running into Jill or Maryanne. He refused to risk an altercation with the two vixens. Now, the only thing he could do was sit and wait for the outcome.

On top of that he and Camille, after an amazing New Year's Eve, seemed to have no time for each other. She was occupied tending to Rita and he was struggling to balance Morgan's weekly routine and regain some type of control. It had been almost three weeks since they'd seen each other. Even their last encounter was seemingly strained from all of the outside pressures.

Sean even felt like she was seeing someone else. He was even more certain that the someone was Ebony. But, he had too much going on to battle something that was out of his reach. He was a firm believer in *'what will be, will be'* and he knew if Camille was meant for him, fate would bring them together.

If that wasn't enough, even him and Nicole were starting to take unexpected turns and not for the better. At first the weekly arrangement they had was copasetic. But soon after, he noticed her personality changing. It seemed she was becoming more and more withdrawn. But, not only from him, it was like she was removing herself from the world.

Every time he saw her, she was dressed plainly with her hair pulled back in a simple bun. She wasn't wearing any make-up at all and was always in an outfit that came all the way down to her wrists as well as her ankles. But, the most obvious thing was her feet. Nicole had always worn some type of heel no matter where she was going. She was the type of "girlie girl" that would not be caught dead in a pair of flats. She'd always said, "A lady should always be sexy, even if she's just going to the drug store." But lately, every time Sean saw her, she had on a pair of loafers.

Now meeting him at the door rather than inviting him in,

Nicole had stopped making eye contact with Sean when he dropped off Morgan. The more he thought about it, the more his mind conjured disturbing explanations. Sean was strictly against questioning Morgan on Nicole's personal life, so he decided today he was going to have a sit down with her himself and find out what he needed to know.

He'd invited her to Dave and Buster's for a family night. At first, she tried to back out, but after some convincing she agreed. Sean had never seen her so beautiful. Her body language peaceful, amidst the may lay of the arcade. She had on an all-brown khaki dress with a tan sweater. On her head was a matching silk scarf, tucked back around her small ears and knotted on the side.

"Hello, dear," Sean bent down to kiss her cheek.
Nicole pulled back slightly. "Peace Sean, how are you?"
He blinked in surprise, laughing at the brush off she'd given him. "I'm okay. What's gwan'on wit' ya'?"
"Not much, you know."
"No," he tried to sound light in his words, but they fell heavily from his mouth. "I don't know. So, why don't ya' tell me."
"Tell you what?"
"What the deal is. I mean, ya' walkin' 'round here like some kind of zombie, dead ta' the world."
Finally, Nicole looked up meeting Sean's eyes, "I'm not dead. I'm finally alive for the first time in forever."
"What the hell is that 'posed ta' mean?"
"I'm changing, Sean. I've found what it is I've been missing all these years."

"What ya' got some new boyfrien' or someting?"

Nicole looked over at Morgan turning in circles under the black light. The virtual reality helmet sagged to one side as her small head fought to keep straight.

"I've been studying Islam for a while now, Sean. I'm about to become Muslim. I'm taking Shahada, my vows, on Friday."

"Oh." Sean felt like he'd just been slapped in the face with a key lime pie. Embarrassment, mixed with confusion etched across his brow, "I see. So, is that why ya've been actin' so funny wit' me 'ere lately?"

"Well, yeah, I guess. I don't really think I've been treating you badly. I hope I haven't. You don't feel like that, do you? I've just been reflecting a lot on my personal life. Re-evaluating a lot of things. And, Sean I've made some serious decisions."

Sean rubbed his forehead, "Whew, tat's a relief. I though' ya' was in some kinda trouble or had a boyfriend or something that was beatin' ya'. Ya' had me worried outta my mind."

Nicole smiled at her ex's obvious concern. "No, I'm good. Can't you tell with Morgan?" She nodded over to their daughter, "I mean, she speaks volumes for both of us. Don't you think she would have said something?"

"Now, ya' know I'm not gwan hound her far no infarmation on you. I don't roll like tat."

Nicole knew full well he was right. This was probably the first time ever she'd wished he would though. At least if Sean asked their daughter, it would've taken the pressure off of what Nicole had to tell him. "Well, I guess you don't know then."

"Know what?" Sean tried to search Nicole's eyes, but they were glued back to the floor.

"I'm getting married."

Chapter 18

Hassan

Hassan sat staring between Ahmed and Mansoor, looking for some sign of approval, "Well, what do you think?"

Ahmed kept silent as Mansoor sat up, clearing his throat. "Hassan, if you're one hundred percent sure about this, I'll support your decision. You know that. But, you need to make sure you're ready to make this commitment. I mean, this is different than with Rita. Granted you were married, but ya'll were married according to man's law. This time you'll be bound according to the law of Allah."

"I know, Mansoor." Hassan was trying to curb his aggravation, "And, I'm *sure*."

"Alright then. Has she taken Shahada?"

Hassan shook his head, "She takes it on Friday."

"Well, I guess in that case - it's time to celebrate masha' Allah," Mansoor stood up and hugged his brother.

Looking over Mansoor's shoulder at the apathy on Ahmed's face, Hassan felt a twinge of sorrow. Why wasn't his father happy for him? No sooner than the thought fell from the brim of his mind was Hasaan reminded of something Ahmed said to him once, "Your faith is not to be trifled with. It is something you are to treat as serious as you would your very own existence. For that is what it is, your existence." And, from that moment, Hassan was determined to prove to his father that he was truly a changed man. He was set on fortifying his role as a worthy son, a devoted husband and a dutiful Muslim.

That night when he got home, there were two messages waiting on his answering machine. The first was from Nicole. She called to tell him she was going to a workshop with Linda in the morning and would link up with him that afternoon. The second was from Camille. She too wanted to get together. Hassan could tell in her voice that the meeting was not going to be pleasant. Camille was pissed and held no punches expressing herself on the four-minute message. Hassan had never heard her so foul and although he was stunned, her words hit him hard.

"You know what Hassan, you ain't shit. And, you take this however you want to, but for-real-real, my girl ain't never do nothing, but love your ass. Fuck all the bullshit and fuck what you can't change. Rita needed you. Bottom line. And, I think it's real fucked up the only person Hassan thinks about is Hassan. Like you the only person in the world with feelings. Like you the only person going through this shit. I never thought you would shit on her like that, but you know what? It's better she found out now than keep going on believing you were something you're not."

Hearing Camille's voice brought back the painful

memories Hassan managed to bury. He knelt to offer salat. He then asked Allah for forgiveness for his treatment of Rita. He prayed she was safe, wherever she was, and that she would soon leave the path of self-destruction on which she was traveling.

As he slept, Hassan's thoughts swam through his head sending him on an emotional whirlpool. He tossed and turned most of the evening, finally getting out of bed before the sun rose. He got dressed and headed out for his daily run an hour earlier than usual. By the time he got back, he was revitalized and ready to face his troubles head on. As he made wudu in preparation for his morning prayer, he knew he had to make a call. Although it was just after six, Hassan was sure Camille would be up getting Jelani ready for school. The phone rang twice before anyone answered.

"Goo-morning," Jelani's carefree morning voice reminded Hassan how it felt to be a child with no concept of daily restrictions like time.

"As'salamu alaykum, Jelani."

"Uncle Hassan! Wa' alaykum salaam!"

"How you doing, akhi?" The first twinge of shame ran through him. He hadn't seen his godson in almost five months. But, Jelani held no grudge. He was just happy to talk to him.

"I'm fine. I gotta brush my teeth. I'm 'bout to go to school."

"Okay, well let me speak to your mom. Go ahead and brush your teeth and I'll call you later," Hassan promised.

His word was gold. "Okay. Hold on!" Before he could respond, Jelani dropped the phone. Hassan could hear his feet pattering across the room. Within seconds he came back out of breath talking to someone in the background, "Heeere it's for you."

"Hello, good morning." Even through the sleepy grog, Hassan recognized Rita's voice. He was stuck in a heavy silence. "Hello?" She repeated. Hassan could not speak. His mouth hung open in shock on the other end. "Jelani who is it?" She asked.

"It's a surprise. I'm not telling you," he sang.

"Well, they hung up babe, maybe…"

That was the last thing Hassan heard before the line went dead. His body started to overheat as acid welled up from the pit of his stomach. Unable to contain it any longer, he didn't bother to try and hold back the tears. He'd been in love with Rita for over ten years. Every part of his life reflected them as a whole. Looking around the empty house, he was struck with grief realizing the rift between them had become too large to gap. Needing to vent, he called his brother, but Noni answered instead, "You just missed him. He left to take the kids to school."

"Oh, ok. Just have him to give me a call."

As usual Noni picked up something in his tone and was concerned, "What's wrong, bro? Anything you want to talk about?"

"No, not really…" Hassan paused, "Well, yeah. I called Camille today and Rita came to the phone."

"Rita?"

"Yeah. Camille left me a message last night, but when I called her back today, Jelani picked up. I guess he assumed I wanted Ree."

"So, what did she say?"

"I didn't talk to her, I couldn't. I was stuck just holding the phone"

"Oh, I see."

"Noni, I'm so hurt and mad at her at the same time. It's like she took my heart and just ripped it out."

"Hassan, you have to think about how she feels, too. This was just as hard on her as it was on you, if not harder. You as a man have love for your child and it's understandable. But, you'll never be able to fully understand the way a mother feels. And, to lose your baby," she took a deep breath, "Ya Allah, I can't even begin to imagine what that was like for her. I know you feel like she deceived you, but you never know exactly what she was going through. Rita has a lot of pain inside her from her own childhood. You have to remember that. I'm sure she blamed herself when she found out the baby was sick. She probably felt like she was less than a woman. I know it's not my place to comment on your home, but Hassan she had a lot going on."

"Man, I just wish I could go back. Now, it's like she's gone, my son is gone, my marriage is gone. I don't know how things got this way."

"Well, you can't go back. No matter how bad you want to-- all you can do is go forward. You've made the decision to be with Nicole, but you have to make sure you're doing this because you love her. Not to replace Rita."

Noni's words smacked him like an open hand. He was so caught up in his anger and himself, he never even looked at it that way. And, what if he was marrying Nicole to try and replace her?

"I know. I love Nicole, I do. I feel like Allah sent her to me. I feel like she was truly supposed to be my wife. We're on the same page; we want the same things out of life. We have the same beliefs. With Rita, I met her when I was unsure about my faith. It wasn't really that important to me then. And, when it was, she was so stubborn she just shut down on me. Then all of this happened. Noni do you know she's started using drugs?"

"Really?"

"Yeah, and that, to me, was just like pouring salt on my wounds. I know it's wrong to harbor these ill feelings, but what do I do now?"

"Talk to her, Hassan."

"And say what!?! I'm getting married in a week?! I can't see us working this out, not right now. I mean, if we're meant to be, Allah will bring us back together."

"Still, Hassan you need some type of closure, especially before you marry Nicole. You don't want that over your soul when you go into this. Even iff you don't do anything but let her speak her mind and you speak yours. You don't have to get back together, but you do owe it to each other to at least talk."

Later that afternoon Hassan's mind kept wandering off, while Nicole chatted on across the table. She looked up and noticed he was staring right past her, "Are you ok?"

"Huh? Um, yeah, I'm fine. How's your food?"

"Hassan, what's wrong? Are you getting nervous?" She dropped her head and started fiddling with her fork. "Because if you need more time, we can…"

Hassan reached for her hand then pulled back. "No," he cut her off, "I don't need any more time. I want you as my wife.

I'm just going through something inside that's all."

"Well, do you want to talk about it?" Hassan was tired of everyone wanting to talk to him about Rita. He just wanted to move on, but Noni's words kept echoing in the back of his mind. *You need closure before you marry Nicole.*

"I'm going to see Rita. I need to clear up this whole situation."

Nicole raised her eyebrow, "Oh." Knowing full well the effect of holding on and harboring, she'd decided long ago to leave that part of Hassan's life alone. She never brought it up unless he did. "Well," she confessed, "I told Morgan's dad the other day and he took it like I expected him to. But you know, it still felt good to let him know what was going on with me." Nicole laughed, "Can you believe he thought I was in some kind of abusive relationship?"

She was glad to see a smile creep up in Hassan's hazel eyes, "What? Why would he think that?"

"Because of the way I've been acting and dressing," she chuckled. "He thought I was hiding bruises."

"What's wrong with the way you dress?" Hassan was confused.

"Nothing, it's just new to him-- that's all. Remember, I was in the world for a long time and believe me I used to *dress.*"

"Oh, okay. Well, at least he knows now what to expect and what not to expect from you."

"Yeah, it's a real weight off of my shoulders. He looked troubled though, like he had a lot on his shoulders. I pray everything with him is ok."

Hassan nodded thinking, *Don't we all.*

Chapter 19
Rita

Time was killing Rita slowly. No matter how much she tried to sleep, the calling remained awake, torturing her fragile body all through the night. It was almost a month now and each day seemed harder than the one before. At first Camille was determined to make her quit cold turkey. Those two weeks were the worst she'd ever been through. The violent tremors accompanied by the continuous vomiting were too much for both of them to handle. So, Camille started taking her to the clinic for Methadone treatment three times a week. It was helping ease some of the pain, but Rita still struggled with the withdrawal.

Today she was having a bad episode. Camille had to take Jelani to the doctor and wasn't able to drive her to the clinic, so she had to take the train. The voices in her head began to whisper as she sat at Allegheny Avenue. She tried to ignore them, telling herself she would be fine as soon as she made it to 5th Avenue. The stop came and Rita stayed on the train as it pulled out and headed for 8th Avenue into Camden. She called Marie and told her to meet her on Broadway with a hit in exchange for some cash. By the time she exited the double doors, Rita's heart was racing in anticipation. Her conscious vowing this would be the last time.

"Ree! Ree!" Marie hurried toward her. The closer she got the more horrific Rita realized she was. She looked as if she'd ran into a brick wall. Her bloodshot eyes were the size of saucers, while deep black and blue tissue covered one side.

"What's up girl? Where you been?"
Rita gasped. A whiff of foul air stole her breath. "I've been chillin." She looked around, "What you got for me?"
"Girl, you don't know what I had to do to get this," Marie stuck her hand in the front pocket of her skintight 1989 stonewash jeans. "You lucky you my peoples. J is gonna kick my ass when he find out I left the strip."
"J? J-Money?"
"Yeah girl, right after you left, I got down. He take real good care of me. I don't even know why you let your peoples pull that *Set It Off* shit." She scratched at her dirty hair, making Rita unconsciously reach up and pat her own, which was finally starting to grow back. "A Ree," Marie lowered her voice to a whisper, "let me get twenty-five instead of the twenty. I need to pick up a few things."

"What?" Rita was disappointed by her sorry attempt to Jew her up.
"Come on man, I got you," she motioned to the goodies in her clenched fist. "This is at least a dub' right here. All I want is five bills." Seeing the look of doubt on Rita's face she added,

"I wanna get me something from Mickey Dees."

The blaring sounds of midday filled Rita's ears like ocean water. She scanned up and down the block, soaking up everything that was going on around her in a flood. Teenage mothers rallied across the street waiting for the bus to take them home from their welfare appointments, while other young girls headed two blocks over to the County. They stood across the street on curb gesturing to the loves of their lives through narrow panes of bulletproof glass throwing hand signs that only true jailbirds and their ride-or-die chicks understood. The homeless were engrossed in their daily schedule of panhandling, while the young boys passed through the area quickly. The station was located too close to the jail for comfort and they wanted no more from the county then the use of its public transportation.

Like a light being flicked into the 'on' position, Rita's sense of self returned in a flash. Her eyes in form welled up washing away the grasp that desire had on her reason. Without saying a word, she turned around leaving Marie where she stood, calling after her.

Her sobs continued as she made the twenty-minute trip back across the Delaware River. She decided to hike it one stop up instead of getting back on another train. The cool air blew against her face, drying her damp eyes as she tread. Her thoughts raced, replaying the events of the past six months. By the time she reached the front door of the clinic, she knew exactly what her plan would be.

Reaching the front desk, "Yes, Rita Abdullah. I had an

appointment at 10o'clock." The clerk eyed her wearily then glanced at her watch. Rita continued, "I know I'm late, I'm sorry. But, I need to keep this appointment and I need some information on long-term rehab centers."

"So, when are you going to check in?" Camille was in the kitchen making dinner as Rita sat at the breakfast bar reading through the pile of information she'd been given.

"I don't know for sure, but I want to get away as soon as possible. They even have a few out of state. I think that would be my best bet. I need a change of scenery."

"Yeah, you're right." Camille turned to the stove, "Ree."

"Hum?"

"How would you feel about seeing Hassan?" The words seemed to reach her ears in slow motion making her body tense. Ebony walked in, "What's up? What ya'll talking about?"

Camille spoke up, wanting to maintain her friend's privacy, "Nothing."

Rita really did like Ebony. She seemed to be genuine and trustworthy. Unlike Sean, she kept a smile on Camille's face, which was all that really mattered. At first, she thought it was going to be weird being around the two of them. But, the more time Ebony spent at the house, the more they all came to be like a normal family.

Rita had to admit Ebony was beautiful and had a shape to die for. She was far from the stereotype Rita imagined a 'dyke' to be. But, as Ebony so patiently explained, the term 'dyke' was just a negative depiction of a masculine lesbian female. Not all gay women were 'mannish' in their mannerisms. Many of them were more feminine than some straight women. She went on to explain the various types, their attractions and supposed 'sexual preferences'. The whole thing, although enlightening, was too much for Rita to try and fully grasp. To her, whatever Ebony and Camille did behind closed doors was their business. She would in no way take the role as either judge or jury. She just knew she could never see herself in that life.

As Ebony sat beside her smiling, Rita filled her in, "I was looking over some information on a rehab and I was just telling Camille I'd rather go out of state."

"Yeah, that's a good idea. You know, a friend of mine back home works for Emory. It's like Virtua Hospital here. Their services are great, in and out patient. But, I can call him and see if he can recommend any centers. I mean, if you don't mind."

"No, not at all. I'll go down south." She looked over at Camille who was staring in Ebony's direction. "Camille you gonna come see me if I move down south, right?"

Eyes still fixed on her girlfriend, Camille sucked her teeth. "Now what kinda question is that? I told you Ebony was leaving me and I was gonna be riding down 95 all the time anyway. What I look like going to see her and not you?"

Ebony laughed, "Damn. Don't make me feel so loved."

Camille went over and kissed her affectionately on the lips. "Oh yeah, Camille you got some type of crazy pop-up. I hope it's not a virus. I was online and the whole screen blanked. Your messenger box came up, but when I tried to close it out it wouldn't let me do anything."

Rita's head whipped over to Camille who was as pale as

a ghost. Dropping the spatula on the floor, she ran out of the kitchen down the hall to the den. Ebony went to go after her, but Rita stopped her grabbing her by the arm, "That's the alert."

Ebony shrugged her shoulders, "What alert? What's going on?"

Rita moved around Ebony then peeped down the hall to make sure both Camille and Jelani were out of earshot. "She didn't tell you about the alert? The thing for Trevor?"

Ebony's eyes widened as it all sunk in. She sat across the bar in silence, while Rita wiped the spilled food from the floor and proceeded to finish dinner.

Camille sat at the desk, crying for what seemed like hours. Ebony tried twice to come in and console her, only to be shooed away. When she finally returned to the kitchen, Rita was washing dishes. Jelani was clearing the table and Ebony was out back smoking her after dinner cigarette.

"Mommie, mommie!" Her son rushed her like a mini linebacker wrapping his arms around her knees. "You missed dinner. It was goood."

"I'm glad you enjoyed it, baby," She scooped him up in her arms, hugging him tightly. Ebony walked in just as Camille was putting him down. "Baby, go put on your pajamas." As soon as he was upstairs, Camille turned to Rita and Ebony who were waiting intently. "There was a match found for the blood. Susan wants me to meet her tomorrow morning." No one knew what to say, so the three of them just stood there in silence.

Chapter 20
Camille

Time seemed to stand still as Camille sat in the lobby of Susan Armand's office. She'd lain awake all night thinking about what this would mean for her life. After all this time of longing to know the truth, she started to dread the reality of it. What if the person was a woman with children of her own? Was she ready to see another home destroyed? Could she sleep at night knowing someone was going to spend a good amount of time behind bars? Was she ready to face them? Would the police even be willing to reopen the case? What would the detective say once he found out she breeched security to get access to these records? Would she be charged with a crime as well?

"Ms. Massey?" The receptionist's voice startled Camille who was entranced in thought.

Susan was solemn as she greeted Camille hugging her sympathetically. "Dear, I know it took a lot for you to come here."

Camille nodded felling her eyes, "Yes, but... I had to,

you know?"

Susan took a deep breath and motioned toward one of the sofas for Camille to sit. Handing her a manila envelope she turned toward the door, "I'm going to step out. Take as much time as you need."

Camille held the folder in her lap, unable to open it as an eerie fear gripped her heart. Sliding the bundle of papers out slowly, she began to shake recognizing the police reports and crime scene photos. The pictures threw her back to the night she stood waling incessantly at the mangled sight of Trevor's white Acura. Still, for some reason she wasn't able to put them down. Her eyes were glued to the painful reminders. She looked at each photo carefully, tracing outlines with her finger as her tears splattered against the prints.

She studied the report of the medical examiner, although she knew each line by heart. Her illegible signature across the bottom of the pages still reflected her indescribable agony that night. At the back of the stack, the final pages documented the findings at the scene. Included was a sample of unidentified blood found in Trevor's car. Scribbled beside them were notes reading: "possible second person...suspect...vehicular homicide..."

The last two pages read almost identical, the first one listing the blood type followed by: NO MATCH FOUND; the second read: MATCH FOUND.

Sample Date: March 8, 2006   Sean Anthony Jeffers
    D.O.B. 6-17-76
Sample Type: DNA Paternity   5824   Centennial   Towers
    P.O.B. St. Croix
Case #: 4444-258641 Jill Delano   Bristol, PA 19007
    D.L.# 0965821476

Camille's whole body convulsed, trembling intensely as she let out a blood curdling shriek. Jumping up, she hurled the papers across the room.

Susan rushed worriedly into the room, followed by her secretary. Grabbing Camille by the shoulders, they struggled to hold her upright as she sank to the ground in despair, "No! No! No! It can't be him. Oh God, nooo!" Camille yanked away from them shaking her head between her hands back and forth. "God no, please no!" Susan motioned to her secretary to leave.

"Camille!" She yelled, "Camille, you have to get a hold of yourself." She clutched Camille's hands, holding her face directly in front of her and stared into her eyes. "Camille, it's okay. It's okay."

All the muscles in her body gave way and she buckled into Susan's arms. She stroked Camille's temple rocking her back-and-forth like a mother rocking her child, while Camille moaned, wriggling in pain until every ounce of her strength was gone.

Ebony peeked in to see if Camille was awake yet. She had been asleep since 11o'clock that morning, when Ebony lugged her worn frame to the den and laid her on the sofa. It was now well after six.

"Hey, you?" Ebony sat pushing Camille's hair from her brow. "How you feeling?" She groaned, rubbing the sleep from her face.

"Like shit. My head hurts real bad," she shrugged her shoulders heavily taking Ebony's hand in hers. Running her fingers lightly across her cheek Ebony chose her words carefully,

"Baby, you know everything is going to work itself out, right?"

"I'd like to believe that. I really would."

"Then you have to, if you don't believe it, it's gonna fester. You'll never heal like that." Ebony thought for a moment, "Do you remember when we first met? You were staring at my tattoo in the elevator." Camille nodded.

"Well, the reason it drew you is because you and I are different. Some people just go through life conforming. With no real connection to whom they are, what they do or how they move. But us, we're more 'in tune' if that's what you wanna call it, with the essence of life." She stared in Camille's eyes to make sure she understood.

"That's why my tattoo fascinated you. People see it and think it's just a flower or some kind of tribal symbol. But, you-- you saw the writing, the message within." She stuck her foot out, "Kismet means…"

"Fate," Camille ended.

Ebony smiled, "Right. Fate. Everything we experience from birth until death is predetermined. Predestined. So, it's like, we may not always understand why things fall the way they do. But, nevertheless things will always fall. It's human nature to analyze everything in an attempt to understand. But, few of us know that not everything is meant to be understood. Some things are to be accepted as just a part of life's natural order. You know what I mean?"

As always, Ebony's words blanketed Camille with comfort. But, still she was shaken. "I just keep asking myself, where do I go from here? I mean should I call detective Grimes and tell him about this or should I let it go. I was so worried last night about the effect this would have on *my* life. Then I realized it's not only going to affect me, but the person who did it, too. And, come to find out its Sean. Sean? I never in a million years would have imagined Sean was the one. I had love for that man. You know what I mean?" Camille shook her head. "I just have so many unanswered questions. I mean what if he knew all of this time and just never told me."

"Well, you told him what happened right? I mean, he knows about the accident and about Susan and all right?"

"You know what Ebony, the crazy thing is I never went into details with him. I mean he asked me once and I kind of brushed it off and he never asked me again."

"Damn, that's a trip."

"Yeah, tell me about it."

"Knock, knock," Rita came through the doorway with Jelani trailing close behind her trying to hide. "Camille, I'm sorry to bother you, but I can't seem to find Jelani anywhere. Have you seen him?"

Camille slowly sat up and looked around. Her sprits instantly lifted as if her son's presence alone had swallowed all of the melancholy emotion in the room. "No, he's not in here.

Ebony have you seen Jelani?"

"No, Camille I haven't seen Jelani anywhere. Maybe he missed the bus and decided to just spend the night at school."

Jelani jumped out snickering and fell into Ebony's lap, "No Eb!! I didn't miss the bus. I was just HIDING!" They all widened their eyes in a fake surprise and laughed at the clever four-year old.

Later that night Rita and Camille lay outside on the grass, staring up at the clear April sky.

"Ree, I'm so hurt. I feel like I've been violated for-real, for-real."

"Man, this whole thing got me trippin' my damn self. I don't know what to think anymore. You think you know people. But in reality, you don't. You only know what they show you."

Camille shook her head, "I know right?"

"And, you said he took a blood test?"

"Yeah! And, the fucking craziest thing is, it's for the broad that came to our lab to get her pregnancy test!"

"No, she didn't Camille."

"I lie to you not. Jill Delano. Young as hell and Italian. Her crazy ass step-mom was going off. Talking about how the daddy was black and married and she wasn't gonna be stuck supporting a baby. And, how they were gonna press charges. All this crazy shit. Do you know she convinced Dr. Merriam to do an amnio on that girl?!"

"You mean she didn't already have the baby?"

"Hell no! Which means Sean got her pregnant while he was still fuckin' with me! Now, if that ain't some shit right there, I don't know what is."

"But, the results you saw weren't from the paternity test were they? It just showed where the sample came from, right?"

"Yeah, but you know what? It don't matter anyway, whether he got her pregnant or not. He had something to do with Trevor dying and I'm really ready to kill his ass. This is deeper than him fucking around."

Rita seemed to be lost in her own thoughts. "You know, Camille, I've been thinking about what you asked me the other day."

"What? What do you mean?"

"When you asked me about seeing Hassan. For a long time, I felt like he betrayed me-- just leaving me like that. But, the more and more I think about it, he probably feels the same way about me. Like I betrayed him. I think he was just acting out of retaliation." She looked at Camille. "And, you see where that leads? I'm not telling you what to do, I'm just saying think before you do something you're gonna regret. Think about the effects it's gonna have in the long run. 'Cause you know how it goes once something is put into motion."

Camille nodded, but Rita could tell her blood was still boiling.

"But, you know I'ma support you whatever you decide to do. Just think about it." Rita rolled over, talking more to herself than to Camille, "'Cause I've sure been thinking about the shit in my life." She was silent for a second, "I'm going to see Hassan." Another pause, "I'ma say what I gotta say and let him get whatever he needs to get off his chest out. Then I'm heading down to the bottom of the map."

"What? You going down south for real? Where, Atlanta?" Camille looked over at her puzzled.

"Nah, even better," Rita smiled, "Macon."

"When did you decide this?"

"You know me and Eb been talking. She made some calls and her friend emailed some info. This one place, man Camille it's like in the middle of the country. It's secluded so I won't get caught up out there. But man it looks so serene. The doctors are all private physicians. And, they offer support meetings out the wahzoo once you leave. It actually looks like a vacation spot. That's what sold me. I wanna get clean, not feel like I'm committing myself to some kinda nut house."

"I know right. That's what's up, Ree. So have you tried to call Hassan yet?"

"No, but I saw he called here. The number was on the caller id."

"I didn't know he'd called back? You know, I blessed him out about a week ago, but on his voicemail."

Rita was laughing at her friend, "You did what? Why you call that man making him all nervous. You know he soft as hell. He probably called his mother crying." She threw her palm up, "You always talking about *'Hassan wouldn't hurt a fly'* and you cursed him out."

Camille huffed then looked at Rita sincerely, "He didn't hurt a fly. He hurt my *sister*. And you know good and damn well I wasn't having that shit."

Chapter 21

Sean

June buzzed in at exactly 9:00. Sean was barely through the threshold of his office, "Mr. Jeffers, there's a Detective Grimes on the line for you." In his haste to settle himself in Sean told her to put the call through without even thinking about it.

"Mr. Jeffers, my name is Paul Grimes. I'm with the Bristol Township Police Department."

"Yes Detective, how may I 'elp you?" Sean was hoping this didn't have anything to do with Jill. He'd not yet seen the results of the paternity test, but he was sure his doctor would've called him immediately had they come back.

"I'd like to meet with you regarding some new evidence found on a hit and run about two years back."

Sean was speechless. *What the hell is going on? Evidence? What evidence?*

"Mr. Jeffers. Are you there?"

"Uh, yes, yes I'm 'ere. I'm sorry you just caught me off guard. I'm afraid I 'ave no idea what ya're talking 'bout."

"I'm sure you don't, Mr. Jeffers. That's why I'd like to

meet with you so we can fill in the gaps. Would you like to come down to the station or would you prefer I come to you?"

Sean looked around as if someone were in the room with him listening to the conversation. He picked up the handset, removing the call from speakerphone. "I'll come to you. That's no problem. But my schedule is pretty much booked far the next couple of deys."

"That's funny; your receptionist said you'd be free all tomorrow."

Fuck, Sean thought, laughing nervously. "Uh, yes yes ya're correct I actually am free per my appointments, but I 'ave a function at my daughter's school. Honor Roll."

"Well, congratulations, Mr. Jeffers, you must be proud. How old is your little one?"

"She's nine and a 'alf set to be tirty on her next bert'tay."

"Yeah, I understand. I've got two of my own." The detective laughed, "So Mr. Jeffers I'll see you tomorrow after the ceremony. Don't forget to take a camera."

With that the detective hung up, leaving Sean sweating profusely behind his desk.

June walked in, took one look at him, and stopped in her tracks. "Mr. Jeffers is everything ok? You look sick. Do you need me to call a doctor or something?" Moving from behind his desk Sean loosed his tie, heading to the bar, "No, June I'm fine. Noting a little 'yak' can't fix. Gwan now leave tose papers 'pon my desk," with his back to her he waived her off. She sat the stack down then left in a hurry, glancing back at her boss pouring a double shot.

"You no good black bastard. You're gonna be sorry you ever laid hands on her, just wait and see. You just wait." Sean erased the message as he had all the others before it-- without an ounce of remorse. He was more than sure he wasn't the father of any baby, especially Jill's who'd become now a walking nightmare. Starting his truck Jay-Z's *Ninety-Nine Problems* reverberated on the walls of the parking deck.

The oxymoronic lyrics of the song brought temporary comfort to the distress of his life. All ninety-nine of Sean's problems were women. While Camille was denying his existence for no apparent reason, Nicole had the audacity to up and plan to get married behind his back. Sean sped toward his lawyer's office with his radio on full blast.

Peter Weinberg sat, fingers crossed behind his cherry wood desk. Sean was across from him perched tensely on the edge of the chair, regurgitating the awful events of that night. Peter's objective facial expression relieved some of Sean's anxiety making it slightly easier for him to confess. "So what do ya' tink? I mean what type of evidence could tey possibly 'ave come across after all tis time?"

"I don't know Sean and quite frankly I'm not going to speculate. Tell me, have you done anything out of the ordinary lately that could have in any way linked you back to the accident?"

"No, noting. I mean shit man if tis comes out I could lose everyting. On top of tat Nicole is about to get married! Can you fucking believe tis? It's like when tings are bad something comes along and just pushes you over the ledge."

"She's getting married? What are your plans for custody of your daughter?"

"Hell, I don't know? I mean we 'ave a decent arrangement now. I take care of Morgan. It's not like she has ta' fight me far suppart. I do right by them financially."

"Yes, but Sean you never know how marriage changes things. I mean I know Nicole is a strong-willed individual, but what about this guy she's about to marry? Have you met him?"

Pacing in front of the enormous window, ignoring the view of the city from the twentieth floor, Sean shook his head. "No. Never."

"See. He may try to pressure her into coming after you in that aspect. You need to keep a close watch on that. This thing with this case is sticky and you don't need to give her any kind of ammunition."

"I see what ya're getting at."

"So what we're going to do is meet with this detective, hear what he has to say and take it from there. Now you said you were drinking, right?"

"Yeah, I had a few drinks at the bar."

"Ok. Keep that to yourself. There's no way to prove that now. Unless you paid for them with a credit card."

"No. Never. Nicole and I were still together. I made sure all of my bases were covered."

"Good, good. Now, you were pretty banged up, right?"

"Just some scratches noting major. I didn't 'ave ta; go to the hospital or anyting." Sean sat back down across from Peter.

"Ok, what about your truck?"

"Minor work, a friend of mine took care of it."

"Did you get a paint job?"

"Yeah," he looked worried, "is that gonna show up?"

"I'm not sure, it could. I'm just trying to get a feel of things." Peter came out from behind his desk resting his hand on Sean's shoulder, "Look, don't worry. We'll go down there, I'll get a copy of the case file and we'll be in and out. I doubt this so-called 'new evidence' is solid anyway. If it were, they would have been able to come up with something before today." Sean nodded, hoping his lawyer was right.

On his way back to the office, Sean found himself unconsciously en route to Camille's house. He was in a state of panic and needed to see her face, even though there was a tiny voice inside telling him this was a bad move.

When he pulled up in the driveway, a fire engine red Dodge Charger sat parallel with Camille's truck. Sean's heart burned in jealousy at the sight of another man's ride parked in his girl's driveway. And, from the looks of the whip, dude was a baller.

The brand new Vogue tires were adorned with chrome and black 'deep dish' 22's. The mirror colored tint added an appeal all its own to the already impressive vehicle. He could tell from the white dust on the rear fender that this was not the car's first trip up Camille's drive way.

Sean sat in his car flipping over the possibilities in his mind. He could get out, ring the bell and face whomever it was trying to take his girl in hopes she would choose him or he could back out and drive away leaving her to the rest of her life.

Before he was able to decide, the front door opened and a short female in money green sweat pants, a 'wife-beater' and an emerald Yankee fitted came out in socked feet storming across the rocks. At first Sean thought the pony-tailed tomboy was Rita until he saw her appear in the screen door behind the chick with a look of concern on her face. His eyes shot back to the figure that had moved close enough for him to decipher the face now inches away from his window.

Sean hopped out vengefully, standing toe-to-toe once again with Ebony. She looked up at him callously, "How could you have the audacity to show up here? What you didn't get the picture when you called?"

"Gwan now wit yar' bullshit. Me' not in the mood ta' tussle wit' ya' lickle'one." Sean tried to step around her but she moved right along with him, blocking his path. From the look on her face Sean could tell she was vexed.

He knew from experience how treacherous an island woman in rare form could be. Ebony cocked her head curling her top lip back viciously, "Just 'oo in da 'ell da'ya tink ya're talkin' to?" Her Trini blood raced through her veins and spilled out of her mouth transforming her words from the studied proper dialect into her native tongue. "Me tink ya' got me mixed up wit' one of yar' American girls. Me not noting ya'wan fuck wit'. Now ya're not welcome 'ere, so leave."

Sean was stunned. Heaving in and out heavily he gaped down on the femme, whose words whacked him across the face as if she'd slapped him with an open hand.

Rita, who was standing by cautiously, had seen enough to know it was time for her to intervene. Before Sean could react any further, she came bounding out of the door placing her body in front of Ebony.

She placed her hands on Sean's shoulders, "Listen man. It's not a good idea for you to be here, for-real for-real." In an effort to divert his attention, she turned him around carefully, "Things are pretty intense right now. You should just step back for a while and wait for all of this to die down. Then when the two of you are both ready to see each other, ya'll will."

Sean looked into her eyes pleadingly, "But I am ready ta' see her now. She's the one with the bulldog." He motioned to Ebony who was pacing guardedly near the steps. "Why the'ell ya girl actin' like I'm the fuckin' enemy far?"

Rita threw her hands up shaking her head, "Man you should just go. Don't make things worse for yourself than they already are."

Sean spun around, slamming his fist on the hood of his car in frustration.

"Tis is some bullshit!"

Jumping in, he gunned the ignition to a start. He purposely made a wide u-turn to exit instead of backing out forcing Ebony off of the narrow driveway and up onto the grass. Infuriated at his blatant disregard for her, she yelled out to him, "Ya' gwan get enough of that shit!" Sean had no idea what she was talking about. He flicked his middle finger at her as he hammered off mumbling, "Crazy bitch!"

Chapter 22

Hasaan

Waiting at the table, Hassan couldn't stop fidgeting. He was more nervous then he'd ever been. The fourth glass of water sent him, reluctantly, to the men's room. As he stood drying his hands, he tried to talk himself calm, "You can do this… you can do this… just relax."

He rounded the corner and saw a woman sitting at his table with her back toward him. Positive the shorthaired lady was in the wrong place he hurried over toward her. "Excuse me, Miss, this table is reser…" Hassan halted in mid-sentence as Rita looked up smiling boldly at him. "Has it been that long?"

Stuttering, he searched for something to say, "No um, I mean…Look at you."

Rita patted her short bob, "Yeah, it sucks, I know."

Unable to take his eyes off of her he tried to remain polite. "No, it's really not that bad," he stared. "Man, I didn't know what I was going to say at first, but now I'm really at a loss for words."

Rita laughed a familiar laugh shaking her head at Hassan.

"You've changed too I see," eyeing his fully grown-in beard and kufi. He shrugged his shoulders, taking a seat. "Well, we all have to change and learn to grow if we're going to accept Allah's will."

"So…" He was silent waiting for Rita to interject as she usually did, but she too said nothing.

She searched his face for some sort of sign, some sort of emotion. Seeing none in his eyes, she was unable to stop the lone tear from streaming down her cheek. A part of Hassan wanted to reach over and grab her in his arms. He wanted to erase the last seven months, but time had created canyons that were now too deep to gap. Overcome with the urge to get up and run he started to feel like the meeting was a bad idea. "I don't know what to say," he confessed.

Rita shook her head, "You don't really have to say anything, Hassan. I just wanted us to end the right way, you know? Without any 'I should have said's'."

They sat staring, the bridge between them growing even more. Finally Hassan spoke up, "Well, I do want to tell you something. And, I want you to hear it from me first."

Rita looked puzzled and worried at the same time, making it hard for Hassan to continue. "Ree, we've been together for a long time and we've never really gone through anything major, until now. The whole timing of everything was eerie to me with me trying to change my life and all. Anyway, I think this was a way of fate showing us we were not meant to be." Rita ran her hands through her hair inhaling deeply. Seeing her reaction Hassan stopped talking. "No, I'm fine," she mustered, "go ahead." Hassan fiddled with the silverware.

"I think all of this happened for a reason, even everything that you went through after the baby."

"You know about that?" She asked turning scarlet in embarrassment. She was sure he just left without ever looking back.

He nodded, "I spoke to your cousin a few weeks after you were there and he told me he thought you were... well, you know. Then Camille called me and went off. She called me everything *but* a child of God."

"For real?" Rita laughed thinking of how much of a solider Camille had been over the past few months.

"Yeah, you should have heard her. But, something she said stuck. She told me I was a poor excuse for a husband. Truth be told, the more I thought about it, the more I saw she was right."

Hassan tried to ease into what he was about to say. He wanted to take on as much of the blame as he could. "Even though it's hard to admit, it's the truth. Something happened when we lost the baby. It was like we, Rita and Hassan, died too. I don't think there's much we can do to get us back on track."

Rita's faced dropped, but Hassan kept going, "Ree I want a divorce. I've met somebody else. I really think it's time for us to move on separately."

The words spilled from his lips so fast he never saw Rita's face contorting into a fiery rage.

"You fucking piece of shit!" She jumped up from the table. "Who in the hell do you think you are? You abandon me, leave me for damn-near dead and now you want a divorce 'cause you're screwing someone else?!!"

The customers at the tables surrounding them gawked shockingly as the concierge hurried over. He got there a second too late. Rita grabbed a glass of water flinging it forcefully at Hassan. He ducked just in time for the goblet to miss the side of his face. It came crashing to the ground behind him in a million pieces as the couple beside them eased back trying to move out of the way.

Oblivious to anyone or anything else, Rita jumped up and swung hard with her right fist. She caught Hassan on the side of his temple with a force that sent him reeling back on the two hind legs of his chair. He grabbed the side of his head in amazement. Rita turned and ran from the restaurant in hysteria, leaving behind a stunned Hassan. He rose up slowly, wiping water from his shirt and pants. Apologizing to the waiter, he paid the tab along with a generous tip and exited.

Hassan pulled up to Nicole's thirty minutes later, still shaken. When she opened the door, the look on her face told him her day was just as sour as his.

"What's wrong?" She asked, holding the door open for him. He walked past the foyer and saw the pink and yellow Bratz bag on the floor. Hassan lowered his voice to a whisper, "Morgan's home?" Nicole nodded. She led him through the kitchen to the living room. Sitting on the couch she buried her face in her palms.

"What is it? What's the matter? Is she okay?"

Nicole sniffled shaking her head, "She's fine it's Sean." This was the first time Hassan heard Nicole refer to her ex by name. Sean, it rang a bell, but Hassan could not place it at the moment. His mind was clouded trying to figure out what she was meant. He sighed heavily. His day had been bad enough, now he had to deal with Nicole's problems with her ex. Agitated, he sat beside her and held his head in his hand, "What happened?"

"He dropped her off today talking about he can't do it anymore. He said there was no guarantee he was going to be in her life forever and he couldn't take losing her. He was talking so crazy I could barely understand him. I don't know what's going on with him."

"Well, what was his problem? Was he drunk?" Hassan asked. "Did ya'll have some kind of fight earlier? I mean what happened?"

"Was he *drunk*?" Nicole looked up at him as if he asked for her Social Security number. "No, he wasn't drunk! He dropped Morgan off. He would never drink and drive with her in the car!"

Hassan pulled back, "Whoa! I'm sorry; I didn't mean to offend you. I just remember you telling me that..."

"What," Nicole stood up with her hands on her hips, "that he used to drink? So what are you taking notes on all of his faults to try and turn me against him?" She spun around throwing her hands in the air. "It's just like he said, you're gonna try and take us away."

Hassan, still reeling from Rita's outburst, was in no mood to try and work through whatever it was Nicole was going through. He came to her for comfort, not to be attacked all over again. He stood, throwing his hands up in defense. "You know what? I'm going to go ahead and leave. We've both had rough days. We probably need some time to gather our thoughts."

"Time, huh? Is that what you told your wife? Nicole laughed with her back still to him. "Is that why you've got that knot on your head and you look like you lost your best friend? You know what Hassan, I see now just how you handle pressure." She faced him, "You don't. You'd rather run. Well, I've got news for you dear-- life isn't always grand! We're real people living in a real world with real problems. Mommie isn't always going to be there to make it all better! You're going to need to stand on your own one day or else you're gonna end up a very lonely 'momma's boy'."

Hassan was astounded. He'd never seen this side of Nicole before. Who did she think she was? How dare she talk to him like that? She had no idea what type of man he was. Here he was leaving his wife to be with her and she had the gall to disrespect him. "Man, whatever. I'm gone. Come lock your door." He walked out without looking back, leaving Nicole in tears.

Chapter 23

Camille

Just like he promised, Detective Grimes called as soon as the meeting with Sean was over saving Camille a trip to the precinct.

"Well, I certainly think he knows something. But, I'm just not sure how much. I've definitely got a feeling he was there."

"Well, of course he was there Mr. Grimes. How else would his blood end up at the scene?" Camille was getting aggravated with the cop's attempts to be neutral.

"Ms. Massey, I know it's been rough, but we are doing our best to try and bring your boyfriend's killer to justice. You have to understand my position. Until we're sure, I don't want to pass any false convictions or get your hopes up."

"Understand your position? How about you try and understand my position, Officer Grimes. You talk about rough! You have no idea what rough is until you see the love of your life laying motionless and knowing he'll never open his eyes again. You have no idea how it feels to look at your four-year-old and break down because he looks so much like his father. So

237

don't tell me you know it's been rough for me, 'cause you don't know!"

Camille slammed the phone down cursing at the empty air in front of her.

She was too tired to cry and seemed to have no more tears left anyway.

The stress she felt, along with the stillness of her empty house, vibrated through her temples painfully. She reached for the bottle of painkillers only to find they were not where she left them. Frustration consumed her spiraling her mind downward into evil plots of revenge. Besides wanting to hurt him physically, Camille decided at that moment to wreak havoc on Sean's 'perfect' world.

June picked up on the first ring as usual, "Good afternoon, Morgan Contracting. How may I help you?"
Camille disguised her voice slightly, "Yes, Mr. Jeffers, please."

"I'm sorry, Miss, he's not available. May I take a message?"

"Um, yes, this is Colette Strickland from Dr. Brown's office. I'm trying to reach him personally. Is he in and just unavailable?"

"Oh well, actually, he just is out, but let me check something." June mumbled as she scanned through the planner, "...School... Weinberg...he should be back by 3 o'clock at the latest. Did you want to leave a..."

Camille had hung up as soon as she heard what she needed. Peter Weinberg was Sean's lawyer. It only made sense that he would be there right now.

Camille jumped up, threw a hat on her head and ran out of the house. Flinging her cargo door open, she slipped a pair of sneakers on her socked feet before checking the duffle bag to make sure she had everything she needed.

By the time Camille made it downtown, the lunchtime rush hour was dying down. She circled the building twice to make sure everything was clear before parking on the opposite side of the street a block behind the Tahoe. She got out and walked briskly toward her target. Her eyes scanned her surroundings meticulously. As she approached the truck, Camille bent down like she was tying her shoe. In one swift move she poked a large hole in the rear passenger side tire with an ice pick the length of her palm. Coming to a stand slowly, she dragged the tip up the panel of the truck running an ugly scratch along the length. Making it just beyond the passenger door, Camille pretended to trip and pierced the front tire just as she did the rear. Walking away casually, she smirked. The hissing sound of escaping air pushed her merrily on her way.

Once in her car, she placed a call before preparing to sit back to enjoy the show, "Yes, account number please."

"Oh, Miss, I don't have my account number with me. Can I give you my address?"

"Yes, go ahead." The representative fell silent.

"5824 Centennial Towers... Bristol... 19007."

"Your name?" She asked.

"Mrs. Jeffers. The account is in my husband's name, Sean."

"Ok, how can I help you?"

"Well, I'd like to disconnect the service on the account."

"Will you need to transfer to another address?"

"No, we're actually moving out of state. It was kind of an on-again off-again move and I wanted to wait until I was sure we were going. That's why I'm calling at the last minute."

"I see. No problem. Can you just verify the last four digits of the social security number?"

"2-6-8-5."

"Ok... great. I'll go ahead and place the order."

After Camille got off of the phone with the cable company, she went on making four similar calls disconnecting the rest of Sean's utilities. Her grand finale call to Sprint as the distraught wife informing them of her husband's stolen phone ended just in time.

Sean came out of the building sporting a stunning mustard yellow linen set with navy Bernini loafers. His eyes were hidden behind a pair of midnight blue Ralph Lauren sunglasses. Around his head a sand colored silk wrap was tied perfectly giving his already fly outfit a sexy neo-soul touch. He strolled coolly toward his truck deactivating the alarm.

Camille watched him get in and roll no more than ten feet before hitting the brakes and pulling back to the curb. Jumping out, he walked around and looked down at his back tire. Kneeling to inspect the damage, Sean ripped the shades from his face. His jaw dropped as he ran his hand along the deep scrape that ruined his once flawless paint job.

Her perfect vision focused on his mouth as he realized

the front tire was pierced as well. "Fuck!" Sean flailed his arms in disgust pitching his glasses onto the ground sending them shattering up the sidewalk.

Seeing enough to satisfy her for the moment, Camille pulled off. From her rear view mirror she watched Sean flip open his cell phone frantically. She laughed to herself, "Yeah, let's see how you like to have your life fucked with."

By the time Camille made it back home, although it was still early, Ebony was there. The two decided since they were spending more and more time together, it only made sense for Ebony to have her own key. Camille walked into the house and was welcomed by the smell of jerk chicken floating from the kitchen. For the first time all day Camille realized she had to eat at some point and time

"Hey, what's..." Ebony turned around raising her eyebrows, "up with you dressed like a thug?"
Camille laughed, removing her hat. "I was doing some working out."
"Shit, you look like you were on a stakeout."
"Very funny. Did Ree call?"
"Nope, there weren't any messages on the machine. How did things go with the detective?" Ebony had been upset that Camille refused to let her go with her to the police station. Little did she know, it was because Camille was dreading having to face Sean and did everything she could to stay home.

"Well, I actually didn't go. And, I'm glad I didn't because the whole thing just pissed me off even more." Seeing the anger returning in Camille's eyes, Ebony instantly regretted opening her mouth. "Detective Grimes claims they're doing everything they can. But he's not telling me anything concrete. I'm just ready for this shit to be over and done with."

"Well Camille, this is just the beginning. We have a long way to go still, so you're gonna have to be patient and understand that there's a process."

Camille looked at Ebony, "Man, whatever." She sulked out of the kitchen with her head hung low.

Ebony came into the den with a steaming plate of chicken, rice and peas. The rumbling in Camille's stomach made her set aside her ego. She sat up, propping her head on Ebony's shoulder, "Can I have some?"

Ebony jerked away as if she were upset, "No. Whatever, remember?"

"Come on. You know I didn't mean it like that."

"Yeah, right. You're mean as hell when you want to be, you know that?"

Camille was silent. She was always terrible at apologies. Ebony turned around and broke a wide grin when she saw the puppy dog look Camille had plastered on her face. "I swear I don't know why I love your crazy ass so much."

Hearing the words form, Camille's heart flip-flopped in excitement. "You love me?" She whispered.

Ebony sucked her teeth. "Don't be silly. You know I love you. I would do anything to see you happy."

Camille couldn't help but cry thinking of all the support and time Ebony had sacrificed over the past few weeks.

"I want you and Jelani to come with me to Atlanta."

Camille blinked hard. "Well, baby, the school year is not over for another three weeks. We would have to wait until his summer vacation starts to take a trip."

Ebony moved back looking Camille in the eyes, "No, not for vacation. I want ya'll to move to Atlanta with me." Camille didn't respond. "You really need a fresh start. Plus, with Rita going to Macon you'll be much closer to her."

No sooner than the words left Ebony's mouth did the telephone ring. Happy to be freed from the spotlight, Camille jumped up grabbing the receiver.

"Hello?" Within seconds Camille's face frowned in alarm. "What?! Where are you? Yeah, I know where that is. I'm on my way right now." Camille threw the phone down and rushed out of the den. "Dammit!"

"What happened?"

"I need you to pick Jelani up no later than 6:30. That was Hassan. Ree done fuckin' flipped! She followed him to his girlfriend's house. He said she got the girl held up in the apartment and locked him out of the house." She rubbed her face nervously. "He said she had a fuckin gun! Where in the hell did she get a...Aww shit!" Camille bolted out the front door to her truck. Ebony watched as she searched frantically underneath the hatch. "It's not here..." she yelled. "She took my piece!"

Chapter 24

Sean

By the time Sean reached his office, June was in shambles, "Mr. Jeffers I've been trying to call you for the past hour. There was some man here asking a whole bunch of questions about you."

Sean's mind was preoccupied as he paced around his office looking for his hidden stash. His bar was empty, his car vandalized and his favorite pair of glasses in pieces on Radcliff Street. "What man, June? What'cha talkin' 'bout?" Reaching under his desk, he punched in the combination to the hidden safe and pulled out a bottle of cognac.

"Joey Delano. He came in with these two guys. They looked like Italians or something. He was asking a bunch of questions about the company at first, like he wanted to do some business. But then he started asking about you, and if you were married and if you had kids. It was weird. He tried to get me to tell him where you were and what time you'd be back. The whole thing didn't sit right with me, so I didn't tell him anything." June handed him a business card. "I just let him know all I could do was take his number."

Sean took the card and leaned back in his chair to think. "Tanks June, ya' did good."

She headed to the door then turned, "Mr. Jeffers, I know it's probably none of my business, but I just need to know I'm not putting myself into any kind of danger."

"Listen'ere, I'm fine, the company is fine. I've just got a few things I need to straighten out." Sean downed the dry bourbon and looked up at the girl. He could see fear written all over her face.

Sean wasn't sure if it was the rush of the liquor combined with the stress of the afternoon, but for the first time he took a really good look at June. Her arms were crossed nervously in front of her small round breasts. They sat perfectly upright underneath an ivory satin camisole. Her black blazer fell open, exposing her flat stomach and petite hips barely covered by the sheer material. Sean felt his dick thump as the heat from the alcohol made its way through his system. *Damn, with all this shit going on, it's been almost a week since I got some head,* he thought.

Before he knew it, Sean was undressing the tense receptionist with his eyes. Jolting back into reality, he had to stand in order to keep from grabbing himself in excitement. Still, he made his way over to June uncrossing her arms, "Ya 'ave noting ta' worry 'bout. Yar' in good hands. Trust." He looked into her innocent eyes masked behind the black-framed glasses. Feeling her body relax, he smiled, "See now tat's better, huh?" June nodded, smiling softly at Sean rubbing his hands up and down her arms.

"I'm sorry, Mr. Jeffers. It's just that you see all kinds of things on the news and all. I guess I'm just being paranoid."

Sean placed his finger on her lips silencing her, "Tere's no need ta' apologize. You're a smart girl and ya' pay attention." He began delicately stroking her face with the back of his hand. "Tat's what I like 'bout you. Ya're very mature far ya' age." His hands traveled easily down her side resting on her hips. His touch shot pulses of desire through her body, racing the speed of June's heart. Before she could even process what it was she was feeling, Sean's large hands were pulling up the sides of her skirt exposing the jet-black stockings followed by the top of her garter. His fingers traveled up the lace to the plush bare skin on the inside of June's thighs.

She raised her arms, pushing Sean lightly while the look in her eyes egged him on. Without a word, he cupped her small round ass forcefully raising both of her feet off the floor at the same time. Grinding her against the head of his muscle, Sean carried her over to his desk pushing the papers scattered across the oak to the side.

As the documents spilled to the floor, Sean perched June carefully on the edge spreading her legs aggressively. She whimpered in delight as he knelt down, pulling the g-string to the side with one hand while parting her surprisingly fat pink lips with the other.

June grabbed at Sean's locks wildly, mashing his face between her legs, urging him to bury his face in her thick juices that were now trickling out steadily. She reached behind her back, grabbing the bottle and took a long swig. Pulling Sean's face up to hers, June kissed him hard. She opened her mouth, allowing the liquor to spill over into his. Sean pulled back in surprise, but June yanked him back. In one swift move she dropped down to her toes, flipping her body with Sean's.

Pushing him down on the desk as she climbed on top of him, she prepared to mount his vertical bullet for a mind blower.

No sooner than she braced herself, did the line ring loudly. The BZZZ yanked both June and Sean out of the heat of the moment and back into the realization of what they were on the brink of doing. Frantically, June hopped up hitting the speaker button on the telephone that in the may lay had fallen to the floor.

"Hello," June cleared her throat. "Hello, Morgan Contracting. How may I help you?" She tried to sound as professional as possible.

"I'm trying to reach Sean Jeffers." The voice on the other end was clueless.

Sean spoke up as he pulled himself together, stuffing his shirt in his pants, "Tis is Mr. Jeffers."

"Mr. Jeffers, this is Faye over at the Children's Academy. Morgan's mom has not made it here to pick her up yet and we closed a half hour ago. We tried to reach her, but haven't been able to do so. Someone needs to come and pick her up."

Sean started to panic immediately. Nicole was never late picking up Morgan, let alone a 'no show' all together. He had no idea what this was all about, but had no time to try and figure it out. Picking the receiver up off of the ground, he spoke calmly into the handset, "I'll be tere in ten minutes." He disconnected the call and grabbed his cell phone dialing Nicole's number from memory.

"Your call cannot be completed as dialed. Please dial *4 for further assistance." The recording pounded in his ears, aggravating the few strands of patience he had left.

"Shit!"

Sean had gotten so caught up with June that he forgot his phone wasn't working.

"I gotta go."

He pushed past the secretary who was searching for her panties. "Mr. Jeffers..." she called out to him, but he was out the double glass doors and in the parking lot before remembering he had no wheels. Sean looked up and down the street miserably. Without having any other choice, he turned back to the building. June was in the lobby as he crossed the threshold, keys in hand.

"You need a ride?" She asked. "I'm ready. I'll take you."

"June, look, ya' don't 'ave to drive me, just call a cab and ya' can gwan'ome far the day."

"Mr. Jeffers," she blushed. "It's no problem. Really. Just let me lock up."

Morgan's puffy eyes and red nose ignited Sean's anger. After apologizing to the director, who was obviously irritated, he grabbed his daughter tightly and left. Sean had told June it was ok to go. He wasn't about to have her drive him home let alone him and his daughter. He'd learned his lesson with Jill and since both he and Morgan needed time to wind down after a hectic day, he decided they could walk home.

"Daddy, where's Mommie?"

"I don't know, baby, but I'm sure she's ok." For a second time, tears threatened to fall down the little one's cheeks. Sean knew she wasn't comforted by his response. He tried again to convince her not to worry, "Maybe she had a flat tire or something."

"Well then, why isn't she answering her cell phone? Even if she had a flat tire, she could still answer her cell phone."

"Yar'right baby, but 'ow 'bout we stop and pick up some pizza?" It was a slick move, but Sean had to change the subject for Morgan's sake.

Hesitantly the twinkle returned to her eyes. "Yeah, let's get some pizza."

After leaving the parlor nearly two hours later, Sean and Morgan set out bellies full on the twelve-block walk home. By the time they reached the building lobby, Sean was carrying his exhausted child in his arms with her book bag dangling awkwardly from his broad shoulder.

Slumping wearily against the wall, he stared up at the blinking lights as the elevator ascended. His mind jumped over the disturbing events of the day like a frog over lily pads. In no time, his thoughts landed on Nicole. Well, my phone isn't working. I'm sure she tried ta' call but couldn't get through. She probably left a boat'loada messages on my machine explainin' herself. She'll be ringing da'ouse as soon as we walk through the door.

Maneuvering his way into the condo with Morgan still lulling in and out of sleep, Sean dropped his keys on the coffee table and looked around his living room suspiciously. There was something strange about his surroundings that put him on edge.

Sean was certain of how he'd left his home that morning; it was the same way he'd left it every day of his life: the lamp over the stove on and his radio playing softly, emitting the aqua blue light that reflected off of the hardwood floors. But today, there was no light coming from the kitchen. There was no reflection greeting him warmly at his feet.

He placed Morgan carefully on the sofa quietly and edged the top drawer of the coffee table open. Drawing the revolver, he tiptoed down the short hall flicking on the dining room light. Nothing happened. Then it hit him like a bullet. The power was out.

Silently, with his pistol extended, he moved through his apartment checking every room. Once satisfied, he headed back into the living room buzzing the doorman from the intercom which, thankfully, was wired through the building, "Sal?"

"Yes, Mr. Jeffers?"

"Are we having problems with the electricity on my floor?"

"No, sir. Not that I know of."

"Well, my power isn't workin' and my cell phone is out'a service…" As the words left Sean's mouth everything seemed to come into perspective. It was too much of a coincidence. His car was vandalized, his cell phone was disconnected and his power was cut off. All of this on the same day he'd met with the detective about the accident. Camille's name was written all over the walls of Sean's cracked glass house.

"Nicole!" She popped into his head again. This time followed by a heavy sense of panic. "Where was she? Why didn't she call if she was going to be late picking up Morgan?" Even if she couldn't call his cell phone, June would've surely said something if she'd tried to get him at the office.

"Mr. Jeffers....sir..." Sal was waiting on a response.

"Huh? Oh, I'm sorry Sal what was tat?"

"I said did you need me to send you up a house phone? I know you have the little one with you."

"Oh, yes Sal. Tank you."

"No problem, right away, sir."

Sal personally brought the phone upstairs to him. After calling Peco Energy, he dialed Sprint's customer service line and found himself having nearly the exact same conversation he'd just had with his electric company. "Excuse me?"

"Yes, Nicole Jeffers. It says here in the notes your wife called in and reported the phone stolen. We immediately turned off the service for your protection."

"Well, that was a mistake. First of all, I'ave no wife. And my phone is not stolen. It's in my 'and as we speak."

"Well sir, I'm going to need you to verify a few things before we can restore the account."

"Verify?!" Sean was boiling. "Did ya'ave 'er verify ne'ting b'far ya' cut my phone off? Tis is ridiculous!"

After spending nearly fifty minutes on the call, Sean's phone was finally back in service. Unfortunately, he could not say the same about his power, which would not be restored until the next morning. Tipping Sal heavily, Sean asked him one last favor, "Could ya' hail me a cab while I get my daughter ta'gether?"

"Sure, no problem. Right away, sir."

By the time Sean laid Morgan's sleeping frame on his mother's bed, it was well past ten o'clock and his fare was well over eighty dollars. Still he refused to take his mother's car. He told her there was no way he was leaving the two of them without a vehicle. The way things were going today he refused to risk anything. Kissing her on the cheek, he zipped down the staircase and out the front door. Inside the rear of the taxi, he instructed the cabbie to turn around and go back in the direction from which they just came.

Nearly thirty minutes later, they pulled up in the parking lot of Nicole's condo. The entire ride Sean tried to prepare himself for the possibility of coming face-to-face with Nicole and her fiancé. Still, his heart skipped when he saw her car parked outside of the building.

Walking past the spotless Accord, he looked up at the windows of the loft. A daunting presence seemed to peer back at him from the windows facing the street. She must be home. Sean was especially certain because the lights were on and no matter how many times he warned Nicole about turning off every single light when she was out, she still did it. She could never seem to break the habit.

Knocking heavily on the door, he braced himself for whatever it was he was about to come up against. He thought he heard movement from behind the thick frame, but no one answered. He knocked again, this time calling out, "Hello?" Still nothing. Frustrated, Sean pulled the Motorola from his pocket and dialed Nicole's home number. He could hear the ring from where he was standing. "Nicole!" **Bang, bang, bang**—he knocked furiously. "Open the damn door. I know yar' home. Nicole!!" **Bang, bang, bang**!

The door opened behind him. A heavyset, middle-aged woman stood in the doorway hands on her hips. Looking Sean up and down, she hissed through the few clenched teeth she had dangling in her crooked mouth, "Now this is too much. I don't know what kinda mess ya'll got going on in there, but ya'll ain't the only people living in this got-damn building."

"I'm sorry, Miss. It's just that…"

The lady threw up her flabby palm, "Nigga. I could care less about ya'll drama. Like I told that other one standing out here, it ain't none of my business." Her voice was tired and harsh. "I could care less about whatever kinda love triangle ya'll got goin on, just keep that got-damn racquet to ya'selves!" She slammed the door hard.

Sean thought for a second. *Who else was here? What was the old lady talking about? Love triangle? It had to be that dude. Who else could it have been?* Nicole had some shit with her that she was hiding from him. Embarrassed and exhausted, Sean headed back outside. Fuck Nicole. I'm not gonna play'tha fool outside this 'ouse ta'nite. Tat's all right, I got me'baby and tat's exactly where she's gonna stey from this dey farward. Wit me! He trudged to the waiting cab, ready to head back uptown and add more expense to his fare that seemed to never end.

Sean sat staring blankly out of the window as the cab reached the top of the hill. *If she put her problems wit that boty'boi before Morgan this time, it won't be the last and I'll be damned if...* Had it not been going over fifty miles per hour at the point of the turn, Sean would have missed the navy Range Rover barreling into the development on two wheels. The truck nearly turned on its side. Sean stared hard at the coffee colored madwoman behind the wheel and shot straight up in his seat when he noticed it was Camille.

"Hold on!" He banged on the hard plastic separating him from the driver, "Turn 'round! Turn 'round!" The cabbie looked back and tapped the meter. "Look man, 'ere!" He stuffed three crisp Grant's through the slot and held on as the taxi spun a one-eighty.

By the time he got back to the building, Camille was already inside and on the elevator. Without a clue as to what the hell was happening and no time to spare trying to figure it out, Sean ripped down the long corridor to the side stairwell. His well-maintained physique had him up the five flights in record time.

Chapter 25

Rita

"Listen to me, Ree. We can talk about this. You don't have to do this. Really! We can work this out."

"Shut up! Shut up! SHUT UP!" Rita shakily held the glock in her hands. Aiming at the air in between the couple on the loveseat across from her, she swung her shoulders back-and-forth. "Eenie, meenie, miny, moe-- Which one of ya'll muthafuckas is gonna be the first to go?"

Nicole trembled in devastation at the psychopath laughing in her face as she toyed with her life. She hadn't said a word since Rita pressed the barrel of the gun to the back of her head in the car across the street from the café. Neither she nor Hassan saw her slouched down in the backseat until it was too late.

Hassan had tried to get in the car once he saw what was happening from where he was parked behind the Accord, but Rita had ordered Nicole to drive.

Now, the three of them were in Nicole's living room and Rita was starting to regret ever letting Hassan in the door. *If he hadn't been making so much noise in the damn hallway, he'd still be out there. He's such a fucking bastard.* Rita thought as the familiar sight of him sent a sharp pain through her heart. *He think he can just go out and replace me? And with this soft-ass corny trick?*

Rita tilted her head to the side, digging her gaze into Nicole's watery eyes. "What are you crying for sweetheart? You got him. I should be the one crying. Oh yeah, I did that already, now didn't I Hassan? But that didn't mean anything to you, did it? You still went ahead and left me like I wasn't shit. Um, um, um," Rita chuckled to herself.

The sound of Camille's voice made her jump in surprise. She thought for sure once Sean left nobody else would disturb her plans.

Her best friend called out to her, "Ree. Ree, it's me. Let me in, Ma." Camille didn't bother to knock. Instead she called softly through the thick panel. Her voice floated in like jasmine, calming the rage in Rita's spirit.

Turning slightly toward the melody of her angel, tears began to well in the corners of Rita's eyes. She knew full well that she'd gone to a point where turning back would be moot. "Camille," she yelled out still pointing the gun at her hostages.
"Camille, I'm gonna kill this son of a bitch!"
"Honey, open the door."
"He did me wrong, Camille. I gave him everything!

Everything I had and he threw me away like I wasn't shit. Who in the fuck do he think he playing with?"

"I know, honey. I know. Open the door so I can handle his sorry ass," she lied.

"Nuh-uh, I got this. I'ma take care of him and his bitch. We don't both need to get our hands dirty. Don't worry about me."

She walked over to Nicole grabbing her roughly by the arm, slinging her hard against the floor, "As a matter of a fact, get the fuck away from him." Rita eased behind the couch leaning over Hassan's right shoulder.

"So tell me," she whispered in his ear with the pistol still extended in Nicole's direction, "how is she in bed? Huh? Is she better than me? Must be. I mean for you to give up damn near a decade, that mutha'fucka gotta be lined in gold or some shit like that. Huh, papi?" Hassan ignored the crude remark.

"Rita, why don't we just leave? She really don't have nothing to do with this. We can go home and talk…" The butt of the gun smashed against his temple so swiftly Hassan didn't realize what hit him until he pulled his blood covered palm from the side of his face.

"Home?!" She repeated. "I don't have no fuckin' home you bastard! Or did you forget?" Rita was so livid she hadn't noticed that Camille was no longer calling out to her. "Your plans were to move this bitch into my home, so what are you talking about Hassan?! You think this is some kinda game? You find this shit you running around doing *amusing*? You getting a kick out of this aren't you? Two women fighting for your love? That's just what your corny ass has always wanted isn't it. Well dear, now you got it!" She slid her tongue up the side of his left cheek.

"As a matter of a fact, how about we make your dream come true. A little "Final Fantasy" fun." Rita turned her attention back to Nicole who was still trembling. Rita moved around and sat beside her husband.

"My, my, my you are a frail thing. I don't really see what Hassan sees in you." She tilted her head to the side, "Sure, you got a nice set of legs on you, but that's about it from what I can tell. How about you take all that shit off and show me what you got."

Nicole's eyes darted toward Hassan only to find his glued in cowardice to the floor.

"Wh... what?" She stammered.

"Bitch you heard me! Take that shit off! You want my man! You want my house! You want my life! Well, show me why I should let you have it!"

Nicole refused to budge. Like a panther, Rita leaped from her seat to the center of the room and onto her. Digging into either side of Nicole's scalp with her nails, Rita brought her to her knees in one swift move. Once atop her, she thrust her hand onto her neck cutting off her air supply. Spit flew from her lips into the air as she spoke, "Escuchar pendejo-- Don't try me."

Hassan jumped up and tried to yank Rita aside. But surprisingly the adrenaline racing through her system paired with the narcotics gave him a run for his money.

"Rita! Rita!" He yelled, tugging forcefully at her arms. The BOOM that sounded through the house from the front door made all three of them freeze. Nicole looked up through her tears to a face she'd never seen, stretching out her arms as if in slow motion she pulled Rita's grip from her tender throat. A gush of air flooded into her lungs like cool water soothing the burning in her trachea.

"Huuuuh!" Nicole drew in a second breathe deeply as she scooted back plastering herself against the wall. She tried to stand, but her legs gave way like warm jelly.

"Get off me! Let me go!" Rita's arms were flailing wildly, slapping Hassan across his head as he tried to restrain her. Camille squatted in front of Rita, close enough for their foreheads to touch.

"Ree... Listen to me. Relax."
Her voice was calm, but firm enough to pull Rita from her violent state. Slowly, she stopped wriggling. Her body went limp as she crumpled over sobbing into Camille's waiting arms. Hassan eased away and looked over at Nicole. Standing with her head pressed against his broad chest, Nicole too wept in the arms of someone who truly loved her-- Sean, it seemed, had come out of nowhere. Hassan hadn't even noticed him in the room.

He glanced up catching his eye. Sean glowered down heatedly as he stroked Nicole's quivering back. His hair hung passionately around his dark face like the mane of lion, reflecting the emotions pulsating through his guarded frame. Like a dog out of place, Hassan stumbled around disoriented feeling like less than a man.

"Get up, Ree. Let's go home," Camille spoke softly, wiping tears of anger from her own eyes. Brushing past Hassan,

Camille didn't look twice at Sean as everything fell absurdly into place in her once confused mind.

"I didn't know who she was, Camille. All I know is when I saw the two of them walk out of the masjid, I lost it."

"Shhhh," Camille fastened her seat belt without looking up. "Don't even worry about that shit. It's over now." Before the words could set in, a glare of blue and red lights shone into the car through Camille's rearview mirror.

"Oh shit, oh shit, oh shit!" Camille tried to relax, but her heart was flipping around in her chest like fish on a line. With one hand on the gearshift and the other gripping the steering wheel tight, she prepared herself.

"Ree, where is my piece?" She almost forgot about the Smith and Wesson.

Without a word, Rita pulled her shirt up flashing the black handle. That was all Camille needed. She backed out of the parking space as if the commotion didn't concern her. Hitting her left blinker, she pulled out onto the two-lane street. Rita was so exhausted mentally and physically she didn't even flinch as the fire truck blazed past them. By the time they reached the interstate, she was slumped over with her head against the glass snoring heavily.

Chapter 26

Hassan

"Now boarding rows 11 through 21, Flight 2895 express to Los Angeles. Now boarding Flight…"

It had been a little over a month since the debacle at Nicole's apartment took place. Hassan shuffled his way down the narrow aisle and took his seat in silence.

"Do you want to switch?" Ahmed twisted and turned attempting to find a comfortable position against the window.
He looks like a stuffed potato, Hassan thought to himself.
"Yeah, that's fine dad." As he unbuckled his seat belt, regret ran through his mind for what seemed like the 100th time. *Why am I going on this trip? I don't feel like being bothered with anyone. All I want to do is go home.*

But that, his parents told him over and over, was Hassan's problem these days. All he wanted to do was sit locked up in his empty house, hating the world. Linda promised this trip was just what he needed to get him back on track. But to him, the combined fourteen hour flight felt more like a punishment than a vacation.

He couldn't stop thinking about Nicole. Where was she? It seemed like she just disappeared from the face of the earth. Two weeks after that horrible night, all of her phone lines were disconnected and she'd moved without a trace. Hassan had even stopped by her job a couple of times, but her car was never in the parking lot. He'd thought about going to Morgan's daycare but figured it would be too risky. He didn't want to take the chance of running into Sean again.

On top of feeling ultimately responsible for placing Nicole in danger, he felt abandoned by how she vanished from existence. Rita, on the other hand, was still very much a part of his life. He regretted not saying anything when the cops showed up more and more every day. *If only I'd spoken up.* But at the time, Nicole swiftly pulled herself together and met them at the door, without so much as a hair out of place. She played the role of 'everything is fine officer' so well that Hassan knew she'd done it before.

Now, it was too late. Other than an anonymous disturbance call that turned out to be a false alarm, there was no record of the night ever taking place. If there was, he may have been able to put up a fight against his psychotic wife who was still on a warpath set to destroy him.

Rita beat Hassan to the punch and filed for divorce under the terms of irreconcilable differences. At first he was relieved. He thought this was the end, which was all he'd wanted for the last eight months. But, as time went on and Rita began throwing accusations of infidelity and desertion into the mix, the whole picture turned very ugly, very quickly. The icing on the cake was the day his attorney called and told him she was blaming him for her drug addiction. And because there was never any prenuptial to cushion Hassan from the falls of Rita's blows, he fell flat on his behind.

He'd stopped working completely and Ahmed had to hire someone to run the lab. Hassan turned into a hermit, confining his mind and body to his barren shell of a home in hopes to disappear himself. But Linda wasn't having it. She'd bullied her way into the dark foyer three days ago announcing that enough was enough. She had booked Hassan and his father round trip tickets to Zahlè, Lebanon.

Linda ordered Hassan to pack as she rambled on and on about the change of pace being what he needed to regain control of his life. The town, she told him, was located about an hour and half outside of Beirut in the foothills of Mount Sannine. Linda had it all planned out, from the tour of the Lebanese Mountains to the reservations at some of the finest bistros the city had to offer. Hassan was to use this time alone with Ahmed to regroup and return ready to start anew. Now, under the deep drone of the plane's engine, he perched reluctantly in the seat and closed his eyes praying that his mother was right.

Chapter 27
Camille

"Well, Ms. Massey it looks as if we have enough evidence to form a case. Sean Jeffers was definitely at the scene. The DNA matches one hundred percent."

Camille could not believe what she was hearing. *How did they get Sean to agree to a blood test? No doubt his lawyer talked him into it. But what now? Does this mean he's going to jail? Of course not. There has to be a trial first. What to do about a lawyer? Was the state going to file charges since this was a criminal case?*

"Ms. Massey? Hello? Are you there?"
"Oh, yes. I'm sorry Detective. I just…"

He interrupted, "No need to apologize ma'am. I understand. I just wanted to call you myself with the good news. Maybe now you and your family can rest easy. I'll be in touch."
Ebony, who had been standing outside, peeked in the room. Satisfaction must have been written all over Camille's face

because she didn't need to say a word.

"They got his ass, huh?" Camille nodded unable to speak. Closure streamed down her cheeks as she buried her face in her girlfriend's arms.

By the time the sun set over the peaceful house that spring evening, everyone was gathered around the dinner table in good spirits. This practice had quickly become a normal routine for the four of them, but today held a dual reason for celebration. Not only did the law finally prove just, but today Rita was 120 days clean and still going strong. They never spoke of that night or the dark place where Rita's addiction had led her. They instead held onto each other for the support they needed to make it through one day at a time.

Camille stared at her best friend, finally able to see the radiant woman that she'd known all her life-- the one who was trapped under a cloud of addiction for far too long. She couldn't think of a better time to make her announcement.

"Okay, ya'll. I've got a surprise. And it's something for all of you." Jelani bounced up and down, grinning from ear-to-ear as if he already knew what his mother was about to say. The word surprise was a gift all its own in his eyes, no matter what was about to materialize. Ebony on the other hand, sat back and braced herself for the unexpected. She had no idea what to think. While Rita was unresponsive, she couldn't help but wonder what Camille had to say that was going to affect all three of them.

"It's been a hell of a year for all of us. Really. And I've

been doing a lot of reflecting lately," looking at her son, she repeated, "reflecting means thinking back, Jelani." She spoke again to all of them, "I made up my mind today that it's time to get a fresh start. A new beginning." She looked over at Ebony, "Remember when you asked me to move down south with you?" Ebony nodded, unable to believe her ears. Camille continued, "Well, I've decided to go ahead and take you up on that offer. That is, if the offer still stands?" Ebony's face flushed a bright red. She turned to Jelani and scooped him up out of his chair twirling him around.

"Did you hear your mom? We're moving to Georgia!"

"Oh cool! Are we leaving tomorrow?"

"Not quite, shorty, but soon. Right?" Ebony looked back to Camille.

"As soon as possible." She looked at Rita for the approval only she could give. When she saw the go-ahead in her homie's smile, Camille knew she'd made the right choice.

The next few weeks were more of a blur to Camille than anything else. She spent most of her days battling with her mother on what Carroll called 'the most ridiculous decision she'd ever made'; her dad, as usual, was all for it.

There was so much that needed to be done she didn't know where to start. She decided that instead of trying to sell her house, the best thing to do was to rent the property. That way she had guaranteed income and could still come back home if need be. She placed an ad and in no time began setting up showings. She spent hours on end surfing the net for all types of information on 'Hotlanta' from schools to jobs to beauty salons.

There was so much for Camille to try and take in, she soon found herself in a mental overload.

Ebony suggested they fly down for a weekend so that Camille could at least see what she was in for and since she'd stopped working already, time off was no issue.

"Well, the only thing is the pretrial on the seventeenth of next month. After that we can roll out," she told Ebony.

The seventeenth came before either of them knew it. Camille stood in the mirror brushing down the front of her outfit the same way she always did when she was nervous.

"Relax."

Rita handed her a pair of pearl earrings Trevor picked out years ago.

"You'll be fine."

"Man, I just keep thinking what am I gonna do when I see his face. Am I gonna cry or try and kill his ass right there in front of the judge? Or am I gonna break the hell down?"

Rita tried to laugh off the heaviness in the room, knowing her friend was as serious as a heart attack. She was glad Camille asked her to go with her. This way if she did get the urge to wild out, Rita would be there.

Chapter 28
Sean

"Daddy! Daddy!" Morgan's voice rang through the apartment, jolting Sean from his sleep in alarm.

"What! What 'appened?" He stumbled into the bathroom where Nicole was squatting down unsuccessfully trying to comb through her daughter's thick mane. She threw her hands up in desperation.

"See. Now you woke up Daddy. Doing all that hollering like somebody is trying to kill you."

"But Mommie, it hurts!" Morgan winced as the comb came close to her scalp.

Sean shook his head clutching her chin tenderly, "Listen lickle girl, yar' gonna 'ave ta' get yar' hair combed. It's part of bein' a lady so ya' might as well get used to it. I'm sure Mommie is bein' as gentle as possible, so cut tat noise. Ya'eard?" With that Morgan nodded, sniffling up her crocodile tears. Sean turned and headed back through the closet.

So much for getting one more hour, he thought, pulling a

pair of socks from the huge armoire. Having Morgan and Nicole living back with him was heaven. It was like a dream come true. Even if that dream was the result of a nightmare he wished Nicole never had to live through.

Finally, Sean felt like he was back in control of his life and today he would take the first step in clearing the very last skeleton he had hanging in his closet. There was no doubt the last four months were hell, but it was all about to end one way or another.

He wasn't sure which was worst, confessing to Nicole about his involvement with the hit and run or the look on her face when he showed her a picture of the curly haired baby girl he'd unknowingly conceived with an under-aged psycho.

Maybe it was her own near-death experience, but Nicole handled the whole situation totally differently than Sean ever imagined she would. He even thought he saw a hint of guilt flash across her face when he recalled the night he came home, bloodied up and bruised. She did, however, question him extensively about the ordeal with Jill. He could tell she was disappointed with his nonchalant attitude toward the child. But what was he to do? He didn't feel anything for the mother; hell, he didn't know Jill from a can of paint. It was just a one-night stand gone bad. The kicker was, even though Jill's family had been hounding him to take responsibility, not once did anyone offer to let him see the baby. It was no bother to Sean. For the past two and a half months the only indication to remind him of his newborn daughter was the monthly support check he had to sign.

Today, however, Sean had bigger fish to fry. It was the first pretrial hearing and he was facing vehicular homicide charges. Not only was he tense as hell, but he was dreading having to face Camille. Never in a million years did he imagine it would all pan out the way it did. Fate, he thought, was a crazy thing and life seemed to be ruled by it.

Sean pulled up in the parking deck nearly an hour before the hearing was set to begin. The glare of the early morning sun shone in vigorously through the gaps in the cement walls. The musty smell of the concrete mixed with morning dew was oddly refreshing as he walked. Hitting the alarm button on his key ring, Sean was stopped in his tracks as the device failed to 'chirp' signaling activation. He turned and took a few steps closer to the truck, pressing the button again. Still nothing. *Me poor truck*, he thought. *It's been trough 'ell. I see why the shit ain't workin' right*. Still he refused to leave it unarmed. Punching the security code on the door handle, Sean never saw the three hundred pound Sicilian wrap his arms around his navy silk blazer until it was too late. With his torso restrained, a smaller but equally strong accomplice hammered at Sean's knees with what had to be a metal baseball bat. The sound of his bones cracking echoed against the empty walls of the deck like surround sound in a theater. The pain shot up his right side in a bolt until it knotted in the pits of his abdomen where it was joined by a thunderous blow to the base of his skull. Within seconds Sean blanked out as his sturdy frame fell to the ground incapacitated.

"A yo! Wake the fuck up," The ice cold water and throaty voice startled Sean to consciousness. He blinked hard trying to clear the tears from his eyes. The darkness of the room, however, made it hard for him to focus. As everything came into view, he realized he was not in a room, but in the back of a huge van strapped to an aluminum bench. A thick iron chain bound his ankle. Sean's hands were bound tightly at the small of his back. His mouth was gagged with electrical tape.

"I said, wake the FUCK up!" With that, the fat guido bitch smacked Sean across the face, yanking the tape from his mouth. His blood boiled in anger, but there was nothing Sean could do.

"Man, wha'de fuck is gwan'ere?! Do ya' know who de'fuck I am?" Sean spewed.

This time the slimmer of the two spoke, "Yeah, I know who the fuck you are, tough guy. You're the moolie who stuck his cock in the wrong girl. You fuck my sister,'eh? Then send her back pregnant with a fucking SWIRLIE MOOK that me and my family gotta look at! Yeah I know who the fuck you are. Your one dead nigger!" He swung hard. His left fist hammered into the side of Sean's jaw. Grabbing a handful of his tousled hair, he pulled Sean's head back violently. "You want to go around fucking with minors then you need to do it in your own neighborhood." Speckles of saliva flew in Sean's face. "You don't see me coming down to the ghetto trying to pick up little brown honeys, do you?" Sean didn't reply. "Then what in the FUCK makes you think you can screw around with my sister and get off by paying a lousy couple hundred dollars a month!" Another blow, this time to Sean's exposed rib cage knocking the wind out of him. Sean looked around for something, anything that could help him free his hands. But there was nothing other than himself and the two brutes that obviously intended to kick his ass for as long as they could.

For what seemed like forever, they took turns pounding away. They beat him in the head endlessly and stomped him in his already broken knees, as they worked him over and over. At first he tried to resist, grunting and shifting his body weight while tightening his muscles at each point of contact. But that, along with the effects of the blows, wore him out quickly. And once again, Sean lulled off into a state of unconsciousness. He never felt them stop. Nor did he feel them pull his battered body from the van. He never felt the bumps and scrapes along the length of his back as they dragged him by the ankles down the long wooded trail to an abandoned cabin somewhere in the pine barren South Jersey woods. Sean didn't feel them rip off his five hundred dollar snakeskin shoes and replace his Gucci socks with a tweed hunting rope. Sean didn't hear them laugh as they laid out a host of weapons they planned on using to torture him until he begged for death. What Sean did feel, however, was the stinging sensation of his exposed flesh hitting the air as the fat one drug the edge of a Bowie Hunter's Blade down his right bicep. He woke to the sadistic stares of his abductors. For the first time Sean was in fear. He took deep anxious breathes trying to prepare himself. Not only for whatever it was he was about to face, but ultimately, for the possibility of not making it out alive.

Chapter 29

Rita

The smell of the courtroom sickened Rita to her stomach. It seemed as if she'd spent all her life inside the same four wood paneled walls, staring at the same pictures of the same Supreme Court Justices, listening to the same lawyers ramble on in the same monotone style.

The first time the back of her legs met the cold deep brown bench, she was seated next to Anna. Her grandmother looked on worriedly as the social worker whispered to the public defender in a language with which Anna had a hard time keeping up. But Rita understood perfectly what they were saying. And even at seven, she knew the severity of phrases like "state custody", "foster home" and "best interest of the child". But how did the two people standing over them know what was best for her? After all she'd only met one of them today and the social worker less than two months ago right after her mother died. From that day on, Rita and Anna spent months in and out of the wood paneled walls trying to convince whatever wrinkled up white man sitting behind the bench in an oversized black dress that she belonged "with her abuela" and nowhere else.

Camille slid into the waiting space next to her friend with agitation oozing from her pores. "His lawyer claims he doesn't know where he is either. This is some bullshit, Ree, for-real, for-real." Camille sucked in some of the stale air through her gritted teeth, "I should have known his punk ass wasn't going to show."

Rita tried to be positive, "Maybe something happened and he's just running late. I doubt he'd skip out on something like this."

"Tsssst!" Camille sucked her teeth again, "I don't see why. He skipped out the night he left Trevor to die under that overpass. He's not a man, Ree. He's a coward. Everything he's done proves it. I just never saw it for myself."

The district attorney walked up tapping a stack of papers against the palm of her ashy hand, "Ms. Massey, we're going to have to reschedule. A bench warrant will be issued against Mr. Jeffers. He'll be served first thing Monday morning at both his home and office. Once taken into custody, the judge will set another date. We'll have someone from my office contact you as soon as possible. I do apologize." Without waiting for Camille to respond, she turned and walked away. "See. What'd I tell you?" Camille slapped her pocketbook strap across her shoulder and huffed out through the double doors. Rita trailed behind, giving her space.

At least she's getting out of here this weekend, she thought. They could all get their minds off of the mayhem they'd been dealing with and on the path of their new lives. Rita had set up a tour of the New Beginnings rehabilitation center. It was a privately funded facility located about one hundred miles south of Atlanta. She'd been consulting with Ebony's connect, Dr.

Orman, over the past three months. He made all of the necessary arrangements for Rita. All she had to do was show up. She kept telling herself this was the best decision she could have ever made. A brand new life. No bullshit this time.

Hassan was finally a thing of the past. She came out of their divorce with more than she's ever imagined. By the time her lawyer finished working his magic, the judge was granting Rita everything, even the house, which she turned down. After all, she wasn't a gold-digger. All she wanted was enough to be able to live on, and she'd gotten just that. She'd heard that Hassan had left the country on a long term sabbatical with his father in the Middle East somewhere. Hell, after all, they all needed some way to cope. Rita's weekly sessions with her therapist were her own life savers. It was in those sixty minute discussions that she could be exactly who she was without judgment or restraint. Within those four walls Ree could cry and laugh and scream, and be still. For the first time in her life she found a place that would take her away. She found the high without the high and it was wonderful.

The trip to Atlanta later that week came before they knew it. Even the flight was a quick two and a half hour hop, skip and jump, it seemed.

"Oh... my... goodness!" Rita's mind was turning back flips as they stepped out onto the busy sidewalk leaving the terminal. A gush of warm wind blew past her filling her lungs with the freshest air she'd ever smelled. Camille peered up into the crystal blue sky filled with nothing but snow white puffy clouds and deeply inhaled the scent of trees and dirt. For as far as the eye could see the clear ocean of the heavens flowed on without a trace of pollution or murk.

"This is incredible," Camille took the words right out of Rita's mouth, smiling from the inside out.

"It's amazing. Isn't it?" She looked down at Jelani who was squinting under the light of the sun.

He smiled revealing his snaggletooth mouth, "Yep."

The ride to Ebony's house was breathtaking. Everything seemed so wide open and spacious. Even the highways, although heavy with traffic, seemed twice the size of the interstates back home. The skyline was immaculate with intricately shaped scrapers covered in mirrored glass of every imaginable color and design. Turner Field boasted proudly as one of the historical landmarks among the prestigious Westin Hotel, the CNN Center and Georgia Tech's campus.

By the time they reached the exit Camille and Rita had 'oohed' and 'ahhed' like schoolgirls, while Jelani just looked on quietly. Ebony's apartment complex was an impressive gated condominium estate with ivory white units trimmed in what looked like newly laid brick. A sparkling blue twelve-foot swimming pool hugged the curve as they rounded the corner. Jelani bounced up and down in his seat raring to be freed for exploration.

By the time they dropped their bags on the hardwood floors of the condo, Rita knew Camille's mind was set in stone. There would be no turning back. This paradise was the kind of place the two had dreamed of for many years. The sun-drenched skies along with the wide open spaces sealed the envelope.

"No matter what it takes," she whispered to Rita, "me and Jelani are going to be back here by the time school lets out."

After they showered and changed, the four of them piled into the rental and headed back downtown to what Ebony called, "the park". Centennial Park was like a photo straight out of a Home Living magazine. There were people of all shades sprinkled out on the kelly-green grass, like rainbow Jimmies on a vanilla ice cream cone. The blazing sun seemed to melt everyone into a tranquil state. On one side of the park, couples strolled hand-in-hand while walking dogs. On the other, kids of all ages screamed joyfully as O-shaped ringlets of water shot up out of the ground and they pranced in jubilee all their own. Even the teenagers, huddled in groups, were content under the refreshing sky that kept their spirits tamed while out of their parents' watchful eyes.

By the time dusk fell over the square, Jelani had run around barefoot in the fountain laughing with kids you'd think he'd known his whole life. After eating from nearly every snack bar in sight, he was now laid out on the grass holding his distended belly in his small hands, "Mom, I gotta poop."

"I'm sure you do," Camille laughed.

"Aunt Ree, tell her it's not funny. My stomach hurts."

"Awww, come'ere baby," Rita kissed his sweaty forehead with the desired magic only his auntie could give.

It was a quarter after seven the next morning and they had just finished a light breakfast. Everyone was bustling around getting ready for the hour and a half ride to Macon to visit the rehab center.

"Hey Camille, do you think I should..." Rita paused at the sight of Camille on the edge of the sofa, soggy-eyed. "What?" She rushed over, bending down in front of her.

"What happened? What is it?" Camille shook her head and tried to speak, but no words came. Like a zombie she pushed the phone into Rita's palm. The recording was looping the main menu. "To repeat this message press one, to save it press two..." Rita punched the keypad and listened.

"This message is for Camille Massey. Ms. Massey, this is special investigator Ronald Peyton calling on behalf of the New Jersey District Attorney's office. I'm calling to inform you that the body of a Sean Jeffers was found yesterday evening at approximately 6:15pm. Two hikers stumbled across what seemed to be a badly dismembered corpse on a trail in the Pine Barrens. We were able to make the identification from a wallet still on the body and a Nicole Porter came in to confirm. Normally, we don't release this type of information to the public, but I've been in contact with the department over in Bristol and I've come to understand there is a very unique connection between yourself and the deceased. Anyway, if you have any further questions, you can contact my office at 609-733-2937."

Rita, herself in shock, had no idea what to say.

Chapter 30

Epilogue

It was exactly one year and two weeks later when Camille closed the trunk of her new, pearl white Infiniti FX45 locking in her suitcase. The unusual heat of an October sun beat down on the back of her neck like invisible drums. Jelani stood on his toes to kiss her goodbye, followed by a tight embrace from Ebony. She would only be gone overnight, but they said their goodbyes as if her visit to Rita was sure to last way too long.

The drive was a breeze; and, with the help of Jill Scott and Eryka Badu, Camille made it to from Atlanta to Macon in record time. As she pulled onto the grounds of the rehab center, a calming peace flowed over her body. It was no surprise that Rita was doing as well as she was. Turning onto the street where Rita's townhouse was Camille almost forgot for a second that all of the homes were occupied by former addicts fighting to change their lives. Pulling into the empty driveway, the sight of her best friend sitting Indian-style on a porch swing greeted her. Rita dropped the book she was engrossed in and ran toward the car.

"Hey, baby doll. How was the ride?"

"Not bad, actually. Not bad at all."

By six thirty that evening, Camille was sitting beside Rita in the auditorium of the subdivision's community center. Twice a week all of the residents were required to participate in what was called "The Social". They would share their triumphs as well as voice their disappointment on the journey back to a substance free existence. Family members and friends were welcome to come and show their support and were even allowed to speak if they so chose.

Tonight, Camille was there with Rita in celebration of her 365th day of achievement. When the speaker called everyone to order and asked if anyone had anything they'd like to share, Rita was shocked when Camille stood and made her way to the podium.

"Hi, my name is Camille and I'm here on behalf of my best friend, La'Rita. Well, we call her Ree. She's been here for a year and words can't describe how proud of her I am. We've been best friends since we were kids, and truth be told, she's more of a sister to me than anything. Anyway, I um, I wrote something that I'd like to share with you all in dedication to my Ree. It's called Kismet, which means fate." Camille opened her journal to the folded page, carefully creasing the spine and cleared her throat.

"It was Kismet that brought me to you
A power greater than our own
That bound us like glue
So we stuck together and through it all

Kismet determined whether we would survive
Many days I wiped your tears
Countless nights you kissed away mine

It was Kismet that held us in times
We felt alone
For our paths were fated
And our journeys already known
Which is why through it all
We're able to atone for our faults
See Kismet holds our future
Secure inside the vaults of life's bank
And so never curse
But instead thank
The well of Kismet
That in the desert watched quietly as from this fountain
Of life we drank..."

Thank you for reading A Turn of Kismet by Kalandra St. George. Don't hesitate to leave a review on Amazon or Barnes & Noble comment forums. We would love to hear from you! Please check out more titles at PrintHouseBooks.com

PRINTHOUSEBOOKS.com
Read it! Enjoy it! Tell A Friend!
Atlanta, GA.

CPSIA information can be obtained
at www.ICGtesting.com
Printed in the USA
FFOW04n0216190416
23341FF